To Alyssa,

Don't let average people hold you back from the greatness you are destined for. Don't play down to the competition

The Ignorance of the Captive
A Curtus Parker Story

By: Avery Justin

Table of Contents

Prologue (5)
I (6)
II (27)
III (40)
IV (54)
V (70)
VI (88)
VII (115)
VIII (141)
IX (154)
X (168)
XI (180)
XII (196)
XIII (210)
XIV (228)
XV (240)
XVI (252)
XVII (264)
XVIII (276)
XIX (291)
XX (304)

Prologue

In the year 2020 human greed rendered the surface to ash. Bombs rained from the sky wiping out entire cities and ecosystems. The temperature on the surface averaged a staggering 105 degrees Fahrenheit. The sea levels rose to heights that swallowed up coastal countries and states. Experts predicted that 92% of the human population lost their lives as a result of this war. In preparation for this the governments of the major developed nations constructed massive floating cities called Arcs to take their leaders and elites up into the sky out of harm's way. These Arcs were designed to carry the last 8% of the human population above the clouds away from the radiation and rising temperatures.

In the beginning there were 10 arcs. 2 US, 2 Russian, 1 European, 2 Chinese, 1 Japanese and 1 Australian. But bad blood wasn't left on the surface as the leaders of each arc brought their grievances to the skies. These old grudges led to disputes over who should have the most airspace. Eventually this disputes would lead to the Aerospace Wars of 2135. This war took the original number of 10 Arcs and dropped it to 3 leaving roughly 22,500,000 people alive on earth. Before the war would killed off the last of the human race the Treaty of Clear Skies was signed permitting that no one owned any airspace and Arcs were able to fly freely. This act effectively saved the human race and rather that disputing over airspace they were able to focus on creating a way to revive their dying.

Now the year is 2235 and the skies are calm. The scientist on each Arc are working around the clock to figure out how to make the surface inhabitable again. But as with all noble crusades there is an evil force waiting in the darkness ready to do anything to halt their progress...

I

Curtus Parker is a 20-year-old med school student who is living on the last remaining United States Aerial City the USAC Jefferson. He stands at around six feet tall with a medium build. He has a light brown complexion with messy black hair with a white patch in the front. His peers regarded Curtus as an all-around genius. He was the youngest in his graduating class in both high school and college and was an exceptional athlete. Though he had all the tools to be successful his natural talent was often overshadowed by him getting in trouble. Often Curtus found himself correcting professors and students, Which often led to verbal altercations with his professors and physical altercations with his classmates. His constant conflicts would inevitably end in his dismissal from the university.

The day Curtus was sent home he had planned on walking in like nothing had happened. When he walked in both of his parents were waiting for him in the kitchen. They normally were in the kitchen when he came home but this was different. There was no food on the stove and the tv was off. Curtus could tell by the expression on his parents faces that they were already aware of his dismissal. "Curt we told you all of the fighting would catch up to you" his father Marcus began. "Let me explain" Curtus said in an effort to defend himself. "How could you get in a fight with the son of the Dean of Admissions" his mother Tanya asked in a panicked tone. "He attacked me. He was all hopped up on Tonics and charged me. I was defending myself." Curtus explain. "They won't let you in after you after you beat up the dean's son Curtus" Marcus yelled. "Oh god all your talent is going to go to waste" Tanya said beginning to sob. "I have been on the top of my class since I was 13 years old, if they don't want me back it is a detriment to them." Curtus reassured. "Curtus you don't understand. This is bigger than just your academic talent. You've enter the world of politics now, and it's going to be harder to pull strings when everyone at the University thinks you beat up the

Dean's son" Tanya yelled back. The room fell silent. Marcus took a deep breath. "Curtus you said that his son was hopped up on Tonics." he asked.

Tonics are the local street drug on the Jefferson. They have a similar effect to the surface drug heroine in that it makes you hallucinate and can cause people to break out in violent rages. "Yeah everyone on campus knows that Jimmy is a fiend." Curtus replied. "So it would make sense to blame Curtus for the fight because he already has a history and he can protect his son and also his image" Marcus concluded. Tanya's demeanor changed upon this realization. "So you saying that you were set up" Tanya asked. "Not set up... more framed" Curtus replied. "Well I'll see what I can do to get you back in, but until then I need your help in the lab. I think I'm close to that breakthrough" Marcus said. Tanya snapped her head to Marcus. "You don't mean THE breakthrough" She asked. "Yes honey THE breakthrough" He replied. She ran over and gave him a hug. She was so happy she was almost sobbing again. "I'm so proud of you honey" she said. "Well don't be proud of me yet I still haven't broken through" he said jokingly. "I don't know what this breakthrough is but I'm proud of you too dad" Curtus said. "Thanks son. What time are you free so we can finish this thing" Marcus asked. "Well I'm kinda sore so can we go in the evening" He asked. "That's fine. Honey go get the good wine from the cellar" Marcus said.

While his parents were busy celebrating Curtus looked out of the window imagining what this mysterious breakthrough could be. He watched kids playing roller hockey in the driveway, his neighbor from down the street was walking nine dogs for her dog walking business, and the neighbor across the street was mowing his grass. There was something about his across the street neighbors that always made him uneasy. Curtus had lived in the same house all of his life and he had never met them. They never had cars coming and going, the lights were never on, it was as if nobody lived there. That is until the come out to cut the grass every week. Like clockwork he would come out at 4:30 every other Wednesday afternoon.

Curtus began to closely analyze his mysterious neighbor. His or her body was completely covered from head to toe with some form of clothing so Curtus couldn't identify them. His mother returned from the cellar with a bottle of wine. "Hey Curt what are you looking at" she asked. "Our weird ass across the street neighbor mowing their grass" he replied. "Mowing his grass?" she asked. "Yeah they mow their grass around this time every other week. It is the only time they come out." he replied. "But the grass on the Jefferson doesn't grow. It is turf" she said walking over. "Well you can take a look and see he is mowing his grass" Curtus said pointing out of the window.

Tanya took a look out the window to see for herself. "Huh that is weird they are mowing their grass" she said. Then the smile evaporated from her face and she dropped the bottle of wine causing the bottle shatter. As this happens the neighbor rips their headphones off and covered his ears. "Marcus we have a problem" Tanya said running upstairs. Trying to understand what was going on Curtus decided to continue examining the lawnmower. He looked at the lawnmower to see a microphone protruding out the side of it. Tanya and Marcus came running back in the kitchen. "Curtus we have to go now!" Marcus yelled. "Why what's going on?" Curtus asked. "Honey now is not the time for questions. Just listen to your father okay" She said nervously. Curtus noticed his mother had returned in a cold sweat. Curtus looked out the window to see the eavesdropper putting back on his headphones. "Curtus lets go" Marcus said grabbing him by his collar. As he was getting yanked he could see the mysterious man pulled a radio out of his pocket and began speaking into it. Then within seconds three armored trucks pulled up in front of the house and several men in full riot gear came pouring out of the back of them.

Curtus didn't understand why they were running to the back of the house. If they were trying to escape why wouldn't they go to the garage and take a car to get out. "Where are we going" Curtus asked. "We are getting you to a safe place" Marcus answered. Marcus opened the closet and pushed the coats aside. He tapped the wall six time and it opened revealing a set of stairs. "PARKER FAMILY WE NEED YOU TO VACATE THE PREMISES" a voice yelled from outside. "Quickly down the stairs" Marcus yelled running down the stairs. Curtus's mind was racing in a million different directions. Just 5 minutes ago they were celebrating on his father's potential breakthrough and now there is an army outside of his house ready to arrest them. "Curt there will be plenty of time to answer all questions later, but now just listen to your father" his mother repeated. Even though his mother was shaken to the core she still managed to put a smile on her face.

The stairs led to a short hallway with a door at the end. "I prayed I'd never have to use this room" Marcus whispered to himself. "THIS IS YOUR LAST WARNING. EXIT THE PREMISES OR WE WILL COME IN. YOU HAVE 2 MINUTES TO COMPLY" the voice yelled again. The sound was muffled from them being underground. "2 minutes that's awful generous. Normally they would just kick the door down and barge in" Tanya said. "Well that is because we aren't normal and they are well aware of that." Marcus murmured. Marcus reached into his pocket and pulled out a singular key. They key looked like a relic out of a museum. All the locks on the Jefferson were unlocked by badges or a smart device. This key was and old earth tumbler lock key. He put the key in the hole and turn it twice to the left to open the door.

On the other side of the door was a fully stocked doomsday panic room. There was a command center with nine computer screens mounted on the wall each with a separate camera feed on it. "Wow how long have you guys had this" Curtus asked. "We had this installed after you were born" Marcus replied. "Better to be prepared than to be unprepared" Tanya added. Curtus walked into the panic room. It was the size of a class room and was stocked with food water and entertainment. "Don't you guys think this is kind of extra. Wouldn't cryofreeze have been cheaper" Curtus asked. Marcus turned on the tv and display the view from the front of their house. There was 40+ men with fully automatic weapons and full riot gear. "Compared to that I feel like this is just right. Plus, in cryofreeze you can't move so it would be a matter of time before they found you." Tanya said pointing at the tv. "OKAY TIMES UP WE ARE COMING IN" the voice yelled. "Hold on have you guys tried knocking rather than just yelling at the front of a house." Another voice asked.

On the security feed the can see a man in a long black coat walking to the front door. "It can't be" Marcus said. He sprinted to the command center and began ferociously typing on the keyboard. Then the feed changed to a camera right above the front door. Curtus looked at his mother the expression on her face turned to one of pure horror. Curtus looked at the screen to see a bald white man with a scar over his left eye. "Why did they send him" Marcus asked nervously. The man knocked on the door twice before he noticed the camera over the door. "Oh hi. I know you guys are watching from whatever bunker you have set up in there, but we kind of need you to come outside" the man said with a smile. The man's calm demeanor made Curtus nervous. There was something unauthentic about it. Curtus could also tell by the expression on both of his parents faces that there was something truly horrifying about the man on the tv. "We have to go out there" Marcus exclaimed. Tanya looked at Marcus. "That is out of the question" she yelled. "Tanya he is grown now he can handle himself. If we don't go out he is going to come in and it is only a matter of time before they find this place" Marcus argued.

Curtus continued to look at the man on the screen. He stood there staring into the camera with a menacing smile. The more Curtus looked at him the more nervous he became. He could tell just by looking at him that this man was unstable in some way. "How could he just sit there in a situation like this and hold a smile like he is taking a school photo" Curtus thought to himself as he stared at the screen. Curtus looked at his mother who was now in tears. "Why him why did they have to send him" she sobbed. "Tanya we have to go" Marcus said. Tanya turned to Curtus and gave him a big hug. "I know you have so many questions and I will answer them later, but we have to go now" she said sniffling. "Where are you guys going" Curtus asked. "We don't know but don't worry we are going to be alright" She reassured. "C'mon you guys. I'm not hourly. Come out here before I let myself and my friends in" the man said. Marcus walked over to Curtus and gave him a hug. After the embrace Marcus put his hands on Curtus's shoulders. "Curtus I need you to listen to me very carefully because what I am about to tell is essential for your survival" Marcus said. Curtus nodded his head. "You are going to need to go to the Market District and find a man named Juice and tell him the phrase 'The Last Train Departs at Midnight ok" Marcus said. "The Last Train Departs at Midnight got it" Curtus repeated. Marcus gave his son another hug. "Be safe out there Curtus" he pleaded before he made his way down the hall. His mother gave him another hug. "I promise I will answer all of your questions," She said again. She let go of him and stepped backward into the hall. She pressed a button on the wall closing the panic room door.

Curtus ran to the command center to keep tabs with what was going on outside. He watched his parents on the feed from the camera in the hallway. He could see his mother locking the door behind her. When she locked the door she broke the key off in the lock so no one could come in if they found the secret bunker. After breaking off the key she ran down the hall and up the stairs to join Marcus. Curtus changed the feed to the foyer of the house. There was nothing going on there. His father hadn't come to open the door and the army outside hadn't blown the door down. Suddenly there was a loud explosion and a cloud of smoke covered the door. Men came flooding into the house running out of the smoke with their guns drawn. "GET DOWN NOW" one of the men yelled. Curtus changed the view of the camera to see both of his parents walking into the foyer. They were surrounded by the mysterious militia with their guns trained on them. The mysterious man who knocked on the door was the last one to come through the smoke. "So you guys were just going to stand by the front door and not let me in. Kinda rude don't ya think?" the man said walking toward his parents.

Curtus's heart began to beat a thousand miles an hour. He had no idea what this mysterious man was capable of. The man began to walk in circles around Curtus's parents. "It has been a long time hasn't it Carolyn" the man asked. "Carolyn…" Curtus whispered to himself. He began to think maybe the man had barged into the wrong house. His mother's name was Tanya not Carolyn. She stood silent with her eyes fixed on the ground refusing to make eye contact with him. "Aww c'mon after all these years I thought you would be happy to see me Carolyn." The man said. "Don't call me that, and I don't know who you are." She replied keeping her eyes fixed at the ground. The mysterious man did not take too kindly to her response. "YOU DON'T REMEMBER LEAVING ME IN THAT HELLHOLE!!!" he yelled in her right ear. The man had become physically distraught losing his menacing yelled. After one look at his father the mysterious man regained his smile. "Oh-ho-ho well isn't today just my lucky day. Not only do I bag the Tonic queen herself but I get one of the most wanted men on the Jefferson as well. How are you Kirkland" the man asked regaining his menacing smile.

Curtus sat down in the chair. Everything he ever knew was being put in question. He didn't even know if he knew his parent's real names. His parents had pasts that they had kept from him and now they were catching up to them. "So this can end one of two ways you could either 1.) come with me peacefully and we will replace your door free of charge or 2.) this gets messy and violent and I drag you out of here. Which is it gonna be?" the mysterious man explained. The room fell silent. Both of his parents continued to look straight at the ground. "We are gonna come peacefully but I have one question." His mother began. "Oh and what is that?" the man asked. "What are they calling you now?" She asked.

The man became enraged again. He became so enraged that he drew his hand back and backhand slapped Curtus's mother across the face knocking her to the ground. "Leremy... they are calling me Leremy." He yelled. "Hey we said we are going to go peacefully!" his father yelled back. "Oh sorry Kirkland it just slipped" Leremy said. "Honey change of plans we are going with option B" he said. "I was hoping you would say that" Leremy said with a smile.

This was it, the moment Curtus was waiting for. It was the moment he got to see what he was going to be up against once he left the bunker. He looked on in awe at Leremy's display of power. It began with his legs disappearing in a cloud of smoke. It looked as if he was floating in the air..

Curtus mother, bleeding out the mouth, looked mortified at Leremy's power. "What did they do to you?" she asked looking a Leremy in horror. "They did what you refused to do. They took a chance on me!!!" he yelled. "Honey get behind me" His father told Carolyn. "YES YES!!! SHOW THEM WHY THEY CALL YOU THE KILLER FLASH!!!" Leremy said. Suddenly his father's arms began to glow a bright white. Then electricity began to spark out of his hands. "COME ON" Leremy yelled. Curtus father charged are Leremy screaming like a madman. He drew back his right arm with murderous intent. He intended to end the fight with that one punch. As he began to throw the punch Leremy lifted his right hand and drew a wall of smoke up from the ground. That wall of smoke didn't deter him as he planned to punch straight through it and put a hole in Leremy's chest. His fist made contact with the wall and pierced it with relative ease.

Curtus couldn't help but get fired up. "There we go dad" Curtus yelled out. Curtus was thinking that this man did all that trash talking and turned out to be no threat at all. Curtus began to laugh at how worried he had been. "They got this" Curtus said. Then Curtus notice something that was unsettling. He zoomed in on some of the soldiers that were in the background. They didn't look like they just watch their leader get killed right in front of them. They were smiling and even some were laughing like they had been there before. Then Curtus looked at his father and noticed what was going on.

When he went to punch Leremy he had jumped in the air to get the added boost from the gravity. When he punched through the cloud of smoke he was still on the way down, but even after the Leremy seeming demise he still hadn't reached the ground. Curtus looked at his father's and could see his arm had gotten stuck in the wall of smoke. Then Leremy suddenly appeared in behind him out of a cloud of smoke. "You almost had me there, old timer" Leremy said. Without hesitation Curtus's father chopped at Leremy's neck with his free hand, and just like last time a wall of smoke came from the ground and grabbed his arm mid chop. Leremy disappeared for a split second before reappearing in front of Curtus's father. "Damn you have gotten rusty in your old age haven't you" Leremy said popping his knuckles.

Keeping his menacing smile, he let loose a ferocious barrage of punches into Curtus's father abdomen. With both of his arm restrained he had no way to defend himself from Leremy's onslaught. "Come on old man you wanted a fight now put up a fight." He yelled as he continued hammering away at his midsection. "STOP" Curtus's Mother cried out. "Not a chance Carolyn. Kirkland picked this fight, now Kirkland is about to get this ass whoopin" Leremy panted. He continued beating on Kirkland until he was passed out from the pain. Once he was unconscious the smoke dissipated and Leremy returned to normal. Curtus's mother crawled over to his father and held his unconscious body. "You're a monster!!!" She yelled. Leremy disregarded the comment. "Load them up. Father will be pleased with tonight's catch" Leremy said walking out of the door. "Sir there are reports that there was a kid in the house with them." One of the soldiers yelled. "We are only here for these two I can give two shits about that kid. Load them up and blow the house sky high." Leremy said as he exited the house. Curtus shot to his feet, and ran to the door in an effort to escape. When he got to the door he realized he there was no way to open it. There was no knob to turn or keypad to unlock the door. He was trapped in the bunker with no way out.

Curtus was in full panic mode as the soldiers began to line the house with C4. "Where am I gonna go" He thought to himself. He ran around the room looking for any type of exit. He opened every drawer ripping papers out and skimming them for answers. All while the soldiers were steadily bringing in more and more C4 into the house. He began pulling books off the shelves hoping there was a switch that opened a secret door. "How are they gonna lock me in here and not tell me how to get out of here" Curtus said to himself. While he was ripping books off the shelf a folded piece of paper flew out from in-between two books. Curtus opened the piece of paper to find it was a map of the Jefferson with several different routes highlighted. They all started at the house and ended at the Market District. "Finally something I can use" He said to himself. At the bottom of the map the was another folded piece of paper taped to it. Curtus unfolded it and saw it was a letter from his dad. Hoping that it would give him answers he began to read it.

Curt,

If you are reading this, they are probably wiring the house with explosives and paying off our neighbors to say that we never existed. What you need to do is wait out the explosion. The room will shake but don't worry it is blast proof so you will be okay. After the fire dies down make your way to the

Market District and find Juice. You can get out through the door behind the Tv. It will automatically out once it is dark outside. It is imperative that you do this as fast as you can. I suggest you go to Lincoln Lake and steal a boat to get across or you could take the sewers and exit through the waste treatment plant on the other side. However, you choose to get there do so discreetly. The Family has eyes everywhere and once they figure out you are alive they will be hunting you. Be safe out there

P.S. Remember The Last Train Departs at Midnight

Curtus folded the letter up and put it in his pocket and ran back to the monitors. Knowing that the room was blast proof eased his panic for the moment. He looked on the monitors to see the last of the soldiers running out of the house. "This is it" Curtus said to himself gearing up for the explosion. He changed the camera to the view outside. He saw two soldiers pulling his dad by his arms letting his feet drag on the ground with his mother handcuffed around her hands and ankles walking beside them. They chucked his father into the back of one of the vans like he was a 50lbs bag of rice. They were about to load his mother when Leremy stopped them. "NO… Turn her around I want her to watch" He yelled. They turned her around to face the house. "You left me in that hole to rot where I felt nothing but pain and despair and now it is time for you to feel that same." He said. One of the soldiers ran to Leremy and handed him a remote. "It's all ready for you sir. All you have to do is hit the button." The soldier said. "Splendid" Leremy said snatching the remote from the solider. "Now we can get this firework show on the road" he added. He turned and looked at his mother. "Do you have any final words for that son of yours Carolyn" Leremy said. She looked in the camera. "Curt I know I will see you again so I won't cry. This is not goodbye it is see you soon" She yelled. "Odd choice of last words" Leremy said as he pressed the button.

After he hit the button the feed suddenly cut off and the room began to rumble. Curtus could tell that the soldiers did a poor job wiring the explosives because instead of one large explosion like they wanted it was several small explosions and Curtus felt every last one of them. There were roughly 17 explosions that violently shook the bunker for about 10 seconds each. Once the explosions stopped Curtus began clicking through the feeds to see if any of the cameras survived the blasts. One by one Curtus panned through the cameras trying to find one with a live feed. He kept going through the cameras until he finally found a camera with a live feed. It was a camera that was in what was left of the kitchen and to Curtus's fortune it was facing toward the front of the house. He could see Leremy going ballistic on the soldiers that wired the house. Then suddenly Leremy shot a cloud of smoke over all of their faces and lifted them into the air. Curtus watched in horror as Leremy held 12 soldiers in the air until the suffocated. One by one each of the soldiers fell limp after they were struggled for their lives. "Get these bodies cleaned up" Leremy yelled as he dropped the bodied and walked towards one of the vans.

As he began to step into the front of the van Leremy caught a glimpse of the camera Curtus was looking through. Then a cloud of smoke came barreling toward the camera. Once the cloud was in the kitchen Leremy seemed to just walk out of it. He picked up the camera and looked directly at the lens. "Huh the light is still on. It must still live" Leremy said in a dishearten tone. He let out a large sigh before continuing. "Curtus is it? I know you are watching this. Those idiots didn't wire the damn bombs properly so you probably survived. I want you to know one thing. This is going to end one of three ways. You killing me, me killing you, or you killing yourself. I am going to hunt you down because you have seen too much and are a threat to the very existence of life on the Jefferson. And don't worry we will deal with all your friends. It will be like you never existed. I hope you make this a fun chase" Leremy said. Curtus noticed a change in Leremy's voice. It was deeper and more raspythan before. It was as if another person was talking from the same body. After he gave his speech he dropped the camera on the ground and stomped on it ending the feed.

Curtus sat down on the couch that was in front of the tv. The only thing he could do now was wait for the door behind the tv to open. He pulled out his phone to check the time. "6:45... it'll be dark in about 30 minutes" Curtus said to himself. He was going to utilize this time to plan the perfect route to the Market District. He could tell the routes on the map he found were out of date because the map was 15 years old. It didn't account for all the new construction that had taken place on the Jefferson. "None of these route are gonna work" Curtus thought to himself. "There is no way I can make it to Lincoln Lake without one of the security cameras catching me. I have to go through the sewers" he concluded.

Curtus dreaded the thought of going down in the sewers. There were several rumors going around that the people who went down in the sewers would never come back and those that did told stories about a race of cannibals that inhabited the sewers. Another rumor is that there was a beast that roamed the sewer. It is said to be roughly nine feet tall and about 450lbs and killed all that entered the sewer. As much as he didn't want to go down there he knew that the only shot he had to get to the Market District.

As he was getting his mind right, Curtus looked down at the clothes he was wearing. He was still wearing the slacks and button down shirt he wore to school that day. "If I'm going to be running from a super powered psychotic mercenary and his army I'm gonna be comfortable doing it" Curtus said to himself. Curtus walked to a dresser to the right of the tv. He opened the top and found one of his father's hoodies from college. It was all grey and read "Class of 2205" across a big letter U across the chest. "this will do" Curtus said unbuttoning his shirts. He took the shirt off and put the hoodie on. The fibers had gotten stiff with age as they scratched against his chest and shoulders. "Ok now time for some pants." Curtus said opening the next drawer. He wasn't as lucky as the next drawer was full of assorted underwear and socks. There was something about seeing his parent's underwear and socks mixed together that made Curtus uncomfortable. He closed the drawer and prayed that the third and final drawer had a pair of pants in it. Curtus opened drawer number three and saw that his prayers were answered because in drawer number three sat a pair of black sweatpants.

He jumped out of his slacks and in to the sweatpants. Just like the hoodies the fibers from the old sweatpants scratched his legs as he put them on. He didn't need a change of shoes because he wore sneakers everywhere. Any social setting no matter what the dress code was Curtus would wear sneakers. Curtus tightened his sneakers up, put his phone in his pocket and was ready to head for the sewer. "Well I'm ready" he said as he stared at the tv waiting for it to open. After five minutes of staring at the tv Curtus let out a loud groan. "This is taking forever" he yelled out falling on the couch. He pulled out his phone. "7:10" it read. "Five more minutes" he thought to himself. Curtus started to become nervous. Even though he was trapped in this bunker he knew he was safe. He knew no one could get in. No one could harm him in here. Once he left the bunker he knew everyone from this mysterious organization would be after him. That is what made Curtus uneasy. He didn't have the slightest clue who or what was chasing him. Their uniforms are unlike anything he had seen before. The government uniforms were white and the had "USAC" embroidered on the front. These uniforms were all black with no distinguishing marking on them. Though he didn't know who they were Curtus knew not to underestimate them. From the super powered mercenary heading the operation to the government grade explosives used to blow up his house Curtus knew he had to be on his toes at all times.

Suddenly Curtus heard a loud "clunk" coming from behind one of the walls. Curtus nearly jumped out of his skin in fear. He immediately thought that Leremy had come to finish what he started. Then the was a second "Clunk" and the door behind the tv slowly opened. Curtus slapped himself in the side of the head. "Get it together Curtus. You can't be scared of a door" he muttered to himself. He opened the door to reveal a ladder in the other side. Curtus took a deep breath and began up the ladder. Half way up the ladder Curtus realized he had forgotten something important. He slid down the ladder and ran back to his slacks. He reached into the pocket and pulled out the letter his father had written him. "Okay now I can go" Curtus said to himself before heading back up the ladder

II

Curtus climbed until he reached a hatch at the top of the shaft. He pushed it open and found himself in the toolshed in his backyard. He opened the shed door and looked out to make sure the coast was clear. Once he felt it was safe he opened the door and stepped out of the shed. Curtus always wondered what that shed was for because his family had it for as long as he could remember but they never once went in it. Curtus turned and looked at the remains of his house. The unsynchronized explosions left parts of the houses framework still standing. As much as he wanted to stay and reminisce about the good times he had Curtus had to get moving because they were most likely sending a patrol to find him. He took his last looks at what was left of the house he grew up in before making his way toward the sewers.

Curtus made his way through his neighbor's backyards in order to avoid being caught on the street cameras. As he made his way through the yards he could hear the sounds of the soldiers terrorizing his neighbors ensuring that they would not talk about what they may or may not have seen earlier today. Sounds of breaking glass and people begging for them to stop echoed through the neighborhood. "Keep moving" Curtus whispered to himself. Curtus was making his way to the Sewer Maintenance access that was located at the end of the street. That is where all the junkies and kids went to enter the sewers. Curtus maneuvered through five backyards before he reached the house on the corner across the street from the sewer access. "Okay so far so good." He whispered to himself. After he said that three armored vans pulled up in front of the sewer access. "Perfect" Curtus said sinking deep in the bush he was hiding in. Soldiers came pouring out of the vans wearing the same uniforms as the ones that took his parents. They lined up in three rows of 10 facing the vans. Then from the front of the second van Leremy came walking out.

A chill ran down Curtus's spine. How was he going to get past this army to get to the sewers now? "Why him... why now?" Curtus thought to himself. He watched as Leremy paced in front of the soldiers barking out orders. Curtus noticed something different about Leremy. Something had changed in his personality since he stomped on the camera. When he was capturing his parents it seemed that he was having fun with it. He was like the Joker from the Batman comics in that he was getting a pure thrill from the chaos he was creating. Now all that joy was gone. He seemed cold and evil. When he was yelling at his men it seemed like he was trying to put a hole their chests with his words. "Look here. Right now we are on the hunt for this little bastard that goes by the name of Curtus Parker. Father says to bring him back alive but if I find the little shit I'm putting a hot one in his ear." Leremy barked. Curtus stomach dropped into his knees. Leremy was talking with so much anger and passion that Curtus knew he was good as dead if he got caught. "He has unofficially been missing for three hours which means he could be anywhere in this neighborhood by now and I want you to search every inch of it until you find him." He barked.

Once he finished he turned his back to the soldiers and Curtus. Curtus knew that if he was going to make a move now was the time to do it. He knew he wouldn't be able to make it all the way across the street without being spotted. He had to come up with a new plan before the army went on their search. Then Curtus noticed a storm drain on his side of the road. He had no idea where it would drop him off in the sewer but he would at least be in the sewer. He began to creep quietly through the grass until he reached the grate. He gripped it and pulled with all his strength. The grate was lighter than he anticipated and flew up and out of his hands towards the streets. Without hesitation Curtus covered his nose and jumped feet first into the storm drain.

Curtus landed in a rapid current of treated cloud water. The current was so strong Curtus seemed to be floating on top of it. Curtus rode the flow until it dropped into another drain and threw Curtus off. He tumbled down a hallway before coming to a stop. "Huh, that was kinda fun" He said brushing himself off. Just as he said that the metal sewer grate hitting the metal street echoed throughout the entire sewer. "What was that" one of the soldiers on the surface said. "It was that storm drain you idiots HE'S IN THE SEWER! GO AFTER HIM" Leremy yelled. "What about you boss?" one of the soldiers said. "I have to report to Father on other matters. You guys should be able to handle one kid" Leremy said. Knowing that Leremy wasn't leading the chase him made Curtus feel a little better, but that sense of comfort quickly disappeared at the sounds of boot echoing through the sewers. "Ok no big deal. Just got to avoid 30 mercenaries armed with automatic weapons while I run through a maze with no map." he whispered to himself. Then to add insult to injury his phone began to ring. His phone may have only been on medium volume, but in the sewers it whaled like a church choir on an Easter Sunday. Curtus quickly hung up the call and threw the phone in one direction and sprinted in the other. He needed to find a map of some sort. He couldn't keep running around blind in the labyrinth or he would get caught for sure. He needed to make his way to a sewer access junction and gain access to one of the offices. There he could find a map of the tunnels and find the quickest way out.

Curtus continued to sprint blindly through the system of tunnels trying to find a junction. He had been running so long that he caught a cramp in his side. If he kept running like this, he would end up pulling something and he would be in real trouble. "I need to take a minute to regroup" He thought to himself. Curtus found an out cove where he could stop and rest. "How hard is it to find a junction I see them on literally every street corner on the surface" Curtus wheezed. "Well that is 'cause they aren't all for sewer maintenance" A voice said. Curtus jumped to his feet. His heart was racing. He thought that one of Leremy's henchman had found him. "Woah slow down there. I'm not one of those armored idiots down here looking for you" the voice said. There was something about the voice that was different from the voices of the soldiers. Even though he didn't see the he couldn't see all the soldiers faces he could tell by their build that they were all men. This voice belonged to a woman. "Who goes there?" Curtus asked. "Who goes there? Who are you John W. Campbell." The voice answered. As the voice replied a woman walked into Curtus's line of sight.

She was one of the most beautiful women that Curtus had ever seen. She had light brown skin with black hair that was bone straight. She was wearing tight blue jeans and a black Henley shirt. "Who is John W. Campbell?" Curtus asked. "John W. Campbell the author of Who Goes There. You don't know who that is" The woman asked. "No" Curtus replied. The woman looked at Curtus's hoodie. "You must be one of those smart dumbasses huh. You one of those that go to University and gets good grades but don't really know shit" The woman asked. Curtus was so confused and made it visually apparent by tilting his head. "I can tell from that confused ass look on your face that you are one of em" she said with a smile. "Ummm who are you" Curtus asked. "Oh I'm sorry let me introduce myself. The name is Glade, Glade Stanford." She replied. "Curtus. My name is Curtus Parker" Curtus said reaching his hand out. "Curtus the smart dumbass. You look lost." She said shaking his hand. "What gave it away" Curtus said grabbing his pants. "Well I watched you run in a giant circle twice. I thought it was common knowledge that four lefts equal a circle." Glade said chuckling. "Well the people chasing me are making it hard to think properly" Curtus replied.

"Where are you headed Dumbass" Glade said with a smile. Normally Curtus would get angry at someone calling him outside of his name but there was something about the way Glade said it the came off as fun. "The Market District" he replied. "Why do you want to go to a dump like that" she asked. "I am meeting someone there" Curtus replied. "Well if you take the sewers it will take you roughly 13 hours to get there and that is without having to avoid the maniacs with guns." Glade said.

"13 HOURS!!!" Curtus yelled. Glade quickly jumped and put her hand over his mouth. "Are you trying to get caught" she whispered. "Hey did you hear that" a voice said. "Yeah I think it came from down this way" another voice replied. "Come on Dumbass you got to have a little bit of situational awareness." Glade whispered digging in her pockets. The sound of footsteps grew louder. "What are we going to do" Curtus asked. "Lay down on the ground" Glade replied. Curtus looked down at the sewer floor. He had been so focused on not being caught that he forgotten that he was in the sewer. The floor was covered in a mixture of different human waste. "I can't" Curtus said. "What do you mean you can't" Glade whispered. "the ground is covered in…" Curtus began. "Shit, I know" Glade interrupted. "I can't lay down. There has to be another way" Curtus said. "Okay… put you hood over your head." Glade said. Curtus hesitated before putting the hood over his head.

Then Glade shoved Curtus. It wasn't a hard enough shove that would put Curtus on his back, but the feces on the ground caused Curtus to slide on the floor. Then Glade grabbed him by his collar and yanked him to the ground. This happened so fast that he couldn't brace himself for the fall and prevent his face from slamming into the metal floor. His head from slamming into the ground covering his face along with the most of his body in feces. "What the hell was that for" Curtus whispered. "It looked like you needed a bit of motivation and I took it upon myself to provide said motivation" Glade whispered. The footsteps were growing louder. "Okay now that you are already down there you need to go limp like a dead guy" Glade said. She dug around in her jean pocket and pulled out a Tonic pump. Curtus then realized what her plan was. She was planning to make them look like a couple of Tonic fiends that overdosed. Curtus then went into full starfish mode spreading out his arms and legs before letting them go limp. Glade sat on top of Curtus with her back against the wall. She let her arms dangle and gave a blanks stare.

The footsteps belonged to two soldiers. Curtus was facing the wall so he couldn't see what was going on. "It is just a bunch of junkies" One of the soldiers said. "You think they have seen the kid" the other soldier asked. "No way, look at them" the first soldier said poking Glade's face with the barrel of his rifle. "They are half dead already. They couldn't find their right hand if you slapped them with it" The soldier finished. "Yeah you're right. Let's keep looking" the other soldier replied. The two soldiers continued down the hallway making a right at the first intersection. "Alright Dumbass the coast is clear" Glade whispered as she standing to her feet. Curtus rose to one knee before he stood to his feet. Glade looked at Curtus and began to chuckle under her breath. "Okay laugh it up. Since you know your way around here can you take me to a place where I can get this off of my face?" Curtus asked. "Okay follow me" Glade said.

Curtus walked through the hallway extremely slow with a slight crouch. He looked around to make sure nobody got the drop on him. Glade on the other hand was walking like she was going to the store. She looked back at Curtus who was about 15 feet behind her. "What the hell are you doing" She asked. "I'm sneaking around. You walking around like that is gonna get us caught" He whispered. "No you walking like that will get yourself caught. You look like someone who is being chased." She replied. Curtus stopped and thought about how he looked walking like Sam Fisher in Splinter Cell. "Stand up. They are looking for an uptight preppy University going kid not a junkie that is literally covered head to toe in shit" She added. "Curtus looked down to see that his hoodie and sweatpants was covered in human feces. "Yeah can you take me to where I can wash this off" Curtus asked. "Don't worry we are almost there" She said smiling.

They continued down the hall and made a right and came upon a random showerhead. "This is for when people who came to clean up clogs came to clean their suits when they got dirty" Glade said. Curtus ran over to the shower and turned it on. The high water pressure of the water lifted the poop right off of his face and clothes. He stayed under the warm water until Glade cut the water off. "We don't have time for a princess shower. Now come with me" Glade said. Curtus followed her down the same hall to an air duct. "Here you can dry your clothes off. You'll catch cold walking around in wet clothes" She said. Curtus stepped over the duct and hot air shot up around and through his pants. The air was blowing so fast that he could feel the water lifting out of his skin. "Okay princess your clothes should be dry" Glade said pulling Curtus from over the vent. Curtus looked down to see that all of the poop was gonna from his clothes. "This won't get the smell out but hey at least you aren't walking around covered in shit" Glade said. Curtus took a sniff of his hoodie only to be met with the smell of dirty diaper. Then something hit Curtus as he was walking off the air duct. Why did she have a Tonic pump in the first place. "Hey Glade why did you have that Tonic pump?" Curtus asked. "Now is not the time. Let's get a move on" She quickly replied.

Curtus, having never been the sewer before took the time look around take in the sights. Curtus expected the sewers to be a poorly lit dungeon, but in fact the sewers were actually well lit. They looked more like a high school hallway rather than a sewer except the floors were covered in different bodily fluids and garbage. Avoiding two more patrols they continued through the sewers until they reached a fork in the road. "Okay we make a right here" Glade whispered. "HEY THEY ARE OVER HERE" a voice yelled. Curtus turned around and saw one of the soldiers reaching for his radio. "Come on Dumbass lets go" Glade yelled pulling his arm. The lights in the sewer changed from white to red and an alarm began wailing throughout the sewer. The alarm was a deep low torn similar to that of a fog horn. It was so loud the halls began to shake. "This way" Glade yelled making a sharp left turn. Curtus turned down the hall to see Glade waiting at a door.

Curtus read a sign on the door that said "Furnace maintenance". "Is this where we have to go' Curtus said. "yes but…" Glade began. "Then what are we waiting on let's go" Curtus said reaching for the doorknob. "No no no wait" Glade yelled, but it was too late. Curtus grabbed the doorknob which was electrified due to the lockdown. A sharp pain shot up Curtus's arm and through the rest of his body. He yelled out in agony as he let go of the doorknob. "I told your dumbass to wait" Glade said shaking her head. Curtus dropped to his knees grabbing his right wrist. "Yeah during a lockdown all the doorknobs become electrified." Glade added walking toward the door. Curtus was in so much pain his vision became distorted. His vison went through all the colors in the spectrum. Red… Blue… Green, the colors kept changing and the everything began to move in a wavy pattern. He looked up at Glade to see how she was going to get the door open. He saw her reach in her pocket and pull out a pocketknife. She opened the knife and sliced her hand open across her palm. Curtus couldn't believe what he was seeing. He wanted to ask why but he was in so much pain he couldn't speak. He watched as Glade held her hand over and let her blood drip on the knob. The alarm continued to echo through the sewer. Unable to move and, with the alarm screaming Curtus felt helpless and thought that this would be the end. That is until a miracle happened.

Suddenly the knob began to smoke and erode. It was as if her blood was made of acid. The knob continued to erode until it fell off the door. Glade then reached out with her other hand and pulled the door open. "There that is how you open the door during a lockdown" She said with a smile. As the pain began to subside Curtus slowly rose to his feet. "How did you do that" Curtus began. "No time now get down the stairs" She yelled pulling Curtus by his collar. Curtus looked at Glade's hand to see that it was healing at an accelerated rate. One minute her hand it was dripping blood and now it had already healed. "How can you do that" Curtus asked. "It is from a Beast Tonic" Glade replied. That answered the question that was lingering in the back of his mind. He was wondering why she was invisible when they first met, but the fact that she was a Beast Tonic user made complete sense.

In the world of Tonics, the main Tonic that everyone uses is the crystal form where people put it in a pipe and smoke or they can get the pump version that is more concentrated. There is also a rumored Tonic that gives people the abilities of certain animals. These are known as Beast Tonics. Though there has never been a confirmed sighting of a person who has taken a Beast Tonic many stories and tall tales have been made up keeping the myth alive.

Curtus and Glade made their way to the bottom of the stairs and into an office hallway. The hallway resembled more of the inside of a conventional building as the floor changed from metal to a navy carpet. The walls changed from cold steel to drywall coated in beige paint. "Where to next" Curtus asked. "We have to make our way to the other side of the furnace" Glade replied. "Okay how do we get there" Curtus inquired. "Well we can either run around the halls for hours with those idiots chasing us or we can run in the furnace for about 20 minutes with those idiots chasing us" Glade proposed. The alarm in the sewer suddenly stopped which meant the soldiers couldn't be far behind. "Yeah let's go through the furnace" Curtus replied. Glade nodded her head. "Ok, but before we go to the furnace we have to grab something first"

III

Glade led Curtus through a maze of hallways. She seemed to be turning into hallways at random and Curtus was having trouble keeping up. She led him to a large steel door with a large window that spanned the width of the door. Looking through the window Curtus could see that door led to an airlock. "Ok before we can run through to the furnace you need to get your hands on a heat suit" Glade said. "Why do I only need a heat suit" Curtus asked. "All questions will be answered when there is not a chance for me to get shot in my ass" Glade replied. Curtus let out a big sigh. "So where do we get one of these heat suit" He asked. "I honestly don't know" She replied with a smile. Curtus jaw dropped to the floor. Glade's confidence made it seem like she had everything planned out. Learning that she had no plan at all made his stomach dropped to his ankles. "When you said get your hands on a heat suit I thought you knew where one was" Curtus said trying to keep his composure. "I never needed one" She said with a laugh. Footsteps and yelling could be heard coming from down the hall. "Well from the sound of that we better get moving" Glade said.

They began opening every door they could see if they could find a suit. None of the doors were labeled so they had no idea what was waiting on the other side. Curtus opened doors at random until he found a supply closet and saw what looked an Old World space suit. "Hey is this what we are looking for." Curtus asked. Glade walked over behind him and peered over his shoulder. "Bingo" she whispered in his ear. "Hey let's check over here" A voice yelled out. "Shit we gotta hide" Glade whispered as she pushed Curtus into the supply closet and shut the door behind her. She pulled the door shut and put a broom though the handle to lock it in place. Curtus looked around the supply closet in search of a good hiding spot. He knew the broom wouldn't stop them from getting in but it should buy him enough time to get out of sight when it happened. "What are you waiting on. Get in the locker Dumbass" Glade whisper. The locker wasn't very wide but it was about 12 feet tall. Curtus opened the storage locker jumped in.

Curtus jumped in and pressed his back against the back of the locker. "No way you get to turn around" Glade said. "What do you mean turn around" Curtus asked. "I mean the way that you are facing now except do the opposite" She spat back. "I understand that but why" He asked. "Because I don't want you dirty dick touching me" She replied. "Dirty?" Curtus asked. "Yes dirty. Remember about 10 minutes ago you were covered in shit. Now will you turn your ass around"

She pleaded. Curtus shook his head and fulfilled Glade's request. "I think I heard something in here." A voice from outside yelled. Glade quickly jumped into the locker and slowly closed the door behind her. Curtus could hear the patrol struggling to get in due to the broom giving Glade plenty of time to close the locker door without making a sound. "Its locked you idiot." Another yelled out. Suddenly they heard the cocking of a gun and a flurry of bullets that flew through the door. Between 85-90 rounds that were fired into the supply closet. "Well now if anyone is in there they are locked in there full of bullets" A voice replied. The group of soldiers laughed at the remark as they walked away from the closet. Glade slowly opened the locker and stepped out. The closet was in shambles. There was food, office supplies, and bullets all over the floor. The door was riddled with bullet holes and there was a slight haze left from the bullet piercing the wooden door. Curtus jumped out of the locker reaching he arms to the ceiling in an effort to stretch. "Alright Dumbass. Time to get in the suit" Glade said

Curtus unzipped the back of the heat suit and stepped inside. He wasn't sure how he was going to be able to move in it. The suit was bulky and heavy that the only movement he could really do is waddle forward. "How am I supposed to run in this thing. I can barely move in it" Curtus asked. "The suit has its own skeleton inside that moves with you." Glade explained. Curtus looked at Glade in amazement. Curtus had never heard of technology like this except for in movies. "So it is like an exo suit" He said with a massive grin. "That's exactly what it is." Glade said zipping up the back of the suit. "Ok once I put the helmet on you won't be able to hear anything, but once the suit starts up we will be able communicate by radio." Glade explained as she put the helmet on him. She twisted it to the left locking it in place and Curtus found himself in his own personal vacuum. It was so quiet he could faintly hear the blood flowing through his body. He saw Glade talking and laughing hysterically to herself. Curtus could tell she was taking advantage of his deafness to talk as much trash about him as he could. Glade then walked behind him and began pressing buttons on the back of his helmet.

As she began pressing buttons icons started to pop-up on his visor. Things like core body temperature, battery life, and a full layout of the suit were all on display. "Hey Dumbass can you hear me" Glade's voice said through the speakers. Curtus wanted to ask where she got the radio but to avoid being called Dumbass again he just nodded his head. "Okay so it looks like you got version 1.4 so the boot should form to whatever shoe you are wearing." Glade said. After she said that a prompt came on the visor. "Would you like to activate the BootMorph system please say yes or no" A robotic voice asked. "Yes" Glade yelled through the speaker. "Okay… molding" the automated voice replied. Curtus looked over at Glade. "What you were taking too long" She said shrugging her shoulders. It took ten seconds for the molding process to finish and the activation sequence to complete. "Exoskeleton now online. Have a good day at work" The automated voice finished. Curtus took a deep breath and stepped with his right foot. Just like Glade said it would the exoskeleton moved with him making the movement of the suit effortless. "Okay now let's get to an airlock" Glade said

Glade pushed opened what was left of the door and peered her head out. She looked both ways making sure the coast was clear. "Okay let's move" She said before bolting down the hall. As Curtus chased after her he noticed that the suit was very quiet. The hydraulics were silent and Curtus felt light on his feet. Glade began to slow down as she came upon an intersection. She didn't want to just dart across and be spotted by one of the patrols. "Hey you what are you doing here" A voice yelled from behind them. Curtus's blood ran cold as he was able to remember the voice. The voice belonged to one of the soldiers that found him and Glade in the sewer. Not trying to act to suspiciously he turned around to confront the soldier. "What are you doing here I thought everyone was on strike?" the soldier asked. "Everyone is on strike but we can't have the furnace breaking down on us now can we" Glade replied. "Oh so you guys are like scabs" the soldiers asked. "Well we prefer the term Temps but yeah you could call us scabs" Curtus added. "Hey work is work. You guys carry on" the soldier said before walking off in the other direction. Glade looked at Curtus with a look of approval. "Way to be quick on your feet" she said lightly punching him on the shoulder.

They made their way through hallways until the returned to the airlock door. Glade walked over to a keypad on the wall and punched in a sequence of numbers causing the large door to slowly open. Curtus began to become suspicious of Glade. Not only did she seem to know her way around this office building, but she also knew a lot about the heat suit. "Hey Glade you seem to know a lot about these heat suits." Curtus said. "What makes you say that" She said walking into the airlock. "Well not only did you know how it works but you could tell what version suit it is just by looking at it." Curtus said as he walking in after her. "Well I guess you caught me" Glade said pulling a lever on the wall closing the door. Curtus became uneasy. He was trapped in a confined space with a woman whose motive are unknown and had the power of a Beast Tonic at her disposal. "Before we head into the furnace you have to tell me what your motives are and how you know so much about these suits." Curtus yelled. "I told you I'll tell you once we aren't getting chased anymore." Glade said. "When we aren't getting chased? They are only chasing me" Curtus said. "Actually she is right. The Family is after you both of you guys" a voice yelled over the radio. Curtus and

Glade turn around and looked in horror as Leremy stared at them through the window with his trademark smile.

"What are the odds of you two teaming up" Leremy asked with a smile. The smile was the same one he had when he abducted Curtus's parents. "What do you want with us" Glade yelled. "Me personally, I don't want you guys. Personally I would kill you both and be done with it, but the Family told me they need you alive" Leremy explained. Curtus noticed that Leremy's mannerisms had changed also since the last time he saw him. On the street he seemed like a murderous gun for hire with no regard for human life. Now he is acting more like he did when he confronted his parents. "The Family will be so pleased when I bring you in." Leremy said. He began to pace back and forth but he kept his eyes fixed on Curtus and Glade. "How did you find us" Curtus asked. "Finding you was completely by circumstance. I came down here because one of my men told me that the infamous Glade Stanford was seen running around in Furnace Maintenance. Her father will be pleased that I found you" He replied. Curtus looked at Glade who turned her focus to the ground. Curtus could tell whatever she was thinking about was horrible because she looked like she was about to be physically sick. "Why would her father be pleased that you found me" Curtus asked nervously. "Oh you don't know who Glades father is, do you Curtus. I mean it would be hard seeing how because she took he mother's last name" Leremy said. A tear ran down Glades face but her expression did not change. "We'll let me inform you my dear Curtus. Her father is Liam Lopez." Leremy said.

Liam Lopez ran the clothing industry on the Jefferson. Every piece of clothing on the Jefferson were from Lopez's company. "Yup her father is one of the richest and most powerful men on the Jefferson and made that heat suit you are wearing Curtus" Leremy said. "HE'S NOT MY FATHER... He made that perfectly clear..." Glade said with tears running down her face. "OH and here is the best part. Her father is the person who told me to go abduct your parents" he said laughing maniacally. Curtus looked over at Glade. She looked at him with a tears running down her face. "Liam thought you might end up with Curtus and gave me one of these" Leremy said reaching into his pocket. He dug around in the pocket of his long trench coat and pulled out a remote. Glade saw the remote and immediately ran behind Curtus trying to get the suit off of him.

Curtus could hear Glade furiously pressing buttons on the back of the helmet. "What is that" Curtus asked. "This little thing. Well I can show you better than I can tell you" Leremy replied. Leremy pressed the button and Curtus felt the exo skeleton lock up on him. The exoskeleton began squeezing tight on his arms, legs, and chest. "Right now you probably feel like your body is being crushed but don't worry you're not gonna die.

The Family needs you alive." Leremy explained. Glade nervously punched buttons until she was able to unlock the helmet. She twisted the helmet and ripped it off of him. As she threw the helmet she noticed Leremy began to walk over to the keypad. Seeing this, Glade quickly ran to the other end of the airlock and pulled the lever to the right of the furnace door. "Ah quick thinking… I like it." Leremy said. The heat from the furnace began to fill the airlock. The hot wind slapped Curtus in the face and he couldn't do anything to protect himself. Glade ran over to Curtus and began opening the suit. "Don't worry I'll get you out of here" She said as she undid the back of the suit. She worked on the back until the exoskeleton unlocked and Curtus fell out. This victory was only to be short lived as he was quickly engulfed by the heat of the furnace. "Don't worry just give your body time to adjust" Glade said in a soothing voice. "I'll give you guys a 30 second head start before I'm coming after your asses" Leremy said taking a seat on the ground with his back against the airlock door. Glade pulled Curtus to his feet. "C'mon Dumbass we got to go" She said running into the furnace.

Running into the furnace, Curtus found it was not as hot as he thought it would be. It was like running through a sauna at the hottest setting. Curtus followed Glade to a cat walk in the wall of the furnace. Curtus looked down through the grates to the gates of hell. The bottom of the furnace glowed a bright red. The furnace itself looked like the inside of a silo. The wall was dotted with holes to let the hot air travel to all parts of the Jefferson. "We need to get to the top of the furnace before you overheat" Glade said running up the stairs. "It's not even that hot in here" Curtus replied. "That is because your body has adjusted to it, but don't be fooled. Your insides are slowly roasting right now and you need to get out of here" Glade replied. Curtus could sense an urgency in her voice. For her to change from her normally sarcastic tone meant that the situation was truly dire. Curtus wiped the sweat off his for head and took a deep breath of the hot humid air before darting up the steps.

During his track days Curtus had ran his fair share of stadium steps, but none of those workouts could have prepared him for this. This was a full sprint up a super-heated set of stairs felt like he was trying to escape hell itself. He took off the hoodie and tied it around his waist in a last ditch effort for some relief. "C'mon you can't stop until we reach the top" Glade said. "We need a new route" Curtus said dropping his hands to his knees. Then the sound gunshots suddenly echoed throughout the furnace. Curtus looked down the stairs and saw the soldiers flooding in from the airlock. Curtus caught his second wind and broke out in a full sprint up the stairs passing Glade almost knocking her off the stairs. "So the sound of bullets will light the fire under that of ass huh" Glade whispered to herself before chasing after Curtus.

They were about a quarter of the way up when Glade caught up to Curtus. Curtus was shocked to see Glade had caught up to him. Through all of his years of school he had been the fastest person never losing a race in his life. "You look surprised" Glade said. "Yeah I didn't expect you to be this fast" Curtus replied. "Well I guess you never ran with someone who was actually fast." She replied arrogantly. The stair case ended at the halfway point of the furnace where it plateaued to a catwalk. In the middle of that catwalk was another set of stairs that would take them the rest of the way up. "We are almost halfway up" Curtus yelled. "I see that, but do you see that" Glade yelled pointing to the far side of the catwalk. Curtus looked over to see soldiers filing in. "What are we gonna do" Curtus asked. "I honestly don't know. I completely forgot about the other airlocks," Glade replied. Curtus looked at the wall and saw the pipes they were running by were large enough to for a person to fit in. "Glade this way" Curtus said as he jumped over the guard rail and into a pipe 15 feet below. Glade cracked a smile and shook her head before jumping down.

Glade caught up to Curtus who stopped about 100 yards into the pipe to put his hoodie back on. "That was some quick thinking back there Dumbass" She said punching him lightly in the shoulder again. "Well we are going to need more of it because we have no idea where we are going" Curtus said putting the finishing touches on his hoodie. "Hey why are you putting that back on. We aren't on the surface yet" She asked. "I know I thought that too but as I ran down the pipe it became cool" Curtus replied. "That's really weird because we are nowhere near the surface" She said. Glade reached into her pocket a pulled out a small flashlight. "The sewers may have lights, but I'm pretty sure these pipes don't" She said turning the flashlight on. Curtus and Glade looked at each other before making their way deeper into the pipe.

As they continued down the pipe down Curtus began to notice things weren't right. The deeper they went the more it felt like the surface. The air was going from burning hot to a tolerable room temperature. The air in the pipe also began to reek of decomposing flesh. "Hey do you smell that?" Curtus asked. "Mhmm" Glade replied putting her shirt over her nose. "What do you think it is" Curtus asked. "I want to say it sewage, but I know that smell" she said. "What are you trying to say" Curtus inquired. "I'm saying those stories about that race of cannibals that live in the sewer might actually have some merit" She replied. Curtus looked down and noticed that the water had change color from clear to a light red. Curtus's stomach dropped to the floor. He thought he got them out of trouble but in actuality he may have led them into something much.

As they walked Glade suddenly dropped to all fours. "Are you okay" Curtus asked running to her side. "Yeah, yeah I just slipped on something." She replied. Curtus picked up the flashlight and looked around to see what Glade slipped on. After a quick search Curtus looked on in horror upon his discovery. Glade had slipped on a severed human hand with the pinky, ring finger, and thumb missing. Upon closer examination it looked like the finger had been bitten off by and animal of some kind. "What's wrong" Glade asked. Curtus didn't say a word as he silently pointed at the hand. Glade gagged upon the sight of the mangled appendage. "Yeah. Cannibal tribe is definitely in play." She said putting her shirt back over her nose. "So what are we going to go up against. Mercenaries with guns or cannibals who probably don't have guns but have a taste for human flesh" Curtus asked. Glade thought about it for a second before walking deeper in the pipe.

As they walked the pipe the smell of dead body became stronger and stronger. "You ready Dumbass" Glade asked. Curtus couldn't hear Glade. Her voice was muffled from her hand being over her nose and mouth. Her question came out as a series of hums and grunt. Curtus just nodded his head and kept walking until the pipe suddenly went vertical 90 degrees towards the surface. Curtus looked up and to his surprise did not see the sky. "This pipe doesn't lead to the surface" Curtus said. "Well then let's just see where it leads. Hop on my back." Glade commanded. Curtus looked

Glade up and down. She was about 5 inches shorter than him about around 100lbs lighter. "Are you sure you can hold me up" Curtus asked. "I already proved I'm faster than you, now I'm gonna show you I'm stronger than you. Hop on my back Dumbass" She said. With her tone becoming more hostile and with no other option Curtus hopped onto her back. Glade stumbled around trying to balance Curtus's weight. "Shit Dumbass, when I said hop on my back I didn't mean to literally hop" she strained through her teeth. Once she gained control of Curtus's weight she took a deep breath and walked over to the back wall.

Under normal circumstance what happened next would leave a normal person in awe, but when Glade began to climb the pipe wall Curtus wasn't the slightest bit phased. He saw her be invisible, melt a doorknob right off the door, and a gash heal on her hand in a matter of minutes. Everything from here on out was in the realm of possibility. "Bet you didn't see this coming now did you" Glade said. "Eh I've seen cooler" Curtus lied. The top of the pipe was cover with metal grate with nine rectangular holes in it. "Can you see where we are going" Glade asked. "No I can't see anything" Curtus replied. At that moment three shadowy figures ran over the top of the grate. The figures didn't run like a normal human. It ran on all fours like a dog. They made a kind of hissing sound as they ran. "What was that" Glade asked. "I don't know but whatever it is, it doesn't sound friendly" Curtus replied.

IV

Glade climbed until they reached the grate at the top of the pipe. Once they reach the grate Curtus noticed that it was stained a deep red. "You sure you still want to do this" Curtus asked nervously. "No I just climbed all the way up here for shits and giggles. Open the damn grate" Glade commanded. Curtus shook his head and grabbed onto the grate. Once he grabbed it he noticed that it wasn't stained but coated in something he was all too familiar with. Curtus could tell by the crusty texture that the grate was coated in dried blood. This sent chills down his spine. "What are you hourly? Hurry the hell up and open the goddamn grate. You're actually kinda heavy" Glade said. Curtus tightened his grip and pushed straight up with all of his might.

The grate was heavier than Curtus anticipated. He was only able to move it couple inches at a time. As he pushed the grate the crusted blood sprinkled down onto him and Glade like a gentle drizzle. "I hope that's not what I think it is" Glade said shaking it out of her hair. Curtus felt he needed to tell her what it was, but to avoid conflict he decided not to. After three good pushes there was enough room for him and Glade to fit through. Glade climbed out of the pipe and dumped Curtus off her back. She walked two steps before laying on the ground like a dead starfish. "Thank God. I was getting claustrophobic in there" Glade said making an imaginary snow angel. Curtus was ready to take a break but he remembered the shadowy figures that jumped over the grate earlier. "Glade this isn't a time to play around" Curtus said standing to his feet. "I just carried your heavy ass 150 feet straight up. I think that warrants a break." Glade replied. "You go ahead and take your break. You'll end up like those guys over there" Curtus said pointing at a pile of bones. Glade looked at the pile of remains and immediately jumped to her feet. "You know what, you have a sound argument there Dumbass" Glade said dusting herself off. "Thanks. Now let's find out where the hell we are" Curtus said.

They walked down an alleyway until they reached a road in a shantytown. Makeshift buildings made of different scraps of metal and wood lined both sides of the street. The town looked like a scene out of a horror movie. The streets were stained a dark red. The ground crunched with every step as if they were walking on snow. It was so quiet in the town Curtus could hear Glade's heartbeat. Curtis looked up and saw they were still below the surface. "So where are we" Glade asked. "It looks like we are in some sort of pocket where hot and cold air meet" Curtus began. "and from the looks of it people have made a settlement down here." He finished. "Well we got to find a way out of here. It's stupid creepy down here" Glade replied.

As they walked Curtus looked into some of the buildings. Contrary to its rundown primal appearance it seems that the people who were living here managed to have electricity and running water. The current state that the city it looked as if the people who originally lived here left in a hurry. Lights were left on and water was left running in many of the buildings. "Hey Dumbass look at that" Glade said pointing at a pile of rotten flesh. "Why on earth would I want to look at that" Curtus asked turning his head. "It's not about what you see but what you smell" She replied. Curtus took a deep breath and to his surprise he didn't smell anything. Even when he got closer he still didn't smell anything. "You can't smell anything either right" Glade asked. "Yeah" Curtus replied nervously. "Also look up" she said. Curtus looked up to see the same ceiling that he had seen earlier. "I don't see the issue" Curtus answered. "Look at the lights" She said. Curtus looked at the light but they were so bright that he had to look away. "Damn they are bright" he replied. "Exactly. Those are government issued fog lights. The question is why the hell are they hooked up down here." She inquired.

Curtus had only seen those lights in front of government building when someone important was about to speak. They are so delicate and expensive that the government will shut down entire roadways just to transport them safely. Now the question on Curtus's mind was how did such a prized piece of government equipment end up above a shantytown in the middle of the sewer. Glade frantically surveyed the landscape. "Dumbass, I got a bad feeling about this place." She finished looking down the street. "Well we aren't getting any closer to the exit standing here" Curtus replied before continuing down the street.

The deeper they walked into the shantytown the more ominous things became. The deafening silence was now being broken by low animalistic grunts and the sounds of pieces of metal being knocked over. It was very apparent that they were being watched but every time they would look to see what may be following them there was nothing. "Hey Dumbass you know how to fight" Glade whispered. "Yes I can defend myself" Curtus replied half way offended. "This is not the time for us to get our feelings hurt. I'm asking because there is a pretty good chance we are going to fight something in here" She whispered back. "Well I am proficient in Bōjutsu and Krav Maga" he whispered. "Well let's hope either of those are useful if we get into a fight" she replied.

Curtus began looking around on the ground for something he could defend himself with. After a short search he found a pipe that was stuck in a pile of scrap metal. Curtus walked over and pulled it out. It was about a meter and a half in length and around the same weight of the Bō he trained with. The pipe was stained red at one end which meant that someone had used it to fight something. "This will work" Curtus whispered to himself as he spun the pipe in his hand. "Hey you need to see this" Glade said. Curtus grabbed the pipe with two hands getting ready to defend himself as he ran over to Glade.

Glade was standing in the middle of the road with a horrified expression on her face. Her light brown skin had turned white as baby powder. She seemed to be trying to say something but whatever she was looking at was preventing her from doing so. "Hey what's up?" Curtus asked as he ran toward her. "O… O…" she replied. Whatever she was looking at had her at a loss for words. She just stood there stumbling over her words with a look of genuine horror on her face. When he got to her side Curtus saw the reason why she was frozen. She was looking at a town center and in the center of it was a pile of dead bodies. "Oh my god" Curtus whisper to himself pulling his collar over his mouth. He began to walk toward it and he noticed Glade wasn't moving. "Hey come on we have to move" he said. "I… eh… this can't be real… the stories can't be real" She whispered to herself. Curtus could tell by the way she was acting that she was about to go in to shock. He quickly ran over and grabbed her by her arms. "We have to stay calm and keep moving. If we don't we are going to end up like them." he said to her in a soothing voice calming her down. Glade suddenly snapped back to reality. "Sorry about that" She apologized. "It's alright. Now come on we gotta find a way out of this nightmare" Curtus said.

They began walking toward the middle of the square to see if they can find a clue or a map of some kind. They were preceded with extreme caution as whatever made that pile was probably watching them, waiting for them to slip up. "Hey Dumbass we might be able to find some information in there" Glade said pointing ahead of them. Curtus looked passed the pile of corpses to a massive building. It was wide with two floors and about 15 windows on the front wall. It also had a dome roof in the center of it making it look like some sort of capital building. "Yeah let's head over there" He replied.

They walked slowly scanning for any potential threats. The sounds of movement could be heard in the distance and unknown nature of the threat was enough to have the hair standing up on the back of both their necks. Suddenly a piercing shriek came from behind them. Curtus's heart began to race. The shriek was both human and animalistic. Neither Curtus or Glade knew what was waiting behind them. They slowly turned around to see the threat was everything that they had feared as they found themselves face to face with a subhuman creature.

It looked somewhat human in the aspect that its facial and body structure were human. Its eyes were blood red and its skin was translucent. It moved around in an animalistic fashion running around on all fours like a leopard. Curtus tightened his grip on the pipe. The three stared at each other waiting for the other to make a move. Curtus looked at Glade and noticed that she had no way to defend herself. "Hey, you don't have a weapon" Curtus whispered. She dug in her pockets and pulled out two makeshift knives. They were two jagged pieces of scrap metal with cloth on one side forming makeshift handles. "How deep are her pockets" Curtus whispered to himself think about how many things she has pulled out of them. "Trust me Dumbass, you don't have to worry about me" she whispered back. The three of them continued to stare at each other intensely. Sweat began to run down the back of Curtus's neck. The creature seemed to be focusing on him. It would occasionally glance at Glade to keep tabs on where she was, but would immediately refocus on Curtus. "It seems to like you" Glade whispered. Curtus took a deep breath and dropped into a defensive stance.

The creature crouched low to the ground and began a low growl. Glade could tell that the creature was not focused on her so she backed up in an effort not to interfere. "Where are you going" Curtus whispered. "That thing doesn't want me. So imma stand over here out of the way so I don't get any blood on me when that thing starts kicking your ass" She replied as she backpedaled. Curtus shook his head and began to slow his breathing. He was taught to be calm and have a clear mind. His mind had been racing ever since his parents were taken and needed to take a moment and decompress. He closed his eye and continued his breathing. Noticing him closing his eyes the creature growled again before pouncing at Curtus.

Glade watched intensely to see was Curtus continued to have his eyes closed at the creature flew toward him. Curtus took another deep breath. This breath got him in his zone. This breath blocked everything out. There was no shantytown. There was no Glade. There wasn't even a Jefferson. He opened his eyes and it was just him and the feral creature that was flying towards him in a vacuum. The creature seemed to be flying at him in slow motion compared to Curtus. Curtus took his pipe and gave the creature a straight jab to the to the collarbone causing the creature to fly backwards. Curtus then brought his hands to the bottom of the staff, jumped up and performed an overhead downward slash. The force of the strike slamming the creature face first on the ground. Curtus spun the pipe around in hands a couple of times before letting out a final exhale bringing him back to reality.

Glade who was taking a seat on a pile of trash and stared at Curtus with a look of amazement. "Holy shit Dumbass! That was awesome" She said clapping as she walked over to him. Curtus couldn't help but smile. "I've got to give it to ya. The speed that you did those two moves was insane" she added. "I told you I could handle myself" He exclaimed. Glade threw her hands up in the air. "Hey my bad. I'm just used to people from the surface couldn't fight" She replied. "People on the surface? You live on the surface too. You live in the Market District" Curtus replied. Glade began to laugh. "That is what they told you" she said chuckling. They walked over to the creature's body. It laid facedown lifeless on the ground. "Are you gonna finish it off" Glade asked." Curtus looked at Glade with a look of disgust on his face. "NO I am not going to kill it" Curtus shot back. Glade shook her head. "Tsk Tsk that is going to bite us in the ass later" She said.

The duo preceded to toward the capital building when the creature when began move. It was unable to move anything below its neck due to Curtus's attack, it began to violently turn its head until it managed to flip to its back. Once it was on its back it let out a bloodcurdling screech. The screech echoed throughout the entire town stopping Curtus and Glade in their tracks. The creature screamed until it passed out. Glade looked at Curtus with a smile on her face. "Don't say it. You're just gonna make it worse" Curtus said. "Oh don't worry I don't have to say it." She replied. Then the situation went from bad to worse as the Ferals began popping up in all of the windows, doorways, and alleys. They looked around as they slowly became surrounded. "Well I told it was going to backfire. I just didn't know it would backfire this quickly" She said. Curtus, without saying a word broke out in a full sprint toward the capital building. Noticing that he left, Glade mutter a couple of obscenities under her breath before chasing after him. One of the Ferals let a loud roar and the creatures began to chase after them.

"You were just going to leave me back there" She yelled. "Have you ever seen a movie. If we wait for them to assemble, we are as good as dead. At least this way we have a head start" he replied. "Yeah but we don't know where the hell we are going" She yelled back. As they were running Curtus heard a voice calling to him. "Curtus" it whispered. "Who is there" he thought to himself. "I am the guardian of this underground city and I want to help you" the voice replied. "How are you in my head" he thought to himself. "There will be plenty of time to answer that, but right now you guys are headed to a trap" The voice said. "Hey Dumbass who are you talking to" Glade asked. Curtus ignored Glade's question. He was to focused on his conversation with this "Guardian". "A trap" Curtus asked. "Yes. you guy are headed to the capital building right" The Guardian replied. Curtus looked at the capitol building. It was close enough to get a good look at it. "What wrong with it. It looked locked down" Curtus asked. "Well if you guys manage to get in you will only be met with a building full of Ferals" The voice replied. Glade had finally caught up to him. "What's the plan Dumbass." Glade asked. Curtus looked over his shoulder. The mob of Ferals was getting closer to them. The mob was about 45 deep. "Hello!!! Earth to Dumbass where are we going" She asked again.

Curtus thought about what the Guardian had said. "What if they were running right into a trap" he thought to himself. Curtus began looking for another place for them to hide and form another plan. Curtus looked at each of the buildings until he came to one that had a steel front door. "This way" Curtus yelled making a break for the building. They ran into the building slamming the door behind them. Glade spun a rusty wheel on the door to lock it. They both put their backs to the door and slowly slid to the floor. They needed a moment to catch their breath as well as plan their next move. "Okay Dumbass where do we go from here" She asked. "Well I'm not sure" Curtus said. The Ferals reached the building and began banging on the door. "So you are saying we are trapped in here waiting on those things that eat people that probably haven't eating in days to find their way in" she asked. "That is a very pessimistic way to look at it" Curtus replied. "If we make it out of here I'm gonna kill you" she muttered to herself.

The Ferals continued banging on the door and wall trying to get in. Curtus looked around to see if there was another way out. He had led them to a tavern of some sort and lucky for them this building was much sturdier than the others. Curtus tried to open the back door only for it to be blocked from the other side. "Great. No going out the back door" He said to himself. "Wow I didn't expect you guys to pick the tavern. You guys might be smarter than I expected" the Guardian said. Curtus noticed something eerily familiar about the way the Guardian spoke. Curtus wanted to figure out who the guardian may be, but with the army of man eating creatures outside he figured it wasn't that important. "How did you get in my head" Glade yelled. Curtus looked at Glade. She had a shocked look on her face and her nose was bleeding. "Glade your nose is bleeding" Curtus said. "Yeah yours is too" She said pressing her fingers under his nose. She pulled them away and showed Curtus her crimson covered fingertips. "Now c'mon Dumbass we gotta find a way out of here" She said wiping the blood from her top lip.

As they searched around the tavern the Ferals stopped banging on the building. Curtus ran to the window to see what was going on. He looked out to see the Ferals were slowly congregating into a large group. As they moved they maintained their focus on the tavern. Curtus looked and noticed they were all smiling like children getting ready for a field trip. This concerned Curtus. They needed to get out of that tavern before whatever they were planning breaks down the door and rips them apart. "What's going on" Glade asked.

"They are grouping together" Curtus replied nervously. Then the group began howling in unison. It wasn't like the shriek from the earlier Feral this was a deep howl as if they were calling for something. "What's that" Glade asked as she walked to the window. "I don't know, but it can't be good" Curtus said running to find an exit. Without there being an apparent second exit Curtus went looking for a secret tunnel. In many movies he's seen, many creepy places have secret tunnels in case of emergency. Though Curtus knew the movies weren't real, but at this point he was running out of options and needed a miracle.

Curtus jumped over the bar trying to find a switch or button. Glade ran into the bathrooms to see if there was a window they could escape through. Under the bar was one shelf that stretched the length of the bar. It was filled wall to wall with empty bottles that used to be full of alcohol. "Hey I think I found something" Glade yelled. "What is it" Curtus yelled back. "It a door, but there is no knob to open it." She replied. "How do you know" Curtus yelled. "Because there are hinges on the wall and a doorframe." She yelled back. Curtus returned his focus back to the shelf. There had to be a switch here to open that door. Curtus continued his search when he noticed something out of the ordinary. One of the bottles on the shelf was full. All of the other bottle look like they have been empty for years, but this bottle looked like it wasn't never opened. Curtus reached out and grabbed the bottle. As he pulled it out it stopped suddenly. "What the hell" Curtus thought to himself. Then Curtus heard Glade scream. "What's wrong" He asked. "Whatever you did it opened the door" She replied

Curtus stood up and walked to the window. The group had stopped the howling and were just staring at the door. They were smiling like they had just won the lottery. Glade ran back into the main part of the bar. "What are you waiting on we need to go" She said. "Look at them." Curtus yelled. Glade walked to a window and took a look outside. "What they aren't doing anything" She replied. "Look again" Curtus said. Glade looked again at the group this time noticing their facial expressions. She stepped back from the window nervously. "We need to go now before whatever they called comes" She said. As Glade began to make her way to the bathroom a deep roar shook the tavern.

This roar was much deeper than the howl from the group of Ferals and was much louder. It so loud it caused bottles in the tavern to shake and fall off the shelves. "DUMBASS LETS GO" Glade yelled. Curtus didn't budge. Curtus's curiosity kept him cemented in place. Suddenly the large pile of bodies in the center of the square exploded. Bodies flew everywhere and from the center of the pile emerged a creature straight out of a science fiction film.

It stood 12 feet tall and looked to weigh about 700 pounds. Its looked like a cross between an alligator and a gorilla. Its lumbered out of the pile like a person that had just woken up from a nap. The group of Feral were jumping for joy. It was as if their prophet had finally come. Curtus looked in horror as the story of the sewer dweller turned from fiction to reality before his eyes. "Glade you gotta come see this" Curtus yelled. "What we need to do is get our asses moving" Glade mumbled as she walked to the window. "What in the hell is so important that is has you stu..." She stopped midsentence at the sight of the creature. "Where the hell the that juggernaut come from" She asked. "From the pile in the middle of the square" Curtus replied. "It's beautiful isn't it" The Guardian said.

Curtus and Glade looked around to see where the voice might have been coming from. "What stands before you is the next step in human evolution." The Guardian added. "Curtus looked back at the beast. "That thing is human" Curtus said shakily. "Yes it is" The voice replied. "That isn't human" Glade began. "It is a mess of animals that would never naturally reproduce" Glade replied. "I said it was the next step in human evolution. I never said it was natural step." The voice replied. The beast looked around aimlessly before it locked eyes with Curtus. Its sleepy demeanor suddenly changed to one of pure rage. It let out a loud deep roar and yelled out in a deep demonic voice "PARKER!!!" and began sprinting at the tavern.

The beast was alarmingly fast for its size. It ran at the tavern with the perfect running form of an Olympic sprinter. "Yeah it's time to go" Glade said running towards the bathroom. Curtus had a million questions but they decided to put his Q&A session on hold and made a break for the door in the bathroom.

Glade led them to the to the men's bathroom. She kicked opened the door to and they ran to the last stall. The toilet lifted up the wall to reveal a stairwell. The stair well was poorly lit and was covered in feces. "Ladies first" Curtus said. "No after you I insist" She replied pushing him toward the stairs. Then there was a loud boom from the Juggernaut ramming into the front door. "Ok that door has about one more good charge in it before it is blown off the hinges" Curtus said. Glade pulled her flashlight out of her pocket. "Fine I'll lead the way… Scary ass" she whispered to herself as she began down the stairs. "Close the door behind us" She yelled back. Curtus saw there was a button on the wall labeled "Close". He pushed the button but the door didn't move.

Curtus hit the button again and again getting the same result. Getting nervous he began mashing the button and the door didn't move one inch. Curtus heard a roar from outside followed by heavy footsteps. Curtus tried grabbing the door and pulling it down by hand but it was to no avail. The door was locked in place. Curtus thought about how he opened the door and realized the only way to close it would be to move the bottle back. Coming to this realization began running down the stairs. As he made his way down the stairs he heard a loud explosion from behind him. The door had been blown off the hinges and the Ferals flooded the tavern above.

V

Curtus ran into Glade who was walking down the stairs. "What's your deal" She asked almost falling down the stairs. "The door is jammed... we have to get moving" he said. "What" she asked. "I couldn't close the door" he said beginning to run again. Glade shook her head. "You have got to be kidding me" She whispered as she began running after him. Heavy footsteps could be heard above them as the Juggernaut entered the tavern. The Ferals could be heard guiding the it toward the bathroom. "How come you couldn't close the door" Glade asked. "It was locked in place. I would have to go and close it at the bar." Curtus replied. "Again. Why didn't you close the door?" Glade reiterated. Curtus was about to respond before he figured out what Glade was saying. She wanted him to sacrifice himself so she could get away. "You don't have very many friends do you" Curtus asked. "I prefer to keep my circle small" She replied with a smile.

The two reached the bottom of the staircase where they were met with a steel door. Glade tried to open the door but it didn't budge. "Shit this isn't good" Glade said. Curtus looked at the door and saw that it was electronically locked. "We need to get power to this door to unlock it" He said. "Well we aint got time for that" She yelled. "This way... This way" one of the Ferals said at the top of the stairs. The footsteps were becoming louder and louder. It was only a matter of time before it found them. Curtus snatched the flashlight out of Glade's hand. "The hell was that for" She asked. "I'm trying to find a way out" Curtus yelled looking around the doorframe. He frantically looked around the door frame until he found a ventilation duct on the ground. "Hold this" Curtus said passing the light back to Glade. He pressed his feet against the wall, grabbed the grate with both hands, and began pulling.

The footsteps began to shaking the walls of the staircase. "Hurry up Dumbass" Glade yelled. The steel bolts had corroded over time and needed to be replaced. One by one the bolt broke off of the wall until the entire grate came off. Glade dove into the duct the like an Olympic swimmer. Curtus looked up the stairs to see the Juggernaut. Looking at it for a second time a sense of familiarity came over Curtus. Curtus knew he wouldn't forget a beast like that, but there was something about it that was familiar to him. The Juggernaut locked eyes with Curtus and let out a loud roar. Curtus snapped out of his daze and crawled into the duct. He could feel the Juggernaut's heavy footsteps as it ran down the stairs. Curtus reached the end of the short tunnel and looked behind him to see the Juggernaut staring at him with lifeless black eyes. "PARKER HELP ME" it yelled. Curtus stared at the monster for a couple more seconds before crawling out of the air duct.

He exited the tunnel to see Glade staring at him intensely. "First of my million questions. How the hell does that thing know your name? You got some explaining to do." Glade said. Curtus was just as confused as she was. Why would it ask him for help while it was trying to kill them at the same time? "You two are a craftier duo then I thought" the Guardian said. "OK enough of your games. Show yourself" Curtus yelled. "Aww but your prize for playing." The Guardian replied. Curtus looked at Glade. She was wiping the blood that was dripping from her top lip. Suddenly there was a loud bang at on the door from the Juggernaut was trying to punch through it. "Oh it looks like you guys aren't out of the woods yet. You guys better start running." The voice said. Curtus looked back to see the door was welded to the frame. Though it wouldn't hold the Juggernaut back for very long it would buy them enough time to get a significant head start. "C'mon Glade" Curtus said pulling her by her arm.

They ran down the tunnel when Curtus began to notice something strange. As they were running the tunnel began to stink more and more. It was as if his sense of smell was slowly coming back. "Oh god what the hell is that smell" Glade yelled as she pinched her nose. The smell got so bad that they had to stop running to get adjusted to it. Curtus looked around and also noticed that it wasn't just his sense of smell that was affected. His vision had been hindered as well. When he entered the tunnel he thought there was blood flowing on the floor, but the blood turned out to actually be water.

The banging continued to echo throughout the tunnel. "Hey Glade how you feeling" Curtus asked wiping the blood from his lip. "About as good as coming down from a bad high could feel" she replied wiping her top lip. "Yeah... glad to see you're alright" Curtus said. "But the question of the day is what is in the air out there" Glade asked. Suddenly there was a loud bang followed by a crash behind them. The Juggernaut had punched the door right off the frame.

"This is great" Glade began. "I'm running from this 12-foot killing machine with an idiot in a direction that could lead to nowhere" She finished. Curtus looked over at Glade. "We aren't going to die" Curtus said in a reassuring voice. "You're right. While its busy killing you I'm gonna escape" She replied back. "Wow" Curtus yelled. "Right I think it is a pretty good plan" Glade said. The roar of the Juggernaut shook the catwalk they were walking on. "Do you even know your way out of here" Curtus yelled. "No but while it is distracted I will have plenty of time to find a way out" She replied. Curtus just shook his head in disgust as he ran.

They ran until the came to a massive pit. Curtus looked down to a bright orange glow which meant this pipe led back to the furnace. Curtus looked up and saw that the catwalk split into two different paths. Their only two options were to either make a right or to continue straight. "How about was split up" Glade said. "Out of the question" Curtus replied. "Why are you scared" Glade asked. "No. I am just saying we have to work together to beat this thing" he replied. Glade looked at Curtus with a smile. "I like the way you think" She said rubbing he hands together. "I mean even if we split up. What is going to stop that thing from hunting you down." Curtus added. "True. So what is the plan" She replied. "Just follow my lead" Curtus said.

Curtus ran across the catwalk stopping where the two paths split. He looked to the right to see the tunnel was dark and didn't show much promise. Using his better judgement, he decided to continue straight. This turned out to be the wrong decision as the path led them to a dead end. "Well is this a part of your plan" Glade asked in a superior tone. "What are you scared to fight this thing" Curtus replied sarcastically. "HAVE YOU SEEN THAT THING... HELL YEAH" she yelled. "Really I thought you were excited" Curtus asked. "Yeah 'cause I thought you were going to trap it or something." She replied. "No we are going to fight it" He said with a smile. "Oh my god I'm really going to die down here because of you" She said beginning to pace. Curtus looked around the hall and spotted a door on the left. "If we are going to die we are at least going to go out swinging, follow me" Curtus said as he ran toward the door.

He barged through the door to a large room full of bunk beds. They walked into the room and looked upon the sea of beds. Row after row of them lined the large room. "This must have been one of the barracks where the people who built the ship slept" Curtus said running his fingers down one of the bedposts. It was caked in dust from years from neglect. "How many people do you think slept in this one room." Glade asked. "From the looks of it may be around 250" He said. "They were crammed in here like animals. They were practically sleeping on top of one another" Glade added. Curtus looked at Glade. "You think the Ferals are the people who built the ship" He asked. Glade sucked her teeth. "This ship has been in the sky for a couple hundred years. Those people and their children's children are probably dead" She said walking down one of the aisles.

The Juggernaut let out a loud roar from down the hall. It was getting close and they needed to come up with a plan in a hurry. "What do we do now" Glade asked. Curtus looked around before responding. "Uhhh hide" He said climbing to the top of one of the beds. Glade let out a deep sigh before she ran further down the aisle and did the same. Once Curtus was on the top of the bunk, he buried himself under the thin sheet. The sheet was thin, scratchy, and coated with dust. As Curtus moved it he could hear the vintage fibers stretching. He made sure to be facing the same way Glade so they could non verbally communicate. Before she got under the sheet she grabbed one of her makeshift knives and punctured one of the pipes on the ceiling. The pipe let out a loud hiss and began filling the room with steam. "What did you do that for" Curtus asked. "Oh what we both can't have plans" Glade replied. The footsteps of the Juggernauts began to shake the nearby beds. "You just have to trust me" She said before burrowing in the sheet.

Curtus and Glade held their breath as the Juggernaut walked through the doorway. It breathed heavily as it aimlessly wandered throughout the room. "Parker... you said you would fix me Parker" it whispered to itself as it lumbered down the aisle. Curtus's was still trying to figure out how the creature knew his last name. The steam stopped flowing in the room but not before all of the bunks was covered in it. "Hey Dumbass can you hear me" Glade asked. Curtus's heart stopped. He waited on the Juggernaut to go berserk and find the source of the noise, but it never happened. It continued slowly stomping down the aisle. "Ye...Yeah I can" he said shakily. "Well if my hunch is correct. This thing is deaf and works solely on sight to get around" She explained. "How did you come to that conclusion" Curtus asked. "Well it wasn't the sound of the screeching that woke it up but the strength of the vibration. When all the Ferals got in to that group and let out that call they were trying to shake the ground enough to wake it up" She explained. It wasn't until after that explanation that Curtus realized what her plan was. She put a cloud over the bunks of all of the beds. This way they could travel between the interconnected beds without fear of being seen. It was a stroke of genius. "Nice job" Curtus said. "Yeah but we only have a couple minutes before we lose our cloud cover so let's to make them count" She said.

The two stealthily moved between the beds. They didn't want to move to quickly in fear they would knock over the beds and alert the creature. Being that the steam was hot and thick it was hard to breathe and talk. The only way they were able to know where each other was by occasionally snapping. Glade was two aisles to the right of Curtus putting the Juggernaut was in between them. The creature continued lumbering aimlessly through the steam until it suddenly stopped and began to cry. "I want fix. Parker said he would fix" it repeated over and over again. "Okay Dumbass now it is time for phase two of my plan" she announced. As fog began to dissipate Curtus could see Glade's silhouette. "Alright what is it" He asked. "Just follow my lead" She replied with a smile.

She climbed to the top bunk of a nearby bed and grabbed the pipe above her. Curtus not sure where this plan was going did the same. The Juggernaut was still standing in the same spot sobbing and repeating the same phrase. "Alright on the count of three kick your bed over. 1…2…3" Glade said. Once she said three Curtus swung his legs and kicked the bed with all his might. Glade did the same the two beds sandwiched the Juggernaut. The beast screamed out in pain as the two beds clamped down on its neck. The roar was so loud it violently shook the entire room. All of the steam in the room had caused the pipes slippery causing Curtus to lose his grip. He came crashing down slamming his lower back onto the beds. "Shit" Glade whispered to herself as she swung over to one of the other beds. Curtus laid on the ground clutching his lower back in agony unaware of the true danger he was in. The creature busted from the vice with a loud roar. It looked around the room before fixing its gaze on Curtus who was laying on a bed frame. Curtus open his eyes and found himself face to face with the beast.

At first the only thing that made the Juggarnaut seem familiar to Curtus was the voice. There was a certain scratchiness that was familiar to him, and upon seeing its face with a clear head he knew why. The voice belonged to one of his patients he tended to at the hospital. Her name was Maria Sanchez. She had brought her son to the hospital because they both had contracted a case of Mexican Blood Flu. When she came to the hospital she didn't speak much English. The only words she said when she got there was "fix us". "Maria is that you?" Curtus asked. Though she was deaf she read Curtus's lips and could tell he said her name. "Hey I thought she was deaf." Curtus questioned. "She is. She can read your lips" Glade answered sitting on the edge of one of the beds.

As the fog cleared more of her face became clear. Curtus could now see tears were running down her face. "Fix me Parker please" She pleaded. "Maria who did this to you" Curtus asked. "La Bruja" She yelled. "What do you mean la Bruja" Curtus asked. "She is saying the Witch. The Witch did this to her" Glade explained sitting on the bed. "What Witch?" Curtus question. "Well there is a scary story that has some people go to sleep and waking up in the middle of a village hearing a mysterious voice. They say the Witch takes them and makes them play a game of cat and mouse for their lives. I thought it was just a scary story to get children to act right, but I think we actually stumbled into her game." Glade explained.

"Seems like you know each other. Well that won't make the game fun now will it" the Guardian said. Now that Curtus's head was clear of whatever was in the air he could tell that there wasn't actually someone in his head. The voice was coming through an intercom system that was installed throughout the town and hallways. "Who are you" Curtus asked. The voice was being distorted by some sort of voice synthesizing software. "That will information will present itself in due time. Right now you need to worry about Maria" The voice answered. Suddenly Maria grabbed her head and begin to stumble around in pain. Curtus looked around for a something to defend himself with. One of the pipes on the bed he kicked over had broken off. It was rusted it came to a point on both side and would have to do. Glade jumped over to the bed next to Curtus. "Do you know what is going on" He inquired. "If I had to guess La Bruja is playing a high pitch frequency through the speaker system. There must be some sort of machine inside her brain to control her when it hears this frequency." She replied. "How do you come to that" Curtus asked. "Would you let a 12 foot tall killing machine walk around with free will" Glade asked. "Good point" Curtus retorted.

Maria continued to stumble around in screaming in agony. "C'mon Dumbass. This is a perfect chance to leave" Glade yelled. Suddenly Maria stopped moving and fell silent. The room fell cold with fear. Maria stood lifeless like a mannequin in a storefront. Neither Curtus nor Glade knew what was going on, but they could only assume that she was being controlled. "Leave…" Maria whispered to herself. "Oh no. Now you done pissed her off" Glade said. "WHY YOU LEAVE PARKER. IM NOT FIXED YET" She yelled as she charged him. "See you in a few Dumbass" Glade said jumping up and off the bed. Maria snatched him up in one of her enormous hands. Maria snatched Curtus up off the ground as if he was a television remote. Curtus looked into Maria's eye. During their brief chat earlier his eyes resembled a normal human eye with a definitive green iris and pupil. Now there wasn't even white in her eyes, it was just all black. "IF PARKER CAN'T FIX. THEN I JUST BREAK" Maria yelled.

She began to squeezing her large hand crushing Curtus. He yelled out in pain as the vertebrae in his back began to pop one by one. Glade jumped from bed to bed trying to get behind Maria. Once she was able to get behind her she noticed something about Maria's skin. Her back was armored with alligator like scales. Though she was armored the scales seemed to be damaged in some areas. Several of them were cracked and many of them were scarred and burned. "What did they do to you" Glade whispered to herself. Curtus let out a loud scream as his pelvis began to crack. "Maria I'm sorry about this" she said as she drew her makeshift knives. She jumped off the bed driving both knives into soft sections of Maria's back.

Maria let out a loud shriek and let go of Curtus. Curtus landed on his feet but immediately dropped to one knee due to the pain. Curtus watched as Glade held for dear life as Maria tried to grab her. "Are you just gonna watch Dumbass or help" Glade yelled. Curtus picked up the pipe he dropped while he was being crushed. As his adrenaline began to kick in the pain in his pelvis began to fade. As he ran over to aid Glade he noticed that Maria's body was changing. It was slowly being covered with new scales. If they didn't do something now they would have no way to damage her.

Curtus analyzed her body and noticed a pattern. It seemed that the joints were developing armor slower than the rest of the body. Seeing as there is no way in beating her in a fight, their only hope now was to be able to make her immobile long enough for them to get way. "Go ahead and take your time. I can do this all day" Glade yelled sarcastically. As she said this Maria finally manage to grab Glade. She ripped her off and threw her across the room like a baseball. Curtus watched as Glade flew through the air slamming against the wall right next to the door they came in. "Glade are you alright" Curtus yelled. She slowly rose to her feet. Curtus could tell by the way that she stood up that she was really hurt. "Don't worry this is all a part of the plan. Now you just distract her until I give you the signal" she said as she limped out of the room. "Wait what is the signal" Curtus yelled. "Trust me you'll know it" she yelled back.

Curtus turned around and saw Maria was staring at him with a demonic smile on her face. Even though she was smiling her tears continued to run down her face. "Maria you don't have to do this. I can help you" Curtus pleaded. Maria ignored his plea. She began repeating a phrase over and over in a language Curtus didn't understand. "Mátame por favor Mátame" she whispered to herself repeatedly. "I don't understand what you are saying" Curtus yelled. Curtus noticed that the scaled on her arms were changing color. They turned from white to a charcoal gray. He wasn't sure what the change in color meant, but Curtus knew that if he didn't act now that Maria would rip him apart. "I'm sorry Maria" Curtus whispered to himself before charging at Maria. When Maria charged at him this time Curtus could tell something was different. She was running in a more ridged fashion. She wasn't moving as fast or as fluidly as before. The armored scales were preventing her from getting the proper knee bend to pick up speed. Curtus had to take advantage of her lack of mobility. As the got closer to each other Maria clenched her fist and drew her arm back. As she began her punch Curtus began to slide like a baseball player heading for home base. He watched as Maria's punch just grazed the top of his head. Curtus managed to slide between both of her legs without getting stepped on.

Once he was on the other side Curtus popped straight up in the air. He grabbed the rusted pipe like a spear and threw it at the back of Maria's right leg piercing her achilles tendon.

Curtus couldn't help but feel somewhat responsible for Maria current state. He remembered the day when Maria and her son went missing from the hospital. When asked his Professor Tina Ross who is the head doctor at Lee Hospital where they went she said "Don't worry about it. They checked out today." Curtus knew in his gut that he should have researched that further. He knew they were in no state to leave, but he had no reason to believe that his teacher would lie to him so he kept on with his day. He felt he could have prevented all of this from happening.

As Maria yelled in agony she swung her opposite arm backward catching Curtus with a backhand. Curtus was sent crashing into a locker on the back wall of the room. Curtus laid with his back against the locker immobilized by the pain. He was in so much pain he couldn't hear or breathe. The crack in his pelvis was growing with every attack. Curtus looked at Maria as she struggled to pull the pipe out of her ankle. Her struggles weren't due to how deep the pipe was, but it was due to how sensitive the area. Curtus could tell that she was in genuine pain by the way she gingerly touched the pipe.

Curtus opened the locker looking for something that might be able to help with his pain. He opened the locker to find the only thing in it was a small first aid kit. "Wonderful" he whispered to himself sarcastically. He grabbed the kit and once he opened it up his entire disposition changed. He opened it up to find a bottle of Bone Stem-X. Bone Stem-X was a pill that was developed by his Professor Tina Ross to heal broken bones in a matter of minutes. It was developed for people who worked construction. If the broke a bone all they had to do is reset, and take two pills and they would be back to work in 5 minutes. They were made illegal when they CDC ruled that it led to cancer when taken in excess. This was after countless construction workers died of cancer and the CDC claimed there was no correlation. Curtus open the bottle, dry swallowed two pills, and began the waiting game.

He watched as Maria continued to attempt to grab onto the pipe in her ankle while he waited for the pills to take effect. She would look at him and let out an earth shaking roar, but whenever she tried to run toward him she would take one step and one her second step fall to her knees in pain. Curtus felt the pain in his hips turn into a tingling feeling. The pills were taking effect and soon Curtus would be able to escape. With the pain fading Curtus slowly rose to his feet. Maria seeing this, she let out a loud roar and ripped the pipe out of her ankle and stabbed it through a nearby bed. Curtus looked at Maria's ankle and noticed that the gash in the back of her leg instantly healed. "Oh that is going to be a problem" Curtus said to himself. "Hey Dumbass this is the signal" Glade yelled from the hallway. Curtus looked at the doorway and then looked at Maria who was staring at him still whispering the same phrase to herself. "I'll be right there." Curtus yelled back knowing he didn't have anything close to an escape plan. Curtus took a deep breath making a break to the door.

Back in high school Curtus was the top hurdlers on the team so jumping over the mattresses was a breeze. Maria was barely able to run let alone jump over anything. She barreled through the beds like an all-pro fullback. She was so strong she sent the heavy beds flying with little effort. With her mobility limited Curtus's only chance was to outrun her. He ran all the way across the room putting as much space between him and her before making a break for the door. He ran until he reached the wall before making a sharp right turn for the door. Curtus made it to the door and turned around. He saw that Maria not only couldn't run as fast but she lost and ability to turn as well as he watched her slam into the wall.

Curtus made his way to the catwalk where he saw Glade leaning against the wall clutching her right hand. She was in the other hallway that Curtus had chosen not to go down. "Bout time you showed up" She said breathing heavily. Curtus smiled and began to make his way to her. "Be careful" Glade said right before Curtus stepped on the catwalk. He stepped on the suspended walkway and it immediately began to shake. "What did you do to it" Curtus asked. "I'll tell you when we aren't being chased by your friend Maria." She replied. Slowly putting one foot in front of the other Curtus made his way down the catwalk. Curtus was about halfway across the walkway when he heard a loud crash behind him. "I'd hurry up if I were you. Maximum occupancy is one" Glade warned. Curtus put his head down and made a mad dash to Glade. He made a hard left before diving off the catwalk into the tunnel. "Glad you could join me. Now you have courtside seats to watch my master plan unfold" Glade said standing to her feet. Curtus looked on as Glade walked to the edge of the catwalk. She dropped to one knee and waited for Maria to come.

Maria came flying out of the tunnel like a bat out of hell. The catwalk began to buckle as she made her way to the middle. Glade looked back at Curtus with a smile. "I give you Operation Look Out Below" Glade said. Maria grabbed on to the handrail to turn and began running at Curtus and Glade. Curtus slid back at the sight of the 12-foot monster charging at them, but Glade remained poised and stood her ground. Maria was about 10 yards away when the catwalk gave way. She gave one last ditch swipe which came inches from Glades face. Maria fell down into the into the hellish pit. As she fell to her demise she yelled one last word. "Gracias"

Glade turned and looked at Curtus with a smile. "Whatcha think. Badass plan huh. I used my blood to burn enough of the supports so the bridge wouldn't be able to support her weight." She explained proudly. "You are quite the strategist" Curtus replied. "Well someone has to be" She replied sharply. Then something came to Curtus that had been bothering him ever since Glade left. "Hey Glade you understood her language. What does Mátame por favor Mátame mean?" he asked. Glade's eyes open in surprise. "Where did you hear that" She asked. "She began repeating it after she threw you across the room" Curtus replied. Glade took a deep breath. "Mátame por favor Mátame means kill me please kill me" Glade answered. Curtus's stomach dropped. "Are you sure that is what she said" Curtus asked. "Positive. It probably explains her dying words" Glade said. "What were they" Curtus asked. "Thank you" Glade said as she began walking down the tunnel.

VI

They walked down the tunnel for five minutes before the Witch's voice came over the intercom. "All that work literally down the damn drain. You know how many times I failed before I got to her and now I have nothing to show for it. Father won't be pleased" she yelled. Curtus remembered Leremy saying something about bringing him to "Father." "Maria was my biggest success and you destroyed her… Oh well at least I have the research" the Witch finished. Curtus stopped dead in his tracks. There is only one person on the Jefferson who says that. "Professor is that you" Curtus asked nervously. Curtus prayed that the voice on the other end would say no. They waited for a minute or so for the Witch to respond. When she came back the voice synthesizer software had been turned off. "I figured you would find out it was me after that slip up" She said. Glade looked at Curtus to find a look of pure horror on his face. "Do you know her." she yelled. "Yeah it is my Professor Tina Ross" Curtus replied. "Well Tina has some explaining to do because that voice belongs to Alyson Burraza." Glade replied.

Alyson Burraza was a scientist who was determined to cracking the human genetic code and making it so a person could tap into their primal side. She was arrested and charged with 14 counts of murder after she was found experimenting on homeless people and killing them in the process. She was sentenced to death but before she could get the lethal injection she disappeared without a trace. "I'm not a mad scientist" she barked over the intercom. "Not a mad scientist… You have no regard for human life." Glade yelled. "All of my research is for the preservation of human life. If a couple of lives are lost in the process, then so be it" she replied.

Curtus thought back to the countless lectures he sat in. She would end every class the same by saying "Never let your research compromise your humanity." Curtus felt betrayed. He had been taking heed to these words and idolizing this person just to figure out she is a hypocrite. "So all that you said about not letting your research comprising your morals was just smoke and mirrors" Curtus asked. "Absolutely. The best research comes when you check your morals at the door." Burraza replied. "You're a monster" Glade yelled. "IM NOT A MONSTER IM JUST MISUNDERSTOOD" She barked over the intercom. "You know why Josef Mengele was ahead of his time. He didn't let petty morals and ethics get in the way of his research" she added. "Josef Mengele was a psychopath... Do you know why he was called the Angel of Death?" Curtus yelled. Burraza took a deep breath. "You guys are too young to understand. I wish I could teach you guys, but you guy know too much. As much I want you to see you win my little game I cannot let you leave." She explained.

Suddenly the tunnel entrance slammed shut behind them. "I really wish I could see how far you would have gotten Curtus but you know too much. If it makes you feel any better, you were always my favorite student" she said in a soothing voice. "Go to hell" Curtus barked back. "Well then... in five minutes that hallway should be full of water from Lincoln Lake. I have to get back to grading papers... Oh look yours is next I'll grade it really quickly for you as you drown." She said. Curtus looked around and noticed that everything in this hallway was watertight. This hallway was designed to drown people who got too far in her game. Curtus looked around and noticed a closet door that was water tight seal on all four edges. Curtus grabbed Glade and ran to the door. He tried to open the door only for it to be locked. "You got to open the door" Curtus whispered. "Do you have a lock pick" She asked. "No use your blood" Curtus whisper. "You know even though it heals fast it still hurts like hell to cut myself." She whispered back. Then vents in the ceiling opened up in the ceiling and water began filling the hall.

Curtus didn't have time to go back and forth with Glade so he looked around for something sharp. He picked up a shard of glass off the ground and drove it into Glade's palm. Glade bit her lip trying not to make any noise. "You bastard" She whispered through her clenched teeth. Then Curtus rested the other end of the shard in the keyhole so the blood could run to it. Glade's blood burned slower through glass then in did metal making the perfect vehicle to move her blood. Just like in the sewer the knob went up in smoke once it made contact with Glade's blood. Once the lock burned off the door went flying open crashing into a shelf. The sound of the crashing water was loud enough to mask the sound of the crash so Burraza was unaware of what was actually happening. Glade ripped the shard out of her hand and slapped him in the face. "Next time a little warning would be nice" She said clutching her hand. "Just follow me" Curtus said running into the closet. They ran in the closet and Curtus closed the door behind them.

It was so dark in the closet Curtus couldn't his hands that were inches from his face. "Hey do you still have that flashlight" Curtus asked. Glade turned the flashlight on and handed it to him. Curtus looked down at the base of the door to see the seal was holding up. "Huh waterproof door. I have to start giving you more credit Dumbass. Sorry I slapped you" she said. "Better to be slapped by a pretty girl and alive than being drowned by a crazy ass teacher" Curtus replied. Curtus looked around for a light switch. As he looked around he saw a door in the ceiling with a string dangling from it. Curtus jumped and gave the string a strong yank revealing a ladder. Curtus flashed the light in the opening. The ladder led to an abyss of pure darkness. He looked at Glade and cracked a nervous smile. "Ladies first" Curtus said nervously. "Boy if you don't get your narrow ass up that ladder" she commanded. Curtus took a deep breath, Curtus put the flashlight in his mouth, and began up the ladder.

Curtus climbed the short wooden ladder to find himself in an old elevator shaft. Curtus looked around to find a long metal ladder hanging in the center of the shaft. "What's up there" Glade asked. "another ladder and darkness" he replied. Glade cracked her knuckles before beginning up the ladder herself. Curtus waited for Glade to enter the shaft before beginning up the second ladder. Curtus could tell that the ladder hadn't been used in years by the thick layer of dust dust on each of the rungs. As Curtus made his way up he felt it was progressively getting darker. "Hey Curtus I just finished grading your paper. You got a 97%. It was really good but as usual with you the were several spelling and grammar errors. You shouldn't write your papers the night befo…" Burraza began. She stopped mid-sentence when she noticed they had disappeared. "Where did you guys go" she asked. Burraza could be heard hastily typing and clicking over the intercom. "Where did you guys go" she repeated nervously. Curtus continued to climb. Now that he knew about his teacher's transgressions he was determined to bring her to justice.

Curtus sped up his climb wanting to get to the top of the shaft as quickly as possible. "Hey slow down. You are the only source of light in here" Glade said. Curtus turned and he saw that he had built a large gap between him and her. "Sorry" Curtus said before continuing up the ladder. They climbed for a couple more minute before they reached the top of the shaft. At the top of the ladder was sealed with a door that looked like an emergency exit on the room of a school bus. "They must have drowned. There is no way they got away." Burraza said to herself. One thing Curtus knew about his teacher is when things didn't go according to plan she had a tendency to unravel. She had such extensive knowledge of the human body that she really could cure anyone at the hospital. Even though she was a monster she is still a medical genius. She was so frazzled that she was talking to herself trying to calm down. Curtus grabbed the wheel in the center of the door and began to twist it counterclockwise. Curtus twisted it slowly now trying break the old rusty wheel. He continued twisting the wheel until he heard a loud "Clunk". The clunk echoed over the intercom which meant it was close. A nervous feeling cam over Curtus. He was about to confront the person he used to idolize. He began to second guess if he would be able to what needed to be done.

Burraza began to panic. This was not a part of her masterplan. No one had ever gotten this close to her private sanctum and she had to make a quick escape. Curtus pushed the hatch but as it opened slightly before being stopped. It was being blocked on the other side. Curtus was so close and wasn't going to let a blocked door get in his way. Curtus began repeatedly pushing on the door each time the door would open a little bit more. "Come on" Curtus yelled to himself. He gave it one last push using all of his strength. This was now a matter of life and death. Curtus inhaled deeply before lunging at the door.

The force from Curtus's lunge sent the hatch flying open. He flew in the room crash landing on the floor. He quickly jumped up ready to confront his former teacher only for her not to be there. Glade climbed in shortly after to see a distraught Curtus. She looked around the room to find that she had escaped. "Dammit" Curtus yelled out stomping his foot. "Calm down. She couldn't have gotten far." Glade said dusting herself off. Curtus looked around to find a way that she may have escaped. The room had no door but had a large window that stretched the length of the wall. Curtus ran over to see if there was a walkway on the other side of it. He looked to only find the window overlooked the shantytown. Glade walked to Curtus's side and looked out the window. The window was made of Smartglass which magnified on certain spots specific to the user. The window was magnified on the grate they came in through, the street where they fought the first Feral, and the front door of the tavern. "She just sat up here and watched as the people she put through her sick game being killed" Curtus whispered to himself.

He clenched his fist so tight that he popped his knuckles. "We aren't going to find her admiring the view. C'mon let's look for clues" Glade said patting Curtus on the shoulder. Curtus let out a large exhale.

"You're right. I can't let anger cloud my judgement" he said. "Well that's not what I said, but if that helps you then I'm all for it" Glade replied as she walked away from the window. Curtus walked over to Burraza's desk that was against the back wall of the suite. The desk sat under pictures of Josef Mengele, Shiro Ishii, and Vladimir Demikhov. It was a shrine dedicated to some of the evilest men in the history of medicine. The sight of these men made Curtus's blood boil. He had been taught all his life by his parents as well as Prof. Ross that there is no room for cruelty in your research. "Who are you" Curtus whispered to himself. Glade looked over and saw Curtus was visually frustrated again. She walked next to him and put her arm on his shoulder. "Don't worry she won't get away with this. And look at the bright side" she said trying to calm him down. "What bright side" Curtus said glaring at Glade. "At least you got a good grade on your paper" She said handing him the essay off the desk. Curtus snatched the paper out of Glade's hand and threw it away before investigating the desk.

Curtus began opening all the drawers of the desk like a madman. He ripped drawers open until he found the bottom drawer full of files. Hoping to find answers Curtus pulled all of them out and put them on the desk. "What are those" Glade asked. "Hopefully, some answers" Curtus replied rummaging through the files. Curtus picked up a file labeled "Operation Red Tide". Underneath the title read "Report by: Alyson Burraza" and an unknown insignia next to it. It looked like a capital R was on the back of a backwards capital F. Curtus opened the file and looked in horror as it was full of autopsy reports, pictures of men, women, and children littered with bloody noses and eyes. Curtus found a research journal behind all of the photos. It read like a timeline in where everything was organized chronologically. Curtus broke out in a cold sweat while reading the report. Glade noticed Curtus's reaction and began to worry about him. "What is it. Did you find something?" She asked. Curtus didn't look at her. He didn't know how to explain what he what he was reading. He didn't know how to explain that someone he looked up to tried to kill off the entire Mexican race.

In 2185 there was a strain of the flu that ravaged the Mexican community. It was unlike anything the medical community had ever seen. It was a strain of the flu that was only contracted by one race of people. Scientists did their best to create a vaccine but they were unsuccessful. The Mexican population was dying at an alarming rate and they had no way to fight against it. People who were infected by it would have a fever of 105 degrees and had regular flu like symptoms. The longer they were infected the fever would increase to 115 degrees and the would begin crying tears of blood before they died. This is how it got the name Mexican Blood Flu. Curtus was at a loss for words as he read his teacher's firsthand account of the situation.

June 28, 2185

Today is the first day of Red Tide. We introduced my virus into the water supply of the Mexican Market District neighborhood. Since their water supply is separate from everyone else's nobody of importance will get hurt. Can't wait to do good work for the people of the Jefferson.

June 28, 2186

One year in and we are right on schedule. We have introduced the virus to the water supply and people are beginning to contract.

December 15, 2186

The contraction rate is lower than expected. Only about 45% of the people who drank the water actually contracted the virus. Though the contraction rate is low the intensity of the virus is high then we expected. The temperature of the fever is much higher than we planned and there are violent cough attacks that could lead to complications in the future.

March 7, 2187

This is better than I could have dreamed it. We had our first mortality today. A 37-year-old woman by the name of Pita Sanchez. She had a fever of 109 and was reported to die because she was coughing so much she suffocated.

October 17, 2187

The mortalities are rolling in. Each report reads better than the last. The reports are saying the cause of death is Exsanguination. The locals are saying that people are bleeding from their eyes and mouth.

June 30, 2189

They have named it the Mexican Blood Flu. The effective death rate is 100%. We need to try to figure out how to infect the elusive 55%. May have to take one of the healthy ones in and runs some tests on them.

December 31, 2190

The mission is a failure. They figured out that it was in the water supply and the airborne strain is not ready for deployment. The Family is scrapping the project as a whole but I will continue. This project may be dead but I have the research. I guess I will release the treatment and at least make some money off that. I will continue to fight the good fight. The family is giving me another chance putting me on something called Operation Playground. I will not fail again.

Curtus dropped the file sending its contents falling to the ground. He was shaken to his core. He thought this grade of evil was reserved for fictional books. He remembered learning about the MBF epidemic in history class. After reading this knowing that it wasn't a natural epidemic but rather an attempt at genocide made him sick to his stomach. This put everything he ever learned into question. "Hey what's up. You're sweating bullets" Glade said. She reached down and picked up the journal. She began reading it and dropped to her knees. "Sh… she created la gripe de sangre" Glade asked. "Yeah it is some of my finest work" Burraza said over to the intercom. Curtus cold sweat quickly came to a raging boil. "Professor show yourself" he yelled. "Oh Curtus. We both know you stopped being my student the moment you stepped in my playground" She replied.

"Her playground" Curtus thought to himself. The shantytown, the Ferals, Maria were they all apart of Operation Playground" Curtus asked himself. "How could the government fund something this inhumane" Glade yelled. "What's more humane than the preservation of human life" Burraza asked in a superior tone. "You try to kill off an entire culture of people" Curtus began. "THEY AREN'T PEOPLE. THEY ARE THUG AND ONLY HOLDING HUMANITY BACK" Burraza yelled. Glade's face went bone white. She had never heard anyone be that overtly racist in real life. "But Professor aren't you Mexican" Curtus Asked. "DON'T EVER CALL ME THAT. I DIDN'T CHOOSE TO BE BORN LIKE THIS" She yelled.

Then she began to explain the reason behind her hatred for the Mexican culture. "All they did was make fun of me for having white skin. It was disgusting how they treated me. Even my parents made jokes about how I looked. It was white girl this and gringa that so at 14 I left the Market District and found my way into an orphanage topside. From there I went to a Landry family. A good wholesome white family. They were the nicest people I had ever me. They didn't pick on people who were different, and I liked that. Because of my white skin they thought I was Caucasian and they talked very openly about how they felt about other races. Though they didn't make fun of the other races behind closed door they would talk for hours about how much they couldn't stand the others. Listening to the way they talked I vowed I would do everything I could to purge the Jefferson of them starting with the Mexicans." She finished.

The room fell silent. Neither Curtus nor Glade knew how to respond to hearing Burraza's explanation for her actions. Curtus looked at Glade and saw she had tears running down her eyes. "Nico Alverez" She said. "Who" Burraza asked. "NICO ALVEREZ. Did you take him?" Glade yelled. Burraza took a couple of moments before responding. "Oh Nico. He is one of the few I do remember. Yes, I did take him. I honestly thought he was going to survive the playground, but alas he let his humility overcome him" Burraza replied. Tears began to roll down Glade's face. "WHAT DID

YOU DO TO HIM" she yelled. "Well I gave him the option. He could either be the subject of my experiments or I would take a little girl of the street and experiment on her." She began. Suddenly he computer screen changed from the security camera feed to the picture of a little girl jumping rope.

Curtus had never seen the girl before but there was something familiar about her. Curtus turned to Glade to see her crying on her knees. "Hey Glade what wrong" Curtus said running to her side. "Oh you can't tell. She is the little girl in the picture. I wish Nico was alive to see this" Burraza said laughing manically. Curtus looked up at the speaker in the ceiling steaming with anger. "I used to look up to you. I thought you one of the few people who pursued the preservation of health and human life. A person who would burn the midnight oil to save one more person. But you're just a psychopath. A serial killing psychopath" Curtus yelled "Aww Curtus that hurts to hear that from you. You were my favorite student and I was about to asked if you wanted to help me with my next operation" Burraza said. "Shove it up your ass. We are going to find you and turn you in" he yelled. Burraza began laughing hysterically. "Who are you going to turn me into. The police? The government? Even if you manage to get them to believe you, I work for something bigger than all of that. The Family will have me out and I'll be back to work on another project within the hour." She yelled back.

"The Family" Curtus whispered to himself. "Yes the Family. And it is too bad because you won't live long enough to figure out who they are" Burraza replied. Glade slowly stood to her feet. "Know this, I will find you and the rest of the Family and kill all of you" Glade said. "Odd choice of dying words. Curtus it was nice knowing you" Burraza said. Suddenly all of the lights in the playground went out for 2 seconds before red emergency lights clicked on.

Curtus looked around for anything he could use to fight the coming threat. He quickly looked around and found a broom behind a filing cabinet. He snapped the brush-end off the long wooden handle making a jagged makeshift spear. "Glade we need to find a way out of here" Curtus said. "You take one wall I'll take the other" she said. Before he ran to find an exit Curtus realized the files were still spread out on the desk. They could be leaving valuable information about the Family behind by not taking them. Curtus picked up Burraza's satchel that she left hanging on the chair and began filling it with files. "Dumbass what are you doing" Glade yelled. "We are going to need these after we get out of here trust me" He replied. "But you aren't getting out of here so it doesn't matter." Burraza said mocking Curtus. Suddenly all of the windows shattered. "Oh that can't be good" Curtus said to himself as he stuffed the last of the files into the bag. "Hey Dumbass take these too" Glade yelled. She threw over three dusty books. Curtus blew off the dusty and looked in awe on the Aerospace Wars Trilogy. These were the rarest books in the world being there was only 4 copies of each book. "There will be plenty of time to read it later. Now we have to find a way out of here" she said ripping books off the shelf. Curtus put the books in the bag and ran to the opposite wall.

He examined the wall to see if anything jumped out at him as a way out. Knowing his teacher, she would put all her answers in the question, all you would have to do is find them. The tavern was the only building without lights on. The switch was the bottle that was still full. They are very apparent clues in hind sight but in the heat of the moment can easily be overlook. On the wall was a painting of her shaking the hand of the Captain of the Jefferson. Curtus shook his head and ripped the painting off the wall. On the other side of the painting was a keypad. "Good work Dumbass now what is the code" Glade said running over to him. "You'll never figure it out. I never give that code to anyone" Burraza confidently. Little did she know that Curtus had known this the code for years.

Curtus learned that his teacher kept the same code for everything when he had to change his grade. He saw her unlock her phone and he entered the same sequence of numbers to open the gradebook on her computer. Curtus entered 2-2-9-4-3-9 into the keypad. The power was returned to the suite and the bookshelf slid to the left revealing an elevator. "oh nooo" Burraza yelled sarcastically. Curtus got an uneasy feeling. He had seen his teacher freak out over a food order not being on time. They were on the verge of escaping and exposing her for the monster she is and she is uncharacteristically calm.

Suddenly a high pitch screech came from outside the window. They ran to the to the window to see a Feral yelling from onto of one of the building. "We don't have to worry about them there is no way they can get up here" Glade said as she walked to the elevator. Curtus stared at the Feral. It stood on the building like a statue. "What's it doing" Glade asked pressing the button to call the elevator. "Nothing it is just standing there" Curtus replied. Curtus noticed something different about the Feral. It was much larger than the one they met during their first encounter. Its skin was also darker and its eyes were yellow. Then it turned its focus to Curtus. Its face was much more human this time around. It stared at Curtus like with an evil grin on its face. "Glade where is that elevator" Curtus said. "Are we standing in it" she asked sarcastically. Even though Glade was back to her sarcastic self he could tell by her tone that she was still shaken up.

Suddenly the Feral let out a deep "ARGH" and continued staring at Curtus. Then Ferals of all shapes and sizes began crawling out from everywhere. Curtus took a step back from the window. This was three times the number of Ferals that chased them when they were in the town. The new Feral dropped to all fours and pounced toward Curtus. The Feral landed halfway up the wall. Curtus looked in horror as the Feral landed on the wall but didn't fall to the ground. It stuck to the wall like Spiderman and began to climb the wall. The other Ferals took a moment to watch the lead Feral before following.

Curtus ran to the back of the suite dropping the broomstick and grabbed the desk. "A little help here" Curtus yelled. Glade ran over to the other side of the desk and began pushing. "What is going on" She asked. "Climbing… Wall… It's really bad" Curtus said straining to push the desk. They pushed the desk to the window and stood it up to block one of the three large window. Curtus quickly scanned the room. "The bookcase" Curtus said running over to it. They tried to move it only for it not to budge. "Damn it's on a track" Curtus said. "Where is the track at." Glade asked. "Behind the bookshelf" He replied. Glade then bit the inside of her mouth to induce bleeding. She swished it around in her mouth until she had enough bloody spit to melt the bookshelf track off the wall. She put her face against the wall and spit down the track. "That will do it" Curtus said. Curtus looked at the window saw a hand grab onto the window frame. Curtus ran and picked the broomstick off the floor. If he was going to die down here he was at least going to go out fighting.

"You get that shelf off the wall. I'll handle this guy" Curtus said twirling the staff in his hands.

The Feral grabbed the window sill with both hands before jumping into the room. The Feral was as tall as Maria, but it was much skinnier. Curtus didn't want to underestimate this new Feral. Since it wasn't as bulky as Maria which means it is more agile than she was. The creature looked Curtus dead in his soul. Its menacing gaze had Curtus shaking in his boots. It kept a chilling smile painted in it face. The smile looked almost cartoonish as the smiled started and ended where its ears would have been. It been to walking in an arcing path. Curtus walked the same path in the opposite direction maintaining his distance. The two walked in two complete circles waiting to see was the other would do. Noticing she wasn't getting help anytime soon Glade let out a sigh and began pulling the bookshelf by herself.

Curtus stopped his advance and stared at the creature. Like a reflection the creature mirrored Curtus's every move. A sweat ran down the back of Curtus's neck. The first Feral he took out with relative ease, but this one was much larger. Curtus grabbed the broomstick tightly with two hands. He was fully prepared to dive if the creature pounced at him. The creature exhaled and said "Lower back" keeping the Needles Kane like smile on its face. The creature dropped on all fours and pounced at Curtus. Curtus dove underneath the creature, but instead of rolling out of it Curtus chose to land and slide on his back. The creature told Curtus "Lower back" for a reason and he wanted to see why.

As Curtus slid on his back he saw what the Feral was talking about. As he slid by he saw a light flashing in its back. The Feral landed turned around hissing through it clown like smile. Curtus looked at Glade who was had finished pulling the bookshelf in front of the third window only leaving the middle one exposed. "Hey Glade do you see the thing in its back" Curtus asked. Glade looked at the Feral and saw the flashing light. "Yeah" She replied. "I need you to jab one of your knives in it" Curtus yelled. "Maria took em" she replied. The Feral suddenly pounced on Curtus while he was distracted talking to Glade. Curtus managed to tuck the broomstick under the its chin to keep the creature from biting his throat. "Figure something out" he yelled holding the creature back.

Glade ran to the window to see if there were any more coming. She looked down to see a 150 fifty Ferals climbing the wall. Though they had the ability to climb the wall they didn't seem very organized. They were climbing the wall with a crab in a barrel mentality. When one would get too far ahead another would pull it back to the group. Glade turned her focus to Curtus who was still on his back struggling to keep the Feral at bay. She could hear the broomstick cracking under the weight of the Feral. It wouldn't be long before the stick broke and Curtus was out of luck. She looked around on the ground for anything that was sharp enough to pierce the skin. She frantically scanned the ground only to come up empty. "There has to be something" She whispered to herself. She looked around until her eyes focused on the desk. Her panic quickly turned to elation as under the desk was an aluminum bat. She grabbed quickly grabbed the bat and ran over to help Curtus.

Curtus could feel the broomstick giving way. Every time the monster tried to bite Curtus the stick would crack a little bit more. The Feral continue to aggressively snap at Curtus's throat. It was pressing its feet into Curtus's knees so he wasn't able to kick the creature off of him. And with both of his hands on the broomstick Curtus was helpless.

Glade ran to the side of Curtus and the Feral. The Feral was so focused on killing Curtus it didn't notice Glade run up on it. Glade took the bat over her head and slammed it onto the creatures lower back landing a direct hit on the light. The Feral let out and animalistic screech of agony and rolled off of Curtus. Curtus shot to his feet and looked at the broomstick. It was nearly cracked all the way through. One or two more bite and he would have been toast. They watched the Feral as it rolled on the floor in pain. As they did that Curtus noticed something changing in the Feral. The scream was changing from an animalistic cry to human yell.

Glade became disinterested in watching the sight of a wounded animal and looked back at the elevator only to see that it still hadn't come yet. "How deep underground are we" She muttered to herself walking over to the door.

 Curtus continued watching the Feral go through its sudden metamorphosis. The chilling smile slowly returned to a normal human sized. It stopped yelling and laid in the ground unconscious. "About time you put that thing out of its misery." She said letting out a sigh of relief. "I didn't do anything it just passed out" he replied. All of the sudden the Feral's body began twitching. Curtus began slowly began pacing backwards. There was nowhere to escape and he had no way to defend himself. "Dumbass catch" Glade said tossing him the metal bat. Curtus caught bat keeping focus on the Feral. It slowly rose it feet. Curtus was prepared himself for anything holding the bat behind his ear like he was at bat in a baseball game. The Feral stood up and looked at Curtus. Looking into its eyes Curtus noticed a new found softness and humanity. The Feral quickly looked around the room and then looked back at Curtus. "Thank you son" The Feral said.

Curtus was at a loss for words. The Feral was speaking fluent English. It was as if Curtus was talking to one of his classmates at University. "The device in my back taps into the primal instincts and I couldn't control myself" He explained. The roar of the Ferals grew louder. "I know this is not the time for introductions, but I am Isaac. I'm a friend of your parents" He said extending his hand. "Curtus" He replied back grabbing his hand. "Thanks again for giving me control of my body again" Isaac repeated. "Don't mention it" Glade said masking it with a cough.

At that moment the elevator door open. "You guys go. I'll hold them off." Isaac said. "But you are one of them" Curtus said. "I may look like one of them but I am not one of them anymore. I told them to kill whatever is up here. By the time the get up here it will be just me." Isaac explained. "Come on Dumbass" Glade said standing in the elevator. "I owe you one" Curtus said running to the elevator. "Hey Curtus" Isaac began. Curtus stopped running turned around. The room fell dead silent and time seemed to stand still. He looked to see the Isaac was smiling, but this smile was different. It wasn't artificial like the one he had when he attacked Curtus. Curtus could tell that he was genuinely happy. "Remember. The Last Train Departs at Midnight" He said with a smile. Curtus remembered his father telling him that right before he got captured by Leremy and from the note attached to the map. He smiled and nodded before running into the elevator. He turned around and the Ferals began to coming in through the window. Isaac charged at the incoming wave of Ferals as the elevator doors began to close.

The elevator began to heading up and Glade let out a sigh of relief and sat down at the back of the elevator. "Finally we are getting out of that hellhole" She said. Curtus was worried about Isaac. The last thing he saw was him taking on all those Ferals. Glade could sense Curtus's worry and walked over to comfort him. "He will be ok" She said grabbing his shoulder. Curtus looked over his shoulder at Glade who was smiling at him. There was something empowering about her smile. She had just figured out the one of her friends was a subject of testing to protect her and she still managed to put a smile on her face to comfort Curtus. "Aww now isn't that just sweet" Burraza said over the speaker. Glade's smile quickly turned into a stern scowl at the sound of Burraza's voice. Curtus found something unsettling about their current situation. If she really wanted Glade and him to die down, there she would have stopped the elevator from coming to get them. "Why did you let the elevator come" Curtus asked. "I have just come up with a plan and that plan requires you to be alive" She replied. "Why the sudden change of heart?" Curtus asked. "Killing you would only benefit me in the short term. This new plan will have me powerful for generations." She said. "Generations" Curtus thought to himself. Curtus tried to figure out how would keeping them alive ensure her power.

"You know I'm gonna find you" Glade began. "I'm going to find and put you through such hell that death will be sweet relief." Curtus could feel Glade's anger from across the elevator. "I can't wait" Burraza replied arrogantly. Suddenly a tv dropped from the roof of the elevator. "Don't get my kindness mistaken for weakness" She added. The tv turned on and on it was a security feed of the suite. Isaac had stood in the middle of scattered Feral bodies. "So not only do you ruin my crowning achievements but I lose all of my test subjects as well" she said. Curtus looked at Isaac on the screen.

His hands were coated red with blood and his face was covered with cuts and bruises. "What stands before you is Subject 954. He was different in that he was able to order the other subjects around. The device you broke in subject 954's spine was a way for me to control him and the other subjects." Suddenly the windows slammed shut with metal shutters. "Now that you broke that device I have no way to control it making it damaged goods." She finished. Curtus became super nervous. Though he only just met Isaac he was in some way connected to his parents. "What are you going to do to him" Curtus asked. "Oh you guys are in for a real treat" She began.

Curtus stared intensely at the screen. He watched as Isaac began to look around trying to find a way out. "Are either of you guy familiar with Zyklon B?" Burraza asked. Curtus froze. He was well aware of what it was and what it was used for. "Such a primitive and drawn out way to dispose of someone so I thought I would improve it" she said. Curtus began to tremble. Knowing her level of genius that she was he could only imagine what she might have created. "Hold up. What is Zyklon B" Glade asked? "It what Old World Germany used in the second world war to exterminate Jewish people" Curtus explained. Curtus looked at Glade and her expression showed that she had no idea what he was talking about. "Don't worry young lady. You have a front to my new and improved formula!" She said proudly. Then a red gas started flowing into the room which seemed odd to Curtus.

In school when they talked about the holocaust they talked about the blue stains that were left on the wall from the gas. This was different. This gas was blood red. "If you're wondering why the gas is red. I colored it with a special blend of gases. It acts as a signature to my achievement" she said. Curtus watched at Isaac covered his mouth and frantically looked for a way out. Curtus knew the only way out was the shaft him and Glade came in, and there was no way to tell him where it was. All he could do is pray that he found it. Isaac ran to the window and tried to lift the shutter. "That won't work. The shutter has a smart counter weight. The more someone tries to open it the more pressure is added. The only way to open it is to override it" she said. "And you go the override" Glade said. "You catch on quick" Burraza muttered under her breath. Curtus couldn't turn from the tv. He had to see if Isaac made it out. Isaac continued trying to open the when he dropped to his knees. Curtus heart began to race. Then the feed was cut off.

"No!!!" Curtus yelled grabbing the tv screen. "Sorry that is all you get for free" Burraza said laughing manically. "How can you do something like that to another person. You're a demented human being." Glade yelled. "On the surface I'm human, but in my playground I am god" She said. The elevator stopped and the door opened. "Now you kids run along now. We will meet again soon enough" she said as the intercom transmission ended.

VII

The elevator opened up to a classroom that Curtus was all too familiar with. It was the class room where he had his first class with Professor Ross. In an instant Curtus relived every class he ever had in this room. Glade saw the look on his face and could tell that this was her classroom. "So... where did you sit" she asked. Curtus looked at Glade in confusion. "I can tell by the way you're acting that you have been here before, and since I'm just going to guess is her classroom I just wanted to know where you sat" Glade explained. "The back" he said pointing at a chair by the door. Glade shook her head. "Paid all that money to sit in the back" She whispered to herself. "So where do we go from here" Curtus asked. "If we are at University then we shouldn't be far. Follow me" Glade said leading him out of the classroom. They exited to the building to find themselves in the middle of a thriving city center.

University was in the center of the Downtown on the Jefferson. Due to the limited there are designated buildings all over Downtown for University rather than having a traditional campus.

"This way" Glade said as she began down the sidewalk. As they walked Curtus noticed something odd about the people walking through the city. They were giving him and Glade with weird looks. They were a mix of fear and disgust as if him and Glade were criminals. "Just noticing the looks huh" Glade said. "Yeah… why are they looking at us like that" Curtus asked. Glade stopped and turned around. "How many times have you walked around the city not dressed to go to school" Glade asked. Curtus thought hard and realized that he never walked around the city unless he was going to school. Whenever he would go out with his friends it would always be to somewhere in the Residential District. "Now that you mention it I never really have" Curtus replied. "Well look at how we are dressed and look at how everyone else is dressed. Plus, look at your clothes. They are tattered and stained to hell." Glade whispered as she turned around and began walking again.

Curtus looked at how everyone was dress and realized why they attracted so much attention. They looked like they didn't belong. Everyone was either in a business suit or a dress as they walked down the street. "Everyone is looking at us because we look like street rats. They know we don't belong. They also know exactly where we are going" Glade said.

The thought of people assuming they know someone's situation based on their appearance disgusted Curtus. "They don't know what we just went through" he whispered. "Well then be my guest. Go ahead and tell them that there is a city full of cannibals running around in the sewers." Glade replied. If they knew exactly where they were going it would take no time for Leremy to find them. "Shouldn't we move faster" Curtus asked. "If we run they are going to think we stole something which will draw more unneeded attention to us. Just keep your cool, we are almost there anyway" Glade said.

They continued down the street until the came upon an old metro entrance. The entrance was blocked by several pieces of police tape the read "Condemned do not enter". "Welp we're here" Glade said moving the tape out of the way. Curtus turned around and looked to see the people staring at them. Glade stepped through the tap and looked back to see Curtus frozen like a deer in headlights. "Dumbass, you coming" Glade yelled. Curtus snapped out it and stepped through the tape.

All of his life Curtus was told the Market District was just another part of the city, but now he found himself in a dilapidated stairwell trying to find the entrance. "I thought the Market District was a part of the city?" Curtus asked. "It was a part of the city" Glade replied. "Then why are we headed underground again?" Curtus questioned. "The key word is "was". It was a part of the city until the city had other plans and put a lid on it' Glade explained. With each question he asked Glade's responses only created more questions. "What did she mean put a lid on it?" "Why would they put it Underground?" "Did they do it to contain something?" These were just some of the questions that were going through Curtus's head. He followed Glade down a flight of stairs until they reached a door at the bottom. "I gotta warn you ahead of time. Whatever they told you the Market District is a lie" Glade said before opening the door.

In school they were told that the Market District was this bustling hub where people could trade goods and services. The pictures they were shown was this open air flea market looking area full of life and happiness where people could come and spend their day off from work. What waited for Curtus on the other side of the door was anything but that. Glade opened the door to a dreary, gloomy, forgotten pocket of the Jefferson. The lid she was referring to was the new highway that was built to connect Residential District to the hospital. Curtus could tell because of the sound of ambulance sirens starting and stopping above them.

There wasn't much that set this place from the shantytown they just left. The streets were covered in trash and an array of bodily fluid. The buildings were constructed by conventional means but they were in bad shape due to year of neglect. They were either empty with the windows shattered or the had bars on the doors and windows. Kids were running up and down the streets doing what kids do while the adults were doing whatever they needed to survive. The air smelled of feces, sweat, and the smoke of several different drugs.

They walked down toward the main street of the Market District when Curtus remember a question he was saving. "Hey Glade back in the airlock you told Leremy that your dad made it clear that you weren't his daughter. What did you mean by that?" Curtus asked. Glade stopped. "You sure you want to know" She asked. Curtus nodded his head. Glade let out a long sigh. "Follow me Dumbass" She said. Glade led him to a bench on the side of the main street. They sat down and rested for a moment. Curtus looked at Glade and noticed that she was shaking. "Are you okay"

Curtus asked. She didn't respond. Glade took a deep breath and began to tell the story of the last day she saw her father.

"It started the day when the Family sent Liam a package. I didn't know it was from the Family at the time, but knowing what I know now it was definitely them. It came an unmarked box. We knew it was his because he is the only one who got packages. That day I remember I was so mad at him because two days earlier I caught him sleeping with his assistant. So when he got the package I opened it and there was a Tonic pump. I knew it was special because the package was locked, so to get back at him I picked the lock and took the Tonic. Well that didn't go over well..." She said. Glade lifted her shirt exposing scars on her back. Almost every inch of her back was covered in scars similar to the ones slaves had after being whipped. Curtus put his hands over his mouth in shock. "Yeah and I got off easy. You should have seen what he did to my mother." Glade said pulling her shirt down. "Wow... how is your mother doing" Curtus asked. "Well she is better now" Glade began. "Oh that is good" Curtus thought to himself. "I mean she committed suicide a year and some change after that. She couldn't cope with what he had done to her. At least now I know she isn't hurting anymore" she finished.

All of the air left Curtus's body. A steady stream of tears began rolling down Glade's face. "So that is why you chose to help me. You have nothing else." He whispered. "That, among other reasons... if you think about it we are more alike than you realize. We are both alone. You didn't know who your parents really were until a couple hours ago and then they were taken from you." Glade said. "Were aren't alone though. We got each other and that has to count for something" Curtus said with a smile. Glade smiled and wiped the tears from her face. "Now come on we have to find whoever you came down here looking for." She said rising to her feet.

The two of them walked down the street scanning each of the building for any sort of clue. "So who are we looking for" Glade asked. "Before they took my dad he said to find someone named Juice" Curtus replied. "Juice… can we get an actual name please" Glade asked. Curtus reached in his pocket and pulled out the note from his father to see if he could find a name. When he opened the note he saw the ink was smeared all over the page from when he washed the poop off of him in the sewers. "The note from my father got ruined in the sewer" Curtus said. "Great now we are being chased by a what I can only assume is a shadow government that is turning people into cannibal creatures, tried to weaponize the flu, and we have no information" Glade said trying to get a grasp on their current situation. "Yeah that sums it up pretty well"

Curtus replied. "Well then we better get moving. I know someone on the surface probably already sold us out so they will be here in no time" Glade said.

The Market District consisted of one main road with buildings on each side. Curtus looked closely at each building to see if he could find anything that may help them. "Anything else on that note that could help us" Glade asked. "I told you the note is ruined" Curtus replied showing her the black sheet of paper. He looked around at all the signs of the stores to see if they held any clue. He scanned each store until he came across one that read "Midnight Manga". Curtus thought back to what his father and Isaac told him. "The Last Train Departs at Midnight." Curtus knew it was a reach, but with no other leads they had to start somewhere. "I think I might have found it" He said running toward the store.

They ran to the store front and saw a young looking kid organizing books. He was a dark skinned rail thin boy who was about 5'10 with messy black hair. He was wearing a logo less black shirt with black pants and white sneakers. "This is who we are looking for" Glade whispered. "It can't be he is like 15" Curtus whispered back. The kid looked up and a smile exploded on his face. He ran to the door and unlocked it. "Please come in" The boy said as he opened the door. Curtus and Glade entered the store and found themselves surrounded by Japanese Manga. The boy closed the door and locked it behind them. "Sorry if you feel uncomfortable being locked in. There are people who want to see this literature destroyed" The boy said. "Hey kid what's your name" Glade asked. The boy hesitated before responding. "That depends... Who sent you" he asked nervously.

Curtus looked at the kid and saw genuine fear in his face. "Don't worry we aren't from the Family if that is what you are asking" Curtus said in a calming voice. That put the boy at ease. "Okay good I got nervous for a second" He replied walking back to the cash register. "The name is Jaymar. Jaymar Odom" He said opening the register. "Well my name is Glade Stanford and that over there is Dumbass" Glade said quickly. Jaymar chuckled. "Well it's nice to meet you Dumbass" he said trying to hold back his laughter. Curtus let out a sigh. "My name is Curtus Parker" he corrected. Jaymar's eyes lit up. "Are you related to Carolyn Parker" he asked.

Curtus's heart began to race. Maybe this is who they were looking for. "Yes... yes I am" Curtus replied. Jaymar could barely hold back his excitement upon learning Curtus identity. "Please follow me" Jaymar said opening the counter. The three of them walked into a back room and Jaymar opened a cabinet and reviled a safe "She left this here years ago and told my dad to keep it hidden" Jaymar said pulling it out of the cabinet. Glade looked at Curtus. "What was your mother doing down here" She asked. "Well until about 12 hours ago I thought I knew everything about my parents. Now they're strangers so I don't know" Curtus replied. Jaymar looked at Curtus. "So do you know the code phrase" He asked. He didn't know the exact phrase but he had a good guess in mind. Curtus walked up to the safe and pressed the voice recognition button and said "The Last Train Departs at midnight"

That phrase seemed too important to just lead them to a book store. But Curtus was wrong as the screen on the safe flashed red and sad try again. Jaymar looked at Curtus. He was beginning to question who he was. "Are you sure you are who you said you were" He asked. Curtus thought about why the phrase wouldn't work until the very obvious answer came to him. "The only voice that can open this is my mother's" He said. "Well great then I'm never get to see the weapon inside" Jaymar said. "Weapon?" Glade asked. "Yeah. My dad told me about the weapon in the safe the night before they took him. He said it had the power to change the world." Jaymar replied. "And let me guess. When you say "They" you mean the Family" Curtus asked. "Bingo. So you can imagine why I would want to get inside" Jaymar explained.

"Hold on. We are looking for a person named Juice, do you know him?" Glade asked. "Well… my dad calls me Juice. He said he squeeze the nectar of his brain into me" Jaymar replied. Glade looked at Curtus. "This is who we are looking for. He runs a comic book store." Glade asked pointing at Jaymar. "Well this is more of a hobby. What brings in the money is the weapons my father makes." Jaymar explained. Glade refocused on Jaymar. "I knew your last name was familiar. Your mother is Lisa Odom isn't it" Glade announced.

Curtus had heard that name somewhere before. "Where have I heard that name before" Curtus said. "She was the woman who took over the Arms trade after Steve Aug mysteriously passed away." Glade elaborated. "Really then why are you living down here. You are loaded" Curtus asked. "Well just like most of the people down here. We were forgotten about." Jaymar replied. The room fell dead silent. The vibe had turned sour after Jaymar's announcement of his mother abandoning him and abducted his father. "How about we get that safe open" Glade said rubbing her hands together. "Yeah I will get right on that" Curtus said running to the back of the safe.

He walked to the back of the safe and examined the wiring. There was something special about the model of safe his mother used. This model was recalled because they would often permanently lock and you would have to cut the door off the door to get your belongings out. However, his mother figured out a way past this glitch. He scanned the wires until he found a wire that was taped together. "Bingo" Curtus said reaching for the wire. "What you doing back there Dumbass" Glade asked. "There is a reason my mom used this safe. Even if she came back and said the phrase she probably wouldn't be able to get in." Curtus explained. He took the tape off and separated the two wires. The screen on the safe went dark and the safe made a loud "Clunk". Curtus crawled to the front of the safe and slowly opened the door.

There were two shelves in the small safe. The top shelf contained a vile full of liquid, a Tonic pump, a diamond the size of a baseball, and an envelope. On the bottom shelf was a gold device that looked like a handheld vacuum. It was a handle with a trigger connected to a cylinder with a long barrel opposite of the handle. He quickly examined it before giving it you Jaymar. Jaymar's face lit up with excitement. "You're not going to take it?" He asked. "I don't know what it is or how to use it. You'll make better use of it than me" Curtus replied. Jaymar took the weapon and walked over to a worktable to further analyze it. Glade looked in the safe and saw the Tonic pump. "You know what that is right" Glade asked. "I'm pretty sure I know what it is. What I need to figure out is what I'm putting in it." Curtus said picking up the envelope. He opened the envelope and smiled as he recognized his mother's handwriting.

Curt,

In the safe are two things one for you to defend yourself with. The first is the MCH-OMN1T00L. It is a grappling hook as well as a long range ballistic weapon. Juice should be able to make ammo for it. The second is a special Tonic that allows you to take the properties of what you are holding at the time of inhalation. The pump is set for a five second delay after you press the button. Make sure you are holding the diamond with both hands while you are inhaling the Tonic. It will be intense and I'm sorry I can't be there to help you through it.

I know you must be surprised by Jaymar's age but trust me his is one of the brightest minds on the Jefferson. Keep him close he will help you maneuver your way around the Jefferson.

Be careful they have eyes everywhere on the Jefferson. Next you need to go to the Smokebox restaurant in the Gettys and find Mysuki Tran. You have to get her off the Jefferson. You will understand why once you meet her.

Be safe and I promise I will answer your questions when we meet again.

Curtus picked up the vile of liquid. He had never seen the liquid of the Tonic before. He had only seen the pumps a handful of time and all of those times they were empty. "You know what you are doing" Glade asked. "No, but my mom left pretty detailed instructions" Curtus replied as he filled the pump. He put the pump in his mouth, pressed the button, and quickly grabbed the diamond with both hands. He couldn't believe he was taking a Tonic. He had always been told not to take them, and now his mother told him that he needs to take it for his survival.

1 Mississippi:
"Calm down Curtus. Mom wouldn't do anything that would kill you. She is some kind of genius right. If not, they wouldn't have gone to such lengths to kidnap her and dad"

2 Mississippi
"Maybe I shouldn't do it. Maybe I should give it to Glade. She knows more about using Tonics than I do."

3 Mississippi
"Quit being a bitch Curtus. If you wuss out now you won't be able to save your mom or dad and you probably will get yourself killed."

4 Mississippi
"OK here we go. When the pump goes off take a deep breath in and whatever happens, happens"

5 Mississippi
puff

Curtus told a deep breath in once the pump went off, and he quickly learned what his mother was talking about when she said "it would be intense." Curtus felt his lungs begin to burn and his bones get heavy. He spat the pump out and dropped to one knee. "Just remember to breathe Dumbass it will pass" Glade said as she walked over to Jaymar. Curtus couldn't believe that Glade just left him. His body was slowly breaking down and all she could tell him was to remember to breathe. Then Curtus realized that while he was getting mad at Glade he had actually stopped breathing. "Ok Curtus focus. Inhale... exhale" he told himself. Curtus turned his complete focus to breathing because there was no chance of him saving his parents if he was dead in the back room of a comic book store.

Glade walked over to Jaymar who was at the table practically jumping for joy. "What's got you so excited" Glade asked. Jaymar picked up the device and held it in front of Glade's face. "Do you know what this is" He asked. "No, but I know you're going to tell me" Glade replied. "This is the legendary Omnitool" He said pointing it around the room. "Okay... what's so special about this thing" she asked. "Well you're not into weapons junkie like I am. It is known as a perfect weapon. It is perfect in every situation" he explained.

"How is it perfect in every situation" Glade asked. "It can shoot any type of bullet with no sound, built in grappling hook, it has a radar, can give off a smoke screen, and has a scope with 25+ viewing settings" Jaymar began. Glade rolled her eyes yawned from boredom. "Your just jealous because I have a cool ass weapon and you're hella lame" Jaymar yelled.

Curtus dropped to his knees and began yelling out in agony. He continued to squeeze the diamond like his life depended on it. Jaymar looked back at Curtus to see him rolling on the floor. "First time huh" He asked looking at Glade. "Yeah" she replied. "It might be good for all of us to be Tonic users. Can't have anyone holding the group back" He said messing with the Omnitool. Glade looked in surprise that not only he knew that she was a Tonic user, but that he was a user as well. "How did you know" She asked. "Your eyes slightly resemble those of a reptile. So I can only imagine you got a lizard based Tonic." He said. "Good Eye" she replied punching him lightly in the shoulder. "The only person who has access to those types of Tonics is the Family. So who is in your family is a member" Jaymar questioned. Glade looked down at the ground before she answered.

"My father is Liam Lopez. I mean biologically he is my father, but he doesn't see me as his daughter" she clarified. "Well we have that in common" Jaymar said. Glade looked up at Jaymar in shock. "Let me guess.

You got a mysterious package in the mail with a weird logo and no name on it. So you opened it and inside there was card and a Tonic pump inside. You sneak and take the Tonic just to try it and your dad finds out and leaves your family. Then your life goes to hell because there is no income in the house." Jaymar hypothesized. "You're close. I didn't sneak it just to try it. I did it because I was mad at my dad. I caught him cheating on my mom and when I told her he beat the hell out of me. So when that package came I knew it was his. Then when he found out what I did he beat the hell out of me and my mother before he disowned us." Glade explained. Jaymar nodded and smiled. "After I did what I did she left us, but she still needed ideas to run the cooperation. So once a month she would send goons down to work over the workshop and take some weapons with them. My father would just build weapons for fun. It was one of the few things that brought him genuine joy. So when the thugs would come down and cause hell the only way he could cope with it was to make more weapons." He finished.

He chuckled lightly. "Now that I think about it. Her plan was genius." Jaymar said chuckling lightly. "I thought I was the only one with shitty parents" Glade said. "Ha-ha no we are on that boat ttogether" Jaymar said. They looked back at Curtus who had fell silent. Glade walked over to him and put her finger under his nose to see if he was still breathing. "Okay he is through the hard part now we just have to wait five minutes for him to wake up before we can go" Glade said. "Okay where are we going next" Jaymar said. "What do you mean we" Glade asked. "I'm going with you guys" He said. "Oh no this mission is much too dangerous for a kid your age" She said. "How old are you" Jaymar asked. "19. How old are you kid?" She replied. "I actually just turned 19 today" He said digging in his pocket. He pulled out his wallet and handed her his ID to confirm his birthday. Glade let out a discouraged sigh. "Well happy goddamn birthday. Welcome to the team" She said throwing his id on the ground. "What was that for" He yelled. "Trust me kid. Where ever we go next you won't need that" She replied putting the diamond in Curtus's bag.

Suddenly there was a loud knock at the door. Jaymar walked over to the computer that was on the workbench. "Aren't you going to get that" Glade asked. Jaymar ignored her and began typing on the computer. The person at the door knocked again, this time more aggressively than the first set of knocks. "You should probably go get that" Glade said. "With you guys back here not a chance" Jaymar said. "Why. no one should go back here right" Glade asked. "There is only one person who knocks on the door when they come here and that is Tyrann" He said turning the screen towards Glade. Her stomach dropped as she looked at the screen and saw Leremy standing at the door with a gang of masked goons.

Jaymar ran to a bookshelf and pulled a green book off the shelf. Removing the book caused the bookshelf to sink into the floor revealing a secret room. "You guys get in here. The button on the wall to close the door" Jaymar said pulling a set of earbuds out of his pockets and putting them in his ears. Glade dragged Curtus by his feet into the secret room. Jaymar picked up the letter and Tonic pump and threw it into the room. Once she had gotten Curtus fully in the room she looked up at Jaymar. "Ill knock twice once the coast is clear. All you have to do is hit the button again to open the door" Jaymar said. Glade nodded and pressed the button bringing the bookshelf from the ground. Jaymar took a deep breath, plugged his headphones into his phone and began to the store front to confront Leremy.

Jaymar had seen these guys rough his dad up pretty good on numerous occasions so he knew they weren't anyone to mess with. He walked up to the door and unlocked the door. "Sorry I didn't hear you guys knock" He said opening the door. The group said nothing as they stormed into the store. "There have been reports of two fugitives that were caught running down here. We are just going door to door to see if anyone knows anything" Leremy said aggressively. "Fugitives? No I'm just here protecting my father's collection until he gets back" Jaymar replied. He had to act like everything was normal and there weren't two wanted criminals in the back. Leremy walked over to a wall of books and picked up a volume of One Piece off the shelf. "You know, I never understood why your father was so into the Jap bullshit" Leremy said fingering through the pages. "They masterfully incorporated beautiful art with great story telling" Jaymar explained. "Whatever you say" Leremy replied putting the book back on the shelf. He turned and looked at Jaymar dead in his soul. "I'm going to ask this once. Have you seen the fugitives or not?" Leremy barked at Jaymar. The aggressive tone of the question made Jaymar nervous. Leremy seemed to be in no mood to hear no as an answer. "Sorry Tyrann, I haven't seen anyone come through here. And trust me if someone came through I would tell you" Jaymar replied. Jaymar saw the look on his face and he could tell that didn't believe him. "Spitter!!! Get 'chur ass over here" He commanded.

One of the masked ran up to the side of Leremy and stood perfectly erect. "Yess commander Tyrann" He said. "Tell our friend here what I think about liars" he yelled. The man removed his mask to reveal a massive grotesque scar that crossed his face. The red scar was in large contrast with his pale white skin. "Thiss iss what happenss when you lie to him" Spitter said. He talked with a noticeable lisp and from the look of his eyes he was a Tonic user as well. "You see what happens. You get hurt" He began. Jaymar was genuinely scared of Leremy, but he put on a good bravado act. "You have nothing to live for so killing you is not a threat." He said pacing back and forth. "What do you have that I can leverage over you" he muttered to himself. He paced for a couple of minutes talking to himself before coming up with a devious idea. "You actually have something to live for and we are surrounded by it" Leremy said with a devilish smile.

Jaymar's stomach dropped to the floor. His father's collection is the only thing he had that made him feel close to his father. "Tell us where they are or we burn the collection" Leremy said pulling a lighter in his pocket. Jaymar found himself in-between a rock and a hard place. If he gives up Curtus and Glade, he can keep his father's collection, but he loses out on any chance to save his father. On the other hand, he can protect them and save his father, but he will lose his father's prized possession. "I'm telling you the truth I don't know where they are" he pleaded. Leremy was not a fan of his answer. "Light it up" He said putting the flame to the shelves and setting the volumes ablaze.

One by one he watched as each volume burst into flames. Spitter spit an acidy spray that dissolved the entire series of Naruto. The others took small handheld flamethrowers to the rest of the collection. "The building is made of aluminum so it won't catch on fire but I do advise to leave the premises inhaling all this smoke is bad for you. If you do hear anything you know how to contact us" Leremy said handing him a card before he and his gang of thugs left the store.

Jaymar ran to the back of the store, grabbed the Omnitool and banged on the bookshelf. Glade opened the door to Jaymar shoving the Omnitool in her stomach. "Hold this" He said before running to his computer. He dug through the drawer until he found an old hard drive. He plugged it into the computer and began to downloading files. Glade peered out of the of the panic room with her collar over her mouth. "Hurry up. You're going to die if you stay out here any longer" she yelled. "Almost done" He yelled. The smoke was growing thick. If he didn't act fast they all would die of smoke inhalation. The moment the download was complete Jaymar grabbed the hard drive and made a mad dash to the panic room.

On the way he saw Glade on her knees choking on the smoke. "Aw come on. You talk too much trash to be TKO'd by a little smoke" He said playfully as he picked her up. He carried her into the panic room closing the door behind him. He set her in a chair and walked over to the computer and began typing. He activated a ventilation system that purged the room of the remaining smoke. Glade continued to cough profusely, but that didn't stop her from voicing her opinion. "What the *cough* Hell" She yelled. "Sorry I had to do something before we left" Jaymar said handing here a bottle of water. She took a big gulp of water and poured the rest on Curtus's face.

Curtus sat straight up from the shock of the cold water. "Ahh momma I don't wanna join the swim team" he yelled. Curtus looked around and found himself in an unfamiliar room with Glade laughing at him. "When were aren't getting chased you are going to tell me that swim team story" She said chuckling. Curtus wiped his face and looked at Jaymar who was still typing. "Hey, what happened" Curtus asked. "Leremy came and burned the store to the ground" Glade said. Curtus looked a Jaymar. He could tell his heart was broken from the way he sat in his chair. He stood to his feet and almost lost his balance. He felt that he had gotten slightly heavier. "You okay Dumbass" Glade asked. "Yeah I just need to get my bearings is all" He said as he stumbled about. He walked over to Jaymar and put his hand on his shoulder. "You alright" Curtus asked in an effort to comfort him. "This is all that's left" He said holding the hard drive in the air. "Every volume, every chapter, every page is saved here" he said. "Well at least you have it" Curtus said. Jaymar looked at Curtus. "I guess I can look at it that way. But there is no feeling like turning the pages of a book" Jaymar said walking over to a lever on the wall. He pulled the lever and the room began to move downward like a freight elevator.

Curtus sat down on the couch and let out a deep sigh. "Finally I can take a breath" Curtus said. "Yeah it has been a minute since we haven't been chased by someone or something" Glade added. "Something?"

Jaymar asked. "Trust me kid you had to be there because you won't believe us" Curtus said. "Hey why do you called Tyrann Leremy?" Jaymar asked. Curtus looked out Glade. "Leremy was here" He asked. "Yeah while you were taking your cat nap he came in and burnt the entire store to the ground. And now we are here" Glade explained bringing him up to speed.

Glade laid on her back putting her hands on the back of her head. "Alright Dumbass where are we going next on our quest" Glade asked. "Well the note my mom left said we have to go to the Gettys and pick up someone named Mysuki Tran" Curtus answered. "Great not only do we have to find our way into the most dangerous part of the Jefferson, but we have to get someone out of there too" Glade griped. "Sound like fun" Jaymar said messing around with the Omnitool. "Where is the Gettys" Curtus asked. "Deep underground. So deep that some people don't even think it exist. It is said that only the government can access the Gettys through a secret entrance but I can get us in" Jaymar said.

Both Curtus and Glade looked at Jaymar. "You… can get us into the Gettys" Glade asked. "Yes indeed" he replied. "May I ask how you know how to get to the Gettys" Curtus asked. "I used to run weapons through an old service tunnel all the time for my father" Jaymar said. His tone gave the impression that his was not proud of his past. Curtus looked at Glade. "The Gettys are named after the old American battlefield Gettysburg. The reason it was sealed off from the general populous is that there was constant fighting there and the thought was that it might leak out" Glade explained. "So to prevent that from happening the cut it off from the rest of society" Curtus said. "Exactly" Glade said. "After they sealed it off the Family turned it into a testing ground for all of my father's weapons." Jaymar explained. Jaymar looked to be on the verge of tears. "Hey it's not your fault" Curtus said. "Well it kinda is" Glade whispered to herself. "None of that matters now. Jaymar can you get us to the Gettys" Curtus asked. "Yeah I already told you I could, but you may want to rest before we going. You both look like you have been through a lot" Jaymar said.

Glade sat up and looked at Jaymar. "Before Leremy came you said you were a Tonic user. What type of Tonic do you have?" Glade asked. "I am the proud owner of the Hawkeye Tonic. It lets me see long distances and land softly no matter how high I'm falling from" he explained. "How does that work" Curtus asked. "When you take a high end Beast Tonic you gain some of the instincts of the animal. Birds when they fly they are in control and never crash land unless they are injured or restrained. So every time before I am about to hit the ground my leg kicks toward the ground and it slows me down for a soft landing" Jaymar explained. "So that explains why I lay down in the sun every time I see it" Glade said. "No you might just be lazy" Jaymar said.

The room came to a stop and the back wall opened up to a massive bunker. The room was the size of a basketball gym. There we four long wooden tables covered in different types of weapons. The walls were covered in racks with several different blades, whips, and trophies. The wooden floors were scorched and carved up. "I give you my father's workshop" Jaymar said walking to the fridge on the wall. Both Curtus and Glade ignored all of the interesting weapons and looked solely at the fridge realizing how long it has been since they last ate. They were too busy getting chased to even think about being hungry. "Do you have any food" Curtus and Glade said in unison. Jaymar looked at them and saw the defeated look on their faces. "Yeah follow me in the kitchen and ill cook you whatever you want" Jaymar said waving for them to follow him.

Jaymar cracked a dozen eggs in a skillet and began to scrabble them. Both Glade and Curtus were drooling like starving dogs at the sight of food. Jaymar added ham, cheese, peppers, and onions to the egg to give it a nutrient and flavor boost. "Y'all need a good meal and a good night sleep before the head out to the Gettys." Jaymar said as gently stirred the eggs in the pan. He cooked the eggs hard and split them three ways. Before Jaymar could finish blessing his food both Curtus and Glade had licked their plates clean. Jaymar put his fork down and began clapping. "That is impressive. If you guys want to sleep, there are beds in the room around the corner" Jaymar said. "Do you have anymore" They both said. Jaymar laughed went back to the kitchen to cooked a dozen more eggs this time leaving Curtus and Glade plenty full. Curtus walked like a zombie to a large room filled with beds. He stumbled over to the nearest bed, jumped on it and immediately passed out.

VIII

Curtus woke up to Glade and Jaymar staring at him. "Welcome back to the world of the living" Glade said sarcastically. Curtus sat up slowly and rubbed the crust out of his eyes. "How long was I out" he asked? "14 hours" Jaymar replied. Curtus smacked his lips, waited a second before jumping at the realization of how long he had slept. "14 Hours" He yelled. "Yeah we thought you died back here Dumbass" Glade said. "Well good thing I didn't" Curtus said sliding off the bed. "Even if you died I would have taken that note out of your pocket and kept it moving" Glade said. Curtus glared at Glade. "Hey you guys. We need to make sure we are prepared before we head to the Gettys" Jaymar exclaimed. Jaymar cleared his throat before he beginning again. "We are headed into a warzone so we need to make sure we all have means to protect ourselves" Jaymar said. He focused his gaze on Curtus. "Do you specialize in any type of weapon" He asked. "I'm proficient in Bōjutsu and Krav Maga" Curtus replied. Jaymar couldn't help but smile. In several of the manga he read there was someone who was skilled with a Bō. "Okay that will work. And before you go you need to understand the basic nature of you Tonic" Jaymar added.

Curtus looked down at his hands. He had no idea what his power was let alone how to activate his power. Glade stood up and began skipping around the room. "Hurry up. We are waiting on you" she said cheerfully. Curtus shot a glare at Glade. "Did Jaymar give you more pocket knives to cut yourself with" Curtus shot back. "Better. Watch this" Glade said ending her skip. She pushed her palms out and two 3-foot-long blades shot out of her wrists.

Curtus's eye grew to the size of basketballs. He had never seen anything like that before. "Cool huh. Her Tonic power allows her to heal wounds quickly. So I installed these blades in her forearms that at made of a special alloy that doesn't erode upon contact with her blood." Jaymar explained. Curtus watched as she walked around the room stabbing random things around the room. "So do you know what my power is" Curtus asked. "Actually me and Glade have a pretty good idea" Jaymar replied. Glade put the palms down and retraced her blades. "Yeah you turn into a giant diamond and shit. It's actually kinda dope" Glade said skipping back to the group. Curtus rolled up the sleeves on his hoodie and took a deep breath. He looked down at his hand and squeezed his fist flexing his forearm. Just a Glade had said his entire fist and forearm turned to diamond. "Woah" Curtus said examining his arm. "From the looks of it your entire arm transforms into diamond not just your skin. This is a very good defensive Tonic." Jaymar explained as examined his arm. Curtus noticed that even though his arm had crystalized it still remained the same weight. "Huh… that kinda cool" he thought to himself as he squeezed his arm returning it back to normal.

Jaymar opened up a wire locker and pulled out a metal pipe. It was the same length of his Bō at home but the material was different. The Bō that Curtus is used to is made of wood which was lighter than the steel rod that Jaymar gave him. He grabbed the Bō and began to spin it around. It was unnaturally smooth, but Curtus felt he would get used to it quickly. "This will work. Thank you" He said. "Good. Now try and turn it to diamond" Jaymar commanded. "Wow Dumbass you gonna let him talk to you like that" Glade instigated.. "Glade shut up… I can do that" Curtus asked. "Yes you can" Jaymar replied. "When you were sleep it wasn't just your body that transformed but your clothes and shoes changed as well" Glade added. Curtus squeezed tightly on the Bō and just like Glade said it turned completely into diamond. Curtus spun the staff around in his hand and to his surprise it was rather effortless. "Huh it seems that it the properties change but the weight stays the same" Jaymar hypnotized. Glade walked over to Curtus. "Lemme see that" She said holding her hand out.

Curtus dropped the Bō and Glade almost fell over trying to catch it. "Holy shit this is heavy" She said slowly lifting it up from the ground. "Really" Curtus asked grabbing it from Glade's hand. "You don't feel any difference" Jaymar asked. "Not even a little bit" He replied. "Huh… So any weapon you make diamond only you can use it" Jaymar whispered to himself. "Neat little power that you got there Dumbass" Glade said shaking her hands. "Thank you" Curtus said returning the Bō and his hand back to normal. "Okay it seems we got that all figured out, we need to get changed before we head out" Jaymar said. "What is wrong with what we have on" Glade asked. "They will be able to tell you aren't from there in a second. Hold on let me get you guys clothes" Jaymar said running into the other room.

He came back with two sets of clothes. He handed Curtus a thick black hoodie with KYL on it and a set of brown pants. He handed Glade a white crewneck sweatshirt with a black check on it and a set of black sweatpants. "Put these on and then we can go" Jaymar said putting on a large white trench coat. "You're worried about us getting found out and your wearing that" Glade said chuckling. "Its Kevlar" Jaymar said fixing his coat. "It's unnecessary" She replied. "Hey you have a healing factor and he is indestructible. All I can do is fall slowly and see well" Jaymar yelled. "And you can't see you look like a jackass" Glade mumbled walking in the other room to change.

Curtus quickly changed his clothes and saw the state of his father's hoodie. It was littered with holes and rips rendering it almost unrecognizable. "Yeah it wasn't going to last anyway" Jaymar said. "Yeah it's just that it's my dad's" Curtus replied. "Well I'm pretty sure he won't want that back" Jaymar said jokingly. Glade walked back in the room in a slightly different outfit. She had on the crewneck sweatshirt but instead of the sweatpants she had on black leggings instead. "I saw these and I thought I could move better in these then those bulky ass sweatpants" She said. Jaymar let out a deep sigh knowing he wasn't going to be able to change her mind. "Okay are we ready now" Curtus asked. "I'm ready to roll" Glade said popping a piece of gum in her mouth. "Yeah I'm ready" Jaymar said clicking the Omnitool to his belt. Curtus looked around and noticed that the satchel he took from Burraza's suite was missing. "Where is my bag" Curtus asked. "Don't panic. I moved it all to this backpack including that big ass diamond." Jaymar said picking up a backpack off a desk. Curtus looked at Glade. "What you don't know when we are going to need it" She said shrugging her shoulders. "And look there is a place you can put your Bō so you don't have to carry it in your hands" Jaymar finished. Curtus locked his Bō into the side of the backpack and put it on. "Okay let's get a move on" Curtus said tightening the straps on his backpack.

Jaymar led them to a door at the back of the bunker. He punched a code into a keypad to the right of the door. When he finished the keypad lit up a bright blue and the door slowly opened. A frigid gust of wind flew through the doorway. "What was that" Curtus asked. "The Gettys are poorly insulated so some of the frigid outside air makes its way in" Jaymar replied. Curtus began to worry about Glade. He didn't think the tights would be enough to keep her warm. "Well what are we waiting on let's get moving" Glade said marching through the doorway. Curtus looked at Jaymar. "Are you going to stop her" Jaymar asked. "I thought you were" Curtus replied back. The both shrugged and followed Glade through the door way.

They walked one behind the other down a narrow hallway. Curtus looked up to see a sea of supports. "Are we in the wall of the Jefferson" He asked. "Yes we are" Jaymar replied. "A better question is how much longer are we going to be like this" Glade asked. Jaymar laughed at Glade's question. "Not much longer just keep moving" He replied scooting down the hallway. All of the sudden the hallway expanded into a massive tunnel. The ceiling was as high as a five story building and the tunnel was as wide as an 8 lane highway. "Come on this way" Jaymar said walking toward a small flatbed cart. "Shotgun" Glade said running to the passenger seat. Curtus shook his head at the thought of sitting in the wooden bed. He let out a sigh of disappointment and began jogging toward the cart.

Curtus hopped into the bed of the cart and they began down the tunnel. "How did this cart get here" Glade asked. "My dad built it" Jaymar replied. Curtus thought about how it was possible for his father to build a cart down here. "So your dad…" Curtus began. "Yes he brought all the parts through that tunnel and built it right here" Jaymar quickly answered. Curtus imagined how difficult it is to build a cart by hand under normal means, and the fact that Jaymar's father brought all the parts to this tunnel and then built it was pretty remarkable. They continued down the tunnel and Curtus began to think about what was ahead. "Hey Jaymar. What kind of weapons are they using down there?" Curtus asked. "They aren't using guns if that is what you are asking" Jaymar replied. "That didn't answer his question at all" Glade whispered to herself. Jaymar cleared his throat before he began. "For the last 3 months my mom has been on this torture binge. She wants to make weapons that don't kill but torture their victim. She also wanted them to have an old earth antique feel to them. So down there you will see twisted renditions on classic weapons. Electrified Crossbows, Flaming Broadswords, Neurotoxin Spears, things of that nature." Jaymar explain.

Jaymar looked over to see Curtus and Glade with their jaws dragging on the ground. "What" Jaymar asked. "Why didn't you just give them guns" Glade asked. "Yeah I'm with her, those are much worse than just guns" Curtus added. "You asked what they were using." Jaymar replied refocusing on the road ahead. "One that didn't answer my question, and two for the record those weapons kill people too" Glade informed.

They continued down the tunnel when Glade had a realization. "Wait if they aren't using guns why do you need a bulletproof coat" She asked. Jaymar opened his mouth to respond but no words came out. "Exactly. It's unnecessary and you look like a dumbass" Glade said. "I don't know I kind of like the jacket. It looks kinda cool" Curtus said. "Plus it is holding all of my ammo" Jaymar added fixing his jacket. "Dumbass when did I ask for your opinion" Glade asked. Before Curtus could reply the cart came to an abrupt stop. "Geez a little warning next time" Glade said rubbing her knees. "My bad... we're here" Jaymar said with a smile.

Curtus looked around and saw nothing but a dark tunnel. Jaymar hopped out of the cart and began stretching. "So where do we go now" Curtus asked.

"You guys aren't going to stretch" Jaymar asked. "What do we need to stretch for" Glade asked. "They are going to be shooting arrows and throwing spears. You don't want to catch a cramp and get killed" Jaymar said. "Jaymar we were chased by a 12-foot super human science project and about 30 of its man-eating friends. I think we can handle arrows and spears" Glade replied. Jaymar looked at Curtus in disbelief. "It was 45 and you forgot to mention that she was indestructible" Curtus said looking at Glade. "How did you guys get away from it" Jaymar asked. "We dropped her in the furnace" Curtus said. "Shit… that's hardcore" Jaymar said finishing his stretch. "Actually I dropped in the furnace you just ran like a punk" Glade corrected. "Well this is our way in" Jaymar said pointing to a grate in the wall.

There was a sign above the grate that read "Waste Water". After reading the sign Curtus instantly smelled a plethora of different odors. "You first" Glade said kicking him closer to the grate. "Why do I have to go first" Curtus asked. "Because you are used to being covered in shit" she answered. "Shhhhhhhhhhh They're everywhere" Jaymar said with his finger over his lips. Curtus looked at Glade and shook his head. "Fine" he whispered reluctantly walking to the grate. The closer he got to the grate the more powerful the scent became. He walked up to the grate and saw it was bolted to the wall. Curtus thought this might be the perfect time to test out his new powers. He squeezed his right hand turning it to diamond and punched through the grate.

In the dimly lit tunnel it was hard to see the color of anything so Curtus couldn't tell the entire grate was rusted. He figured it out when the grate turned to dust as he punched it. The lack of resistance sent him flying through the opening. With no way to stop himself Curtus flew face first into the river of waste water. Glade and Jaymar walked over and peered into the opening. "Did you know that it was rusted" Glade asked. "Yes. I wanted to see how he would approach it" Jaymar began. "And he approached it like how I thought he would with brute force"

Curtus stood up dripping in god knows what. "You okay Dumbass" Glade yelled. "Shhhhhhhhhh" Jaymar said. "Yeah. You know, just covered in shit… again" Curtus yelled back. "What part of they are everywhere do you not understand" Jaymar whispered. "Sorry I didn't hear you. You should quit whispering" Glade said jumping into the waste pipe. She landed on a narrow ledge close to the wall. "You see this is how you do it. You don't just dive in like a professional swimmer" Glade began. While she was in the middle of her speech Curtus splashed a huge wave of dirty water on her soaking her entire outfit. Glade looked down at here outfit in disgust. Here white sweatshirt had taken on a brownish tint from the water. "You're kidding me" She said. "Hop in the water is great"

Curtus said jokingly. Jaymar jumped in to the water also splashing it on Glade. "What... the... HELL!!!" Glade yelled. Jaymar came to the surface with a smile on his face. "And its waterproof" he said grabbing his jacket. Jaymar looked over and saw Glade was so mad she was on the verge of tears. "You might as well hop in" He said. Without saying word, she turned and began walking deeper in the pipe.

Curtus and Jaymar waded through the river of brown trying to keep up with Glade's rage filled stroll. Visibility was limited as their only source of light was from Glade's small flashlight. "We are almost there" Jaymar said pushing a box out of his way. "Where does this tunnel lead" Curtus asked. "It doesn't matter where it leads. The first place we are going in the Gettys is a damn clothing store" Glade barked "Well you're in luck because that is where it actually leads" Jaymar said. "Perfect" Glade said. "Hey do you think they are going to check down here" Curtus asked. "They eventually will, but we have time. They think they are the only ones with access to the Gettys." Jaymar said. Knowing they could find Mysuki without having to worry about Leremy bearing down their necks was a breath of fresh air.

They continued walking until a ladder came into view. "There it is" Jaymar said pointing. The ladder was in the middle of the tunnel hanging over the dirty water. Glade would have to jump and grab it. She lined herself up, took a deep breath, and jumped. As she jumped she slipped on the wet floor and tumbled into the water. Time seemed to move in slow motion as the two of them watched Glade tumble face first mouth open into the river of waste. They looked at each other to see if the other had a plan. Glade slowly poked her head from the water. The water seemed top boil due to Glade's anger. She spat the waste water out of her mouth before barking orders. "Get your asses up that goddamn ladder now" she said slowly. Jaymar pushed Curtus out of the way and practically ran up the ladder. Curtus looked at Glade who shot him a nasty glare. "What are you waiting on and handwritten invitation" she barked. "a p...please would be nice" Curtus said stumbling over his words. Glade scoffed and made her way to the ladder. Curtus waited for her to be completely up the ladder before he made his way up.

He climbed up the ladder to find himself in what looked like a sweatshirt superstore. There were hoodies, crewneck sweatshirts, and jackets of all colors all over the store. "Brace yourselves" Jaymar yelled. He flipped a switched that turned the lights on. The sudden exposure blinded both Curtus and Glade. Once they regained their vison the were met with Jaymar grinning ear to ear with a pair of kid's sunglasses on. "Yeah that light can be a douse. You shoulda had a pair of sunglasses on" He said. Glade snatched the glasses of his face exposing him to the light. "Gahhhh. That was a dick move" He yelled out. "Well I'm a lesbian so

I don't know about dicks or their various movements" Glade said walking over to a rack full of yellow hoodies.

A deflated feeling came over Curtus. He thought that after they weren't being chased anymore he maybe had a shot with her. Glade looked over and noticed the sad expression on Curtus's face. "What's that face for Dumbass?" She asked. Curtus knew he couldn't tell her why he was actually sad because she would ridicule him for it. "I'm just worried about my parents is all" he replied. "Don't worry. If what you told me is true and they sent a mercenary to kidnap them, then they need them alive" Glade explained. Curtus nodded and began looking at a rack of light blue hoodies.

Curtus changed into a logo less sky-blue hoodie, a pair of tight black running pants, and sky blue low top sneakers. Glade put on a black crew neck sweatshirt with some white leggings she found and a pair of white cross training sneakers. "Don't worry we are going to get your parents" Glade said putting her arm around Curtus. They walked over to Jaymar who was you drying off the Omnitool with a pair of boxer shorts. "Are you guys ready to checkout" he said laughing. "Hardy har har. Where is the Smokebox?" Curtus asked. "It's in the middle of town" he replied. "Okay now where is that" Glade asked bouncing in place. After she asked her question an explosion could be heard in the distance. "That way" Jaymar said. "Well we aren't getting any closer standing here. Let's get going" Curtus said. Curtus pulled the Bō off his bag and kicked open the front door.

IX

Curtus expected to see the streets lined with carnage and debris like in all the war movies he had seen, but was met with the exact opposite. The streets were almost spotless and well lit. There was an ominous silence that made Curtus and the others nervous. Curtus walked out on to the street with Glade and Jaymar creeping close behind. "Jaymar I thought you said it was a war zone down here" Curtus asked. "It is. And like most warzones most of the fighting will be done in one concentrated area" He replied. "Where is the fighting happening" Glade asked. "Well from the direction the sound of that explosion they are in the Supply District" Jaymar said. Curtus turned around and looked at Jaymar. "Do you have any type of two-way radio in that jacket of yours" Curtus asked. "As a matter of fact I do" Jaymar said digging his coat pocket.

He dug in his pocket and pulled out two earpieces. "Here we are. Two two-way radios" Jaymar said handing one to Curtus. "Okay I'll use Omnitool to get to higher ground and guide you guys to the Smokebox" Jaymar added as he put the earpiece in his ear. "Good. That will be a huge help" Curtus said putting his earpiece in. Jaymar aimed the Omnitool at a building and fired the grappling hook. The harpoon like hook pierced the metal ledge of the building with ease. Jaymar pressed a button and he was suddenly whisked away at a high-speed. They had never seen anything like the Omnitool before and were mystified by how it worked. "Hey can you guys hear me" Jaymar said over the radio "I hear you loud and clear" Curtus replied pressing his fingers against the earpiece. "Hey wait a minute. where is my radio?" Glade asked. "We only need one on the ground" Curtus replied. "And beside you would just argue with Jaymar anyway" Curtus added. "Okay this is a good spot. You guys just walk straight through that alley. I'll let you know if there is anyone coming" Jaymar said. Curtus nodded. He looked at Glade, pointed at the alley, and they began pushing forward.

They crossed the street into an alleyway. It was in complete contrast to the street they were just on. It was lined with garbage and almost too dark to see. "Stop you guys" Jaymar said over the radio. Curtus lifted his hand signaling Glade to stop. Then all of the sudden four bodies fell lifelessly into the alley. "They were about to get the jump on you guys. Now you can keep going" Jaymar said. "Did he shoot them" Glade whispered. "Yes I did and you should have seen these shots. They were like 125 yards with no scope" Jaymar said proudly. Curtus looked at Glade. "I vote him on the team" he said softly. "He needs to show more than that. He could have just made four lucky shots" Glade replied. "Let he know it was actually six. Two didn't fall into the alley" he corrected.

They continued down the alley when Curtus became curious about how this civil war actually started. "So how did this war actually start" Curtus asked. "Well when I explain it will sound kind of dumb, but okay" Jaymar warned. "Of course you get to hear the history of this place while I walk in silence" Glade mumbled to herself. Jaymar cleared his throat before beginning his history lesson.

"About 70 years ago the Family put a top on the Gettys. They feared the residents of the Gettys. If they organized would be too much for them to handle and they would lose control the Jefferson. But if they were to kill everyone here, they had the potential to miss out on a potential money generating idea. So they did the next best thing. They pitted everyone against each other. They began taking 2-3 people out of the Gettys every year. What happens to them nobody knows, but what they think is they left to get rich." Jaymar explained. Glade let out a huge sigh. "Tell him to summarize" She said. Overhearing this Jaymar began to just tell Curtus the main points. "Well to make a long story short all the people they were taking out were fairer skinned and the dark skinned residents did not particularly like that very much. They began to think that the light skinned people thought they were better than them. So they retaliated with violence and they have been fighting ever since" Jaymar finished.

Curtus thought about the plan and realized how genius it was. You took a couple of people from one side of a demographic and make it seem like they are getting better lives for no reason and the other side of the demographic will begin to get frustrated. This leads to violence within a community and create an auto regulating system of population control. They will never have to worry about them uprising because they will be too divided to ever unite and launch an offensive. "Well what the story about this war" Glade asked. "The Family is at work again" Curtus replied. "Of course they are" Glade replied.

They reached the end of the alley when Jaymar told them to stop and hide. They crouched behind a pile of trash cans. Curtus watched as a patrol of people armed with broadswords walked past. The patrol contained what looked like 15-20 light skinned men wearing beige vest with black pants and boots. "That is the Haske. The light skinned faction of the Gettys" Jaymar said. Suddenly there was an explosion and a bunch of men came flying out of the trash cans and ambushed the Haske patrol. Curtus and Glade jumped back to avoid the violence but stayed close enough to be able to watch the conflict.

The ambush seemed to end as fast as it began. The men who jumped out of the trash bags were armed with crossbow and lit the patrol up with arrows. The entire patrol was wiped out in a matter of seconds leaving no survivors. There was one ambusher who had a sword driven into his lower back paralyzing him from the waist down. He was dragging himself down the street by his hands when he caught a glimpse of Curtus and Glade. "Please kill me. Please don't give them the satisfaction of seeing us as weak" The dark skinned man pleaded. "That weird. I thought he would have tried to kill you guy because of your skin color" Jaymar said. "Vintage Haske. Would rather watch the Duhu struggle than to grant their dying wish. Go to Hell" the man yelled. "That more like it" Jaymar added. Glade walked over to the man and shot one of her blades into the base of the man's neck severing his spine.

Curtus looked at Glade with a horrified expression on his face. "What I was just granting that man's dying wish. That was the most humane way to do it. He went with no pain" Glade explained. Curtus wasn't worried about Glade killing the solider. It was the realization that the two sides that were fighting both African American. "Jaymar is everyone in the Gettys black" Curtus asked frantically. "Just about. 99% of the black population lives down here" Jaymar replied. Curtus did the math about how much that actually was. There were 10 million people on the Jefferson. Of those 10 million 24.1% of them were African American or Black. "so you're telling me there are 2.4 million people living down here" Curtus asked. "Yeah that sounds about right" Jaymar said.

Curtus had always wondered why he didn't really see many other people topside that looked like him. No matter where they went. The store, school, any social gathering Curtus rarely ever saw any black people. Now to find out that the they were all underground killing each other made Curtus sick. "You guys need to get moving. There will no doubt be Haske reinforcements coming soon" Jaymar said. Glade looked at Curtus who was spaced out. Though he had a blank expression on his face, his body language gave the indication that he was angry. She took the earpiece out of Curtus's ear and put it in her ear. "Where do we go now" Glade asked. "If you go straight three more blocks it will be on your right, but you gotta get moving" Jaymar said. Glade heard metal clanking over the radio. "Damn the Haske found me. I will meet you guys at the restaurant" Jaymar said before the radio went dead.

Glade ran up to Curtus and slapped him the back of the head bringing him back to the real world. "I know this whole arrangement is shitty, but we need to get moving" Glade said. "Ok where do we need to go" he asked rubbing the back of his head "Just go straight three more blocks and it will be on the right" she said. They didn't hesitate without seeing if the coast was clear he bolted across the street.

They managed to make it down two blocks without running into any trouble. Curtus was adamant to get to the restaurant and read the files he had taken from Burraza's office. It would give them a chance to learn more about the Family. As they ran down the alley when four men dropped from the rooftops above. With Jaymar dealing with his own problem he couldn't warn them about the incoming ambush. They were ambushed by three masked men and one large unmasked dark skin man. He stood about six foot three and looked to weigh more than 250. Curtus personally had no problem with dark skinned people mainly because he didn't know any, but he knew that down here they had a problem with him. "What 'chall doing round here. Y'all know this Duhu territory" The man yelled. Curtus could tell that no matter what he said the man was in no mood to talk with him or Glade solely based on the color of their skin. "We were just headed to the Smokebox to get something to eat" Curtus said. The man began to get mad. "All the territory y'all got and y'all decide to run through ours" He yelled.

The man began to pace across the alley. "You Haske think that everything down here is yours and aren't willing to share with us just because the government likes y'all" He yelled. Curtus looked at the masked men. They had their hands on their crossbows waiting on the order to shot. Curtus looked at Glade. They knew the only way they would be able to beat them is if they got the jump on them. Curtus nodded and focused on the leader of the ambush team. He had made a couple of passes across the alley and Curtus had figured out his walking pattern. Every time he changed direction he would turn his back to them. The next time he turned around he would make his move.

Before the man began his turn there was a massive explosion down the alley that knocked everybody over. Curtus sat up and looked up for Glade but when he looked over she was gone. There is no way she could have ran out of the alley without anyone noticing. Curtus looked up to see if she was climbing up the side of one of the building only to find that she wasn't there. Then two of the masked men suddenly dropped to the ground. The third rose to his feet and drew his crossbow. "What the hell happened to them" The leader yelled. "I don't know they just dr…" before the man could finished he began coughing up blood. Then as the man began to drop to his knees Glade faded back into view.

The leader was seething with rage as he looked at Glade stand above the lifeless bodies of his comrades. "You're going to pay for that you Haske trash" He said drawing his broadsword. As the man walked over to confront Glade Curtus struck him in the ear with his diamond Bō knocking him unconscious. "Nice job. I thought I would have to do all the work by myself" Glade said wiping the blood off her hands on one of the masked men's pants. "How did you do that" Curtus asked. "You like that huh" Glade said with a smile. "I can't like I'm jealous." Curtus said reverting the Bō back to normal. "Well you have seen me do it before. Remember when I met you in the sewer I did the same thing." She explained. "Oh yeah that's right..." Curtus replied. "C'mon Dumbass. I bet Jaymar has been waiting at the restaurant" Glade said. Curtus put the Bō back on his pack and they continued toward the restaurant.

The Smokebox sat in the middle of a city square that looked completely different from the rest of the city. When enter the city the streets were clean but this was a new level of clean. The streets were made of ceramic tile each of which was a small piece to a much bigger piece of art. "This looks like an exhibit out of a museum" Curtus said. "I've never been to a museum so I'll just have to take your word for it" Glade replied as she walked out into the square. As the moved into the square Jaymar landed softly right next to Curtus. He was cover in sweat and dirt but didn't have any major injuries. "What happened to you" Curtus asked. "I had to fight like thir... forty dudes. You should have seen it." he said clipping the Omnitool back onto his belt. "You know we were about to go and find you to watch, but we didn't want to ambushed again" Glade said. "Smart" Jaymar said pointing to his temple. They walked up to the impressive front door of and even more impressive building. The building looked like a Hindu temple. The two story building was about 50 yards wide with every inch of it being covered in art. The door stood around 15 feet tall and was made of some sort of wood. There was a detailed engraving that covered the entire door that looked to depict some sort of a battle.

Curtus tried to pulled the door open but the door didn't budge. "Well it is obviously a push door" Glade said snickering at Curtus's struggle. Curtus took a deep breath and pushed on the door with all his might, but was met with the same result. "Is this even the right door" Curtus asked retreating back to the group. Jaymar looked around and saw a woman riding a bike. She had a cooler taped to the front of his bike letting him know she was a delivery woman. She rode up to the side of the building and parked her bike in front of a side door. "Hey guy I think that I just found our way in" Jaymar said drawing the Omnitool from his belt.
Curtus ran to Jaymar and grabbed the barrel of the Omnitool. "Look around you. This looks like some sort of safe zone. If we kill anyone here we will be in all sorts of hot water" Curtus explained. Jaymar thought for a moment and then reluctantly put it back on his belt. "Then how do you suggest we get in"

Jaymar asked. Curtus watched as the woman punched in a code and the door opened. "Do you have something in that jacket of yours along the lines of a fingerprint scanner" Curtus asked. A devilish grin grew on Jaymar's face. "You are in luck" He said digging into one of his coat pockets. "Great then let's go" Curtus said.

They waited for the door to completely close before making their move. They crept to the door in a triangle formation making sure not to be spotted. They reached the door Jaymar pulled a device that looked like a cellular phone out of his pocket. He walked over to the keypad and shined a purple like on the keypad. Curtus and Glade looked on as Jaymar worked his magic. The purple light shined on the keypad for about 10 second before it shut off and revealed them woman's fingerprints. There were four fingerprints and Curtus saw the lady punching four numbers which meant it was a four-digit password. "It's a four-digit passcode" Curtus said. "Then that make is easy" Jaymar said putting the scanner in his pocket. "How it could be any combination of those for numbers" Glade asked. "The scanner shows the heat signature of each fingerprint. The more fade ones will be the older ones because they had more time to cool off" Jaymar explained cracking his knuckles. He examined the keypad before punching in the numbers. "6-9-5-7" Jaymar said as he punched the numbers in. The keypad glowed green and the door slowly opened. "You know you might make a great addition to the team" Glade said patting Jaymar on the back. "We can throw a party after, but now we got to find this Mysuki person" Curtus said as he walked through the door.

They walked through the door and found themselves in the distributing center of the restaurant. Coolers were being handed off, filled with food, and sent out through several different doors. They walked down the main hallway of the room trying to find any clues to help them find Mysuki. "What is this girl's last name again" Jaymar asked. "Tran. And how do you know she is a girl" Curtus asked. "I read Japanese comics every day. It isn't the first time I've heard that name Mysuki before" Jaymar explained. "Okay. What did you ask for her last name?" Curtus asked. "To see if it matched the name on the door" Jaymar said pointing at a large steel door. The door was red and on the top of the door frame read "Y. Tran". "Not the name we are looking for but it is a start" Curtus said. He walked up to the door and knocked on it three times.

He didn't hit the door very hard but the metal sound echoed throughout the distribution wing. Curtus looked back and saw that everyone had stopped working. They stared at him like he had just jumped into a lion's cage wearing an all meat tuxedo. "I think this might have been a bad idea" Curtus whispered. "Well keep acting like it is a good idea until shit goes south" Glade whispered back. They could hear footsteps behind the door. "What do you want" A woman's voice said from behind the door. "I need your help" Curtus said nervously. "Your voice doesn't sound familiar who are you" The voice asked. "I am Uhhh Curtus Parker." He replied.

The room felt dead silent. It was so quiet in that room that Curtus could hear his own heartbeat. Then the sound of unlocking locks broke the silence. From the sound of it there were about five locks on the other side of the door. The door flew open and a small round Asian lady walked out. "Are you really Carolyn's son" She asked staring at Curtus. "Yes I am" He replied. "Please come in. You and your friends come in" She said waving them in. They walked into the office and the lady slammed the door behind her.

The walls of the office were lined with swords and other types of weapons. The lady walked over to her desk and she stared at Curtus with a cartoonish smile. "Let me introduce myself. I'm Yuki Tran I'm a friend of your mother's. So how is Carolyn, I haven't seen her in many years" she asked. "Well her and my dad were abducted and they left notes with instructions that led me here" Curtus explained. "Oh no. I hope she is okay" Yuki replied.

Curtus noticed something weird about Yuki. It felt like there was something disingenuous about her. "So what brings you down here Curtus" She asked. "Well like I said about the notes my parents left. The most recent one told me to come here and pick up a girl named Mysuki" He answered. After hearing Curtus's reasoning Yuki's demeanor changed. He cartoonish smile quickly turned into a look of disdain. "Oh you're here for her. Makes sense" Yuki said standing up out of her chair. She walked over to the door and stopped. "I don't know how much use she will be to you" Yuki said as she opened the door.

They followed Yuki to the main dining room. The dining area was divided right down the middle. The Duhu on one side and Haske on the other side. The group receive an array of dirty looks as Yuki led them through the center of dining room. They reached the front of the building and walked up a set of stairs. Once they were up the stairs to a hallway that led to a singular door at the end of the hall. "Is this the attic" Glade asked. "Yes it is" Yuki said. "And someone is living up here" Jaymar asked. "When you meet her you will understand why she is up here" Yuki said. Yuki pulled a set of keys what looked like 75 keys out of her pocket. She fiddled around with them as they walked until she found the right one. Once they reached the door Yuki just put the key in the door. "Aren't you going to knock first" Curtus asked. Yuki ignored Curtus and continued to unlock the door. She opened the door and they walked into a lifeless room. All that was in the room was a bed and one dresser. "Mysuki there are people to see you" Yuki yelled. Suddenly someone rose from the blankets and when she stepped out Curtus realized why his mother wanted him to go out of his way to make sure she got off the Jefferson. Curtus found himself looking at the last Middle Eastern person on the Jefferson.

X

Curtus held back his panic and questions as he didn't want to make a scene. She stood from her bed and walked over to the group. "Nice to meet you guys my name is Mysuki" She said as she walking over. She was one of the most beautiful women that Curtus had ever seen ranking in the top two with Glade. She had flawless light brown skin with long black hair that hung just over her lower back. She had a fit build and the natural curves of her body would make any outfit look good. Curtus and Glade looked in awe as she walked over to them, but as she got closer they notice something wrong. Her eyes were a lifeless grey color. "That's enough. You're close enough Mysuki" Yuki barked. She stopped and focused her gaze at the ground. "Sorry mother" She said. "What did I tell you. You walk off what you hear" Yuki barked. As she was yelling at Mysuki she had forgotten that Curtus and company was in the room. "I'm sorry. She has been blind all her life and she just won't listen when I tell her to listen to what is going on around her." Yuki explained. Curtus could tell that this explanation was disingenuous, but he acted as if everything was normal. "Trust me I know. Working at the hospital we get a whole lot of patients that don't want to cooperate" Curtus said with a fake smile.

Suddenly there was a loud crash downstairs followed by the screams of arguing men. "I have to handle this. You guy do what you need to do up here. If you need me I will be yelling at drunk men downstairs" Yuki said. She ran out of the room closing the door behind her. Jaymar walked over to the dresser and began dragging it over to the group. "Excuse me can we borrow this" Jaymar asked. "Yes you can" Mysuki said with a smile. Curtus looked at Mysuki's smile and he got butterflies in his stomach. Her smile was a perfect complement to her figure. She was so beautiful that Curtus was almost afraid to talk to her. Glade leaned over to Curtus and whispered in his ear. "You better make your move soon. Cause if not she is mine." Curtus looked at her as she walked over to help Jaymar.

They brought the dresser over and laid it face down using the back as a makeshift table. Curtus walked over and helped Mysuki find her seat at the table. He slowly guided her to her knees making sure she wouldn't bang them on the dresser. Curtus looked over at Glade after he took his seat and she was giving Curtus a dirty look. Curtus couldn't help but smile as he felt had a small head start over Glade. "So what are your guy's names" Mysuki asked. "Well I'm Glade, to you right is Jaymar, and to your left is Dumbass" Glade stated. Curtus had gotten used to Glade calling him Dumbass but she had never called him it in front of a woman of Mysuki's caliber. It was only in front of human science experiments and men trying to kill them. Mysuki laughing at the joke did not help Curtus's already shaken confidence. "My name is actually Curtus. Dumbass is more of a nickname" Curtus explained nervously. "Curtus huh... I like that name. It is nice to meet you Curtus." Mysuki said with a smile. Curtus was relieved that Glade's attempt at sabotage was unsuccessful. He had regained his confidence and remembered the reason they were in that attic in the first place.

"Mysuki tell us about your mom. Because I got a weird vibe from her" Curtus said. "Well as you obviously could tell she isn't my real mother, but she is an evil tyrant" Glade began. "She runs her employees into the ground using their safety as a bargaining chip. She sold my brother Ymerel to make a quick buck and will probably do the same to me later when the price is right" She finished. "She sold your brother" Jaymar asked. "Yeah. Evidently there is a rather large price on the head of anyone of Middle Eastern decent. I don't know why but she told me after she blinded me that I was only alive for her to be sold later" She explained. "Wait Yuki said you were blind all your life" Glade said. "She lies so much I don't think she even knows what the truth is anymore" Mysuki replied.

Her story got progressively worse the more she told. "When I was six she sold my brother to a bunch of white men in suits. I saw the entire thing and went to ask her what happened. But rather than lie to me like any decent parent would she took me in the kitchen and poured some sort of cleaner in my eyes and blinded me" she said finishing the sad tale of Mysuki Tran. Everyone found themselves at a loss for words. They had only heard stories this sad in movies, but to hear it in real life and see the results of it made their stomachs turn. "I can't believe you went through that" Curtus said. "Yeah actually telling someone about it, the story doesn't even sound real" Mysuki said chuckling. Curtus grabbed her hand and held it tight. "Don't worry. We are going to do everything we can to get you out of here" Curtus promised her.

Curtus took off his backpack and spread the files out on the dresser analyzing the titles as he moved them around. "Okay I know this isn't all the information on them, but hopefully we will find out what the people are capable of" Curtus said. "Who is chasing you guy" Mysuki asked. "Oh we are being chased by a shadow government. Nothing major." Jaymar said picking up a file labeled "The Rush of 4". "Yeah it is all Dumbass's fault" Glade jokingly added picking up a file labeled "Purge of 2215". Curtus wanted to defend himself, but after he thought about it more they wouldn't be in this predicament if they hadn't met Curtus. "My bad guys" Curtus said apologetically. Glade and Jaymar looked at Curtus in surprise. "If you guys had never met me you would have never met me and your lives would be normal" Curtus said tightening his grip on his bag. "Are you serious" Glade asked. "Yeah what are you apologizing for" Jaymar asked. "If I had just turned myself in to Leremy. You guys wouldn't be getting hunted like dogs" Curtus replied.

Jaymar looked at Curtus with a reassuring smile. "Hey I was getting worked over by them every month for weapons from my dad's stash. I felt there was no way out and my life would only last as long as I had weapons to give them. And then you guys came to my shop and that all changed. Now I feel like I have a chance at life and I began to hope again" Jaymar said. Glade put her hand on Curtus's shoulder. "When I was running through the sewer you know what I was doing" Glade asked. Curtus thought hard but he actually had no idea why she was down there. "I was trying to find a place to kill myself and join my mother. I felt alone. I felt I had no purpose and had given up on life. I filled a Tonic Pump with cyanide and went to the sewer to be forgotten about. Then I saw you running aimlessly around the sewer and thought let me do one last good deed before I die. But it turned out to be more than just one last good deed. When I met you, you gave my life purpose. At first it was to keep you alive and help you find your parents, but the more time I spent with you the more I realized that life wasn't so bad. You became my friend and cured me of my loneliness. You saved my life so don't you dare apologize" Glade said with a smile. Curtus was taken back by their words. "Don't you ever think that you ruin our lives. We actually need to thank you Curtus" Glade added. Curtus had never heard Glade say his real name before. It in a sense was a stamp of sincerity on how she felt. "You guys really feel like that" Curtus asked. "Absolutely" Jaymar said. "And we will do all we can to save your parents" Glade said. Tears began rolling down Curtus's face. "Thank you guys" He said wiping the tears from his face. "Now c'mon Dumbass we got some research to do" Glade said breaking the seal on her file. Curtus smiled and opened up a file named "[Project M41M1]".

Curtus opened the file and was appalled at what he found. It was Burraza's playground but at the scale of a metropolitan city. "Hey you guys come take a look at this" Curtus said pulling a blueprint out of the file. "There is no way she can do this" Jaymar said "The Family can do anything" Glade replied. "No they physically can't. Look at the scale. The city would be twice the size of the Jefferson" Jaymar explained pointing at the paper. "Then where would they put this" Glade asked. "Your guess is as good as mine, but this information isn't teaching us anything" Curtus said throwing the file on the floor. Curtus looked at Jaymar.

"What does your file say" He asked. "It is about the day four people challenged the family a long time ago" Jaymar said fingering through the file. "Give us a synopsis" Curtus said. "What is that" Mysuki asked. "It's a summary of the main points of a story" Curtus explained. Jaymar cleared his throat before beginning.

"There were four people Freto, Angel, Issa bu, and Babie Austin and they led a group called the Kryll that was in direct opposition of The Family. The group was losing trust in its leaders thinking they were fit to lead the movement. So the four of them charged the Keep and tried a head on assault of the Family's HQ. Well they didn't get very far as they were easily defeated by the Family. In a show a strength the four were hung from the wall for all to see."

"Oh my goodness" Mysuki said. "Yeah but that was there plan all along. As the left a note behind that was later found in a raid of a Kryll base" Jaymar said flipping through the file trying to find the letter. As he frantically flipped the file the letter flew out of the file and into Glade's lap. She picked it up and began reading aloud.

> "If you are reading this, they probably have us on display in the city square bloodied and beaten. We knew we couldn't take then on by ourselves that wasn't the point. We were trying to convey two separate messages one to the people of the Jefferson

and one to you guys. To the people of the Jefferson this is not a utopia. There is a true evil out there that they are unconscious of. They are in more danger than they know. And to you guys especially the people that doubted us. We are 100% with the cause and you guys need to be to. Those people need to be liberated and they can't break from an evil that they don't know exist. Your job now is to expose them. Give the people the information they need to think for themselves and be free"

You will not see the changes now but future generations will have you guys to thank.

Give them hell
Angel
Freto
I55A bu
Babie Austin

The room feel silent. After seeing the picture of the four of the hanging from the wall of the Keep everyone felt the emotions of the letter. "What is the date on the letter" Curtus asked. "June 10, 2201" Glade replied handing the letter back to Jaymar. "2201… Makes you wonder where they have been for almost 35 years" Curtus questioned shaking his head. "It wasn't a failure. In the file is says that during the Rush they managed to severely injure the Captain Vladimir Don who was the presumed leader of the Family who would later die from his injuries" Jaymar added. "But it seems that they managed to recover in 35 years" Glade said.

Curtus turned his head to Glade. "Ok Glade. What does your file say?" He asked. Glade looked at everyone and gave them a warning. "You guys are going to need to buckle up for this on. It's really bad" she said looking around. Curtus didn't detect any sarcasm in her voice. This meant that whatever was in that file was an act of pure evil. Glade looked at Mysuki. "Mysuki you especially brace yourself" She said. "I am ready for whatever you have to tell me" Mysuki said adamantly. "Okay" Glade replied opening the file. She cleared her throat but didn't speak. Glade couldn't read what was in the file not because she didn't have the ability to, but because the contents were that disgusting. "Are you okay Glade" Mysuki asked in a soothing voice. "Y… yeah I'm fine" She replied shakily. "Whatever is in that file I can handle it" She reassured Glade. Glade took a deep breath and began reading.

```
           December 25 2215.

       The Operation was a resounding success.
    99% of the Muslims were jettisoned from
       the Jefferson along with all their
            religious manuscripts. We have
        confirmed that all the adults are off
        the ship which means the remaining <1%
```

```
      are children. Even though they won't
      have anyone to pass on their religious
      teachings, we will still need to dispose
      of them before they reach an age where
      they can cause a panic. It is believed
          that the Kryll are harboring the
          remaining children which will make
             acquiring the children rather
          difficult. None the less this was a
          resounding success for the Family.
```

Curtus considered himself a history nerd. While people would go out to party Curtus would be at home looking up history and learning as much about the Jefferson as he could. This is new information to him. No website or book ever talked about a genocide of the Muslim culture. Curtus had learned about the Muslim culture from his research, but they were told that they had gotten on another airship. Curtus looked at Glade and noticed that her face had turned red. He could tell that the content of the file was affecting her. "Does that file tell you how it happened" Curtus asked. Glade snapped out of her trance and began flipping through the folder. Curtus could tell that she didn't want to read anymore but Glade knew that this was not a time to be weak.

She flipped until she found a page that contained a flyer in it. She pulled the flyer out and threw it on the table. It was for the first ever mosque on the Jefferson. "They used their religion as bait" Jaymar said. "Now you see what we are up against. These people have no moral. No standards. No regard for anyone. All they want to do is do whatever it takes to keep a choke hold on power" Glade said. Curtus saw fear in Glade's eyes for the first time. "Don't worry. If they are a government all you have to do is to go to top" Mysuki said. Everyone looked at Mysuki said in surprise. "What do you mean" Curtus asked. "They might be the ones that come up with the idea, but I assume they will never be the ones that do the leg work. Just like Yuki they will come up with a plan but always send henchmen to do their dirty work. Well at least that is how Yuki does it." Mysuki explained.

Curtus thought about what she said and saw that it was brilliant. Back when he was in the sewer he overheard Leremy talking about how the Family wanted his parents and of he had any say in the matter he would just killed him. "So what you are saying is if we cut the head off the snake the body has no choice but to die" Glade asked. "Precisely" Mysuki replied. The plan was much easier said than done. The only way to get into the Keep without being attacked by armed troops is to have an invite or an escort. "So any ideas on how to get in there" Glade asked. Everyone looked at Curtus. Being that he was the only one that lived topside they though that he would have a plan. "That place is a fortress. There is only one way to get in and out and it is heavily guarded" Curtus said. "We could rush it" Jaymar said. "Not the best plan but it has promise.

Let's keep thinking but put that in our back pocket" Mysuki said jokingly.

Curtus looked at Mysuki's eye and noticed something familiar about them. "Hey Mysuki do you know what Type of cleaner your mother used to blind you" Curtus asked. "Formula 561 why" She replied. "Okay that is what I thought" Curtus said. Jaymar and Glade looked at Curtus in confusion. "What are you getting at" Glade asked. "Formula 561 is an old school tactic to blind people and is very effective. Topside we had a problem with gang members blinding people that. So we created a solvent to fix that gave the victims their vision back" Curtus explained. "And you know how to make it" Jaymar asked. "Of course I do. I'm the one that created it" Curtus replied patting himself on the back. Curtus took a pen out of his backpack and picture of one of the MBF victims out of the file. He flipped it over and began writing a list of what he needed to create the solvent on the back of it.

The list was relatively small only containing 5 items. Curtus looked at Mysuki. "Where in the Gettys can I get pharmaceutical supplies and chemicals" He asked. "Warehouse 88 in the Supply District" She replied. "Of course where all the fighting is" Glade said. "Sadly yes" Mysuki said. Curtus stood to his feet. "Glade, Jaymar, you coming" Curtus asked. They both smiled as they jumped to their feet. "I mean you weren't going to go without us" Glade replied. "Wait where are you guys going" Mysuki asked. "We are going to go get the supplies and give you your sight back" Curtus said putting all the files back in his book bag. "You guy really don't have to" Mysuki pleaded. "No offence we kinda have to" Glade said. "Yeah if we are going up against the family everyone on the team needs to have their vision" Jaymar added. "Don't worry about us. What we have been through this will be like running to the store" Curtus reassured her.

He put the backpack on and began the door with Glade and Jaymar close behind. He grabbed the doorknob and before he opened the door he turned around. "Your job is to think of a way out of here and into the Keep" Curtus said. Mysuki smiled. "You got it" She replied. "Okay welcome to the team" Curtus added. He opened the door and they walked out of the attic.

XI

They made their way down the hallway when Yuki met them at the top of the stairs. They didn't want her to know they were aware of her past so they put on fake smiles and kept it cool. "So what do you think of her. She is going to be worth a fortune in 6 months" Yuki said with a smile. Curtus was disgusted. How could someone think of another human being a property.

"What happens in 6 months" Jaymar asked. "Well she turns 21. That means I can price her as an adult." Yuki replied with a smile. Her tone gave the impression that this should be common knowledge in the Gettys. "Well we are going to run to the store really quick" Curtus said trying to walk past Yuki. She sidestepped in front of him stopping his advance. "What are you getting from the store. "We are getting soap and stuff. We have been running for days and haven't had a proper shower" Glade said. They could tell by Yuki's face that she thought they were foul smelling. "Yeah you guys need a good scrub down. Be careful. I want to talk more about your mother when you guys get back" She said looking directly at Curtus. He had no desire to talk to her about anything. "Yes ma'am" Curtus said through his teeth. She got out of the way and they walked down the stairs.

They exited the restaurant and everyone looked at Curtus as he seemed to have taken charge of this operation. "So where are we going Dumbass" Glade asked. "Ummm" Curtus began. As he was answering there was a large explosion to the right of them. "That way" Curtus said pointing in the direction of the explosion. Jaymar unhooked the Omnitool off of his belt. "Okay you guys grab on" Jaymar said. They just looked at him in confusion. "The longer we stay here the more time we give for people to raid that warehouse" Jaymar reiterated. Against their better judgement they grabbed onto Jaymar. He pressed a button on the Omnitool and pulled the trigger firing the grappling hook. The hook pierced the ledge right below the roof of a 15 story building. "Here we go" Jaymar said releasing the trigger. Once he let go of the trigger Omnitool began reeling in at a high speed send the try flying through the air.

The only time Curtus had ever be this high off the ground was in the safety of a high-rise building. He had never flown through the this high and at this rate of speed. Though he had been afraid of heights for most of his life this was a different sensation. The speed they were flying made this more of a thrill. As they approached the building and Curtus realized they had no plan to stop. "Hey Jaymar. How are we going to land?" Curtus asked. "You guys just hang on and let me drive" Jaymar replied. He pressed another button and the hook unlatched falling out of the wall before returning to the Omnitool. "Whatever you are going to do can you please hurry it the hell up please" Glade yelled. Jaymar put the Omnitool in his left hand and aimed it a building about two blocks ahead of them. He took a deep breath and pulled the trigger. The hook propelled at the building until it found a home in-between two apartment windows. Right before they crashed into the ledge of the building Jaymar released the trigger and the Omnitool jerked the toward the hook changing their course.

Curtus was in awe of how Jaymar had become so comfortable with the Omnitool in such a short time. "When did you learn to do this" Curtus asked. "While you guys were playing around on the ground getting ambushed I learned how to fly" Jaymar said with a smile. "Good now fly our asses to the Supply District. I'm not trying to be here any longer than I have to" Glade said. "What are you scared Glade" Curtus asked cheerfully. "No I just don't want to babysit you more than I already have to" She replied. "You guys are great in-flight entertainment" Jaymar said. "Just shut up and grapple" Glade yelled.

They flew through the sky until they reached a large makeshift wall. The wall was made of sheet metal and concrete salvaged from collapsed buildings. "Can you get over that" Curtus asked. "He should drop you for asking a stupid-ass question like that. Of course he can" Glade yelled. "Thank you Glade" Jaymar said. Jaymar examined the wall and found scaffolding on top of the wall. He reeled the hook and aimed for the scaffolding. He inhaled deeply and held his breath to steady his aim. He stared down the scope and pulled the trigger. The hook flew through the air and right through the scaffolding. "Oh god" Jaymar said. "What do you mean oh god" Glade yelled. "I mean oh god what a great shot" Jaymar replied nervously.

Curtus could tell that something went terribly wrong and Jaymar was blowing smoke. Jaymar needed to act fast before the crash into the wall. He let go of the trigger and hook began to reel in. The hook never pierced and took hold of anything. His plan was to wait for the hook to drag against the wood then he would pull the trigger again and hope the hook would catch the wood. If not, they were in for a painful crash landing. Jaymar watched intensely as the hook made its way back to him. Then the moment the hook began flying over the wood he pulled the trigger again. Blades deployed from the side of the hook and dug into the scaffolding.

Jaymar had to contain his relief as he said earlier that there was no problem. He released the trigger again and they began flying toward the top of the wall. As they flew toward the scaffolding it came to Curtus that again they had no landing plan. "Not to sound like a worry wart but how are we going to land" Curtus asked. "Don't worry I got that covered" Jaymar said with a smile. As they flew toward the scaffold they seemed to be picking up speed with no way to protect themselves. If they hit the scaffolding at their current speed the impact would knock all three of them unconscious and the would certainly fall to their deaths. As they approached the walkway Curtus took off his backpack and putting his left arm through both straps. He squeezed his fist and turned the backpack into diamond holding it in front of Jaymar. "A diamond headed battering ram. Great idea" Jaymar said. Curtus watched as they closed in on the scaffolding. He ducked his head behind the backpack and braced for impact.

They blew through the scaffolding as if there was nothing there. Curtus opened his eyes and looked down at the hellish nightmare that was the Supply District. It resembled more of a trash dumb than a city as debris was scattered everywhere. The landscape was spotted with fires and smoke. Faint screams of combatant could be heard all the way up where they were. Curtus and Glade held onto Jaymar as they got to see first-hand his Tonic in action. Rather than falling straight down like a normal person they were gliding. "Jaymar, time to put that eagle vision to the test" Glade said. "We are looking for Warehouse 88" Curtus added returning his backpack to its original form. Jaymar scanned the landscaped intensely. Curtus noticed as Jaymar focused his irises began to turn yellow. "Found it" Jaymar said as his eye returned to normal. He pointed the Omnitool, fired the grappling hook and they flew towards it.

They slowly floated to the ground landing in alley between two warehouses. Curtus looked around at the surrounding warehouses. Many of them had broken window and looked to have been looted. "Okay which one is 88" Glade asked. Jaymar pointed at the warehouse that was in the best shape giving Curtus hope. If they hadn't looted it then they would be able to find what they were looking for. Glade jumped on the wall right above the window and shot the blade out of her right wrist. She pressed it in between the two panes of glass and let her blood run down the blade. He blood eroded the lock causing the window to fall off. Jaymar caught the window to prevent it from shattering and drawing attention. "C'mon Dumbass. You're the one with the list" Glade said retracting the blade into her wrist. Not wanting to leave Mysuki waiting Curtus jumped through the window.

The warehouse was dimly lit by the emergency lights. Rather than their being shelves the warehouse was full of pallets with various supplies on them. Glade and Jaymar entered the warehouse and walked over to Curtus. "Okay what do we need" Glade asked. Curtus unfolded the list and read it aloud. "We need Toral-C, Nitrolyric acid, D-stilled water, Saline, and Alcohol" Curtus said. They both nodded before running off. Curtus ran straight down the aisle looked on either side hoping to find what he needed. He made his way to the end of the aisle where he was able to find a case of D-stilled water. "Bingo" He said as he opened the case and put a bottle in his backpack. As he zipped his backpack he overheard a news report coming from the security office. Curtus's gut told him not to go over there, but he had been out of touch with the world for so long his curiosity got the best of him.

He slowly pushed the door open to find the person who was supposed to be watching the security feed sleep. Curtus wondered how the tv were still working if the power was out for the rest of the warehouse. He looked around and saw a network of cables leading out of a window. "Huh got to give it to him. He wasn't about to sit here bored" Curtus whispered. Curtus refocused on the tv with the news report. It was a breaking news alert about a group of terrorist that were planning an attack somewhere on the Jefferson. "Authorities were able to acquired pictures of the terrorists. If you see them call the police and do not engage. These terrorist are armed and dangerous" the news anchor stated.

Curtus used to watch old terrorist shows with his parents on Friday nights when he was younger. He liked them because of the uncertainty of when and how they would strike created a certain constant suspense. He was also fascinated about their thought process. How could they kill innocent men, woman and children and expect not to be hated by the group they attacked. He hated the terrorist and would actually get frustrated when they would come on the tv. So it broke his heart to see his name and picture being associated with the word terrorist. Curtus watched in horror as him, Glade, and Jaymar's picture were put up on the screen. "These terrorist want nothing but to see the Jefferson fall below the cloud and conventional American values to go with it. Be a good citizen. Don't be fearful. Be vigilant. Think about your neighbor. If you see them help bring them to justice. I am Billie Del

Rey and that is your news at noon" The news anchor finished. Curtus ran out of the office trying to find Glade and Jaymar.

He found them both by the window with items in each of their hands. "Hey we found what you were looking for" Jaymar said holding his hands up. Curtus unzipped his backpack. "Great put it in here" Curtus said breathing heavy. Glade could tell that something was bothering Curtus. "Dumbass what is going on. You're shaking" Glade asked as she put her items in the bag. "Uhhh we have a bit of a problem" He began. "How big" Jaymar asked putting his items in the bag. "A we are now enemies of the state sized problem" Curtus replied. Looks of shock came over their faces. "I saw a news report and it said that we were terrorist and were armed and dangerous" Curtus elaborated. "Damn they know we are down here" Jaymar said. "What do you mean" Curtus asked. "The Family wouldn't risk damaging their utopia they set up topside. They're only airing the terrorist threats down here on a closed circuit because they know the people will do anything for the reward money" Jaymar explained. "How much is it" Curtus asked quietly. "Five million dollars a head" Jaymar said. "Gahd Damn imma turn y'all asses in and buy myself a condo" Glade said jokingly. "Well I just wanted to let you guy know" Curtus said. "Yeah it is good to know that 2.4 million people with nothing to lose are looking for us" Glade replied sarcastically. "Well the longer we stay here the closer we get to getting caught. Let's get moving" Curtus exclaimed as he jumped through the window.

Curtus couldn't even two feet on the ground before being spotted. "Hey their down here" A voice yelled. "Dumbass what did you do" Glade asked as she jumped out of the window. "I didn't do anything" Curtus replied. "Exactly. What you should have done is waited for the coast to be clear before you jumped your stupid ass out of the window" She yelled back. "Jaymar what are you doing" Curtus asked. "I'm coming I just had to grab something" He said as he jumped through the window. They grabbed onto Jaymar and has grappled them to the roof. The buildings were close enough for them to hop across from one roof top to another. "Any plans on getting out of here" Curtus asked "I was actually working one" Jaymar replied loading egg shaped casing into the Omnitool. He aimed the Omnitool and pulled the trigger. Five eggs were sent flying on a line toward the wall. "What the hell did that accomplish" Glade asked. "A good plan is like an onion. There are layers to it" Jaymar replied. The three of them jumped over the alley to the next rooftop. "Now it is time for phase two. Grab on" Jaymar yelled as he flipped another switch on the side of the Omnitool. They grabbed on to Jaymar and he shot the grappling hook at the wall. He released the trigger and they were yanked toward the wall.

As they flew toward the wall the people on the ground began firing arrows and throwing spears at them. Curtus grabbed his Bō and began to deflect the arrows and spears that got too close. Glade erected one of her blades and did the same. "You guys are going to want to look at this" Jaymar said pulling a small radio out of his pocket. Curtus knocked away a spear and two more arrows before looking toward the wall. "We were in the warehouse for 5 minutes. When did you have time to set all this up" Glade asked. "Rule number 10. Never question my genius" Jaymar replied. Glade could tell that whatever Jaymar had planned was about to be over the top. "Here we go. Phase 2" Jaymar said pressing the button on the radio.

When Jaymar first shot those eggs Curtus had no idea what they were, but after pressing the button it was very obvious. There were five massive explosions in the center of the wall. Curtus and Glade looked in amazement as the massive wall began to crumble in front of them. "When did you get time to make that" Glade asked. "ah ah ah Rule #10. Don't question my genius" Jaymar said with a smile. Massive chunks of debris dropped down giving them the opening they needed to escape. "It's not subtle but it sure is effective" Curtus said with a smile. "Thanks Curt" Jaymar replied reeling the hook from the crumbling wall. They continued towards the wall, but without the pull from the grapple they began to descend. "We aren't going to make it" Curtus yelled. "We need to get low enough so I can use the remaining wall as a catapult" Jaymar said. "Okay we will hold off the arrows n shit" Glade replied. As the descended a bright light came from directly above him. There was something different about this light. There was a certain heat that came with it. A light this hot could come from only one source. The sun.

The sunlight was coming through a massive opening in the roof. "They're here" Curtus yelled. "Oh course they are" Glade yelled as she grabbed a spear out of the air and threw it back. "Jaymar we need to go now" Curtus yelled. Jaymar knew they weren't low enough for his desired flight path but with this recent development his plan would need an update. "Okay hang on" He said firing the grappling hook. It latched onto the wall and shot them at a 45-degree angle in the air. Once they were on the other side of the wall Jaymar aimed the Omnitool directly at the Smokebox. "The landing is going to be rough so hang on to your butts" Jaymar said pulling the trigger. The hook sunk into the S of the Smokebox sign and they began flying toward the restaurant. As they were about to crash land something came to Curtus. "Why would they put such a large reward on our heads if they were just going to come and get us" Curtus asked. "When they did capture us naturally one side would blame the other for preventing them from getting the reward money thus leading to more conflict" Glade explained. "Ahhhh" Curtus replied realizing the genius of the whole thing.

Curtus could feel Jaymar's power try and slow them down but it wasn't enough for a soft landing. Curtus put the Bō back on his bag and turned it to diamond to protect the contents inside. Jaymar's feet slid across the ground but he quickly lost his balance and everyone began tumbling down the street. They continued rolling until they came to a stop in front of the Smokebox. "So what do y'all think about that plan huh. Pretty kickass am I right" Jaymar asked. "I can't hate. It was pretty kickass" Glade said fixing her hair. Curtus opened his backpack to see that the contents survived the crash. "Alright let's go. We don't have much time to give Mysuki her sight back" Curtus said.

They walked in to the restaurant to see Yuki standing in the middle of the dining room. The vibe in the room was off. There were trained killers eating in fear from something Yuki either said or did. Curtus walked nervously in the dining room. The only thing that was going through his mind was the reward on their heads. "Back already" Yuki asked. "Yeah I found everything pretty easy. Hey I need a couple of things" Curtus asked. "Oh what do you need" She replied. "I need a Pyrex dish, measuring spoons, and some soup spoons" Curtus stated. "Oh what do you need those for" She asked. "Me and Glade drank dirty water on the way here and I want to make something that will clean our systems out" Curtus answered. Curtus was known for being a notoriously bad liar, but due to the circumstances he focused all his energy on keeping it together. There was too much on the line from them to be stopped right here. "Okay wait here" She said walking back to the kitchen. She came back with a small glass bowl, measuring spoons and two soup spoons. "I want to taste this cleanse when you finish it" She said. "Okay Ms. Tran. If you need us we will be upstairs" Curtus said running upstairs. Glade and Jaymar gave her a small wave before following Curtus.

Curtus ran down the hall and opened the door to find Mysuki still sitting on the dresser. She looked at Curtus with a smile. "Were you able to find what you were looking for" She asked. "Yes we found everything and more" Curtus replied putting the bowls and spoons down on the dresser. "What do you more did you find" She asked. "Well we found out that we are now enemies of the state" Jaymar said smiling. "Yeah and Jaymar here blew up the wall" Glade said punching him in the shoulder. "So that was you guy that were making all that noise" Mysuki said chuckling a little. "Yeah. You can't have a kickass plan without a little kick right" Jaymar said jokingly. The room fell silent at the feet of Jaymar's bad joke. "So are you ready to get you sight back" Curtus asked unpacking al the supplies from his backpack. "I'm kind of nervous. I've been blind so long I can't wait to see how much the world has changed" she said moving the hair from in front of her face. "Well in about 15 minutes you will be able to" Curtus said before beginning to prep the solvent.

The solvent was relatively simple to make. It is just ¼ teaspoon of the four chemical ingredients added 1 teaspoon water. Curtus figured out the solvent worked when he mixed the ingredients while he was bored and seeing how they reacted with different cleaners. When it was mixed with Formula 561 it turns the solution into water. After this breakthrough he began testing it on rats by blinding them and giving them their sight back. He brought this discovery to his professor who tested it on one of the 561 victims. When it gave back the man's sight they began mass producing the solvent. Curtus allowed his professor to take the credit for the discovery which after learning about her dark past and disturbing present he regrets.

He mixed all the ingredients together until it made a bright red colored solution. "That looks like it will make her vision worse" Jaymar said. Glade shook her head. "How can a blind girl's vision get any worse" She asked. "Hey, that is soon to be the girl with sight" Mysuki said. "ooo sassy just like I like them" Glade said taking a seat on Mysuki's bed.

Curtus took the soup spoons and filled it with the solution. "Ok you might feel stinging sensation" Curtus said as he poured the solution in her right eye. His filled the second soup spoon and emptied it in her left eye. Mysuki laid on the back of the dresser with a childlike smile on her face. Curtus watched as the solvent began to immediately take effect. The red liquid turned from red to green and the clear. Once the liquid turned clear Curtus could see the color of her eyes. Her eyes were a beautiful blue green. Curtus had done this procedure hundreds of times that he knew when exactly the patient's vison returns to them. Her eyes were clear and her vision should be back but she stared at him.

"You enjoying the view" Curtus asked jokingly. Mysuki began to blush. "Sorry it's been so long since I've see anyone and you're cuter than I pictured you" Mysuki said wiping her eyes. "You do have an ugly voice" Glade said laying back on the bed. "Oh and sorry Glade I am not a lesbian" She added. A look of genuine defeat came over Glade's face. The thought of her losing out on the Mysuki sweepstakes to Curtus made her stomach turn. "It's alright. I'm happy you can see again." She said turning her back to them. "Yeah welcome back to the world of the seeing" Jaymar said with a smile. "I'm glad to be back" She replied continuing to wipe her eyes. "Sorry to cut the celebration short but did you come up with a plan" Curtus asked. "I did but you're not gonna like it" She said. "Honestly in our current situation there is no such thing as bad plan" Glade said spinning around. "Well the plan is that we turn ourselves in" Glade said

XII

"I stand corrected there are bad plans and that is one of them" Glade said beginning pacing around the room. "No hear me out" Mysuki pleaded. Glade took a deep breath before joining the rest of the group as they gathered around Mysuki. "I don't know what you guys did but if they labeled you enemies of the state they wouldn't just kill you. They'll want to make an example out of you guys to show the people that nobody can oppose the government. If we turn ourselves in, we will be able to get up to the Keep without having to fight anyone" Mysuki explained. "Okay but what do we do when we get up there and we are handcuffed" Jaymar asked. "Well I have more of an organic thought process. I think of ideas when we need them most" Mysuki said with a smile. "Okay so we are up in the Keep and we somehow break free. What can you do to defend yourself?" Curtus asked putting his backpack on. "Before I was blinded Yuki trained me in the art of dual Shinwa Shirasaya Katanas and I was pretty good. I just have to find them" Mysuki replied. "Well that settles it. Mysuki will get changed, grab her swords and we will turn ourselves in" Curtus said rising to his feet.

Jaymar and Curtus lifted the dresser upright and Mysuki began to look through the drawers. "It has been so long since I have pick an outfit. I'm so excited" Mysuki said. "Well make sure you like it because it's gonna be the last one you pick out" Glade said. "We'll be outside if you need us" Curtus said as him and Jaymar walked out of the room. They walked down the hall when Curtus noticed something weird about the wall. It looked as if someone had taken the knob off a door and put wallpaper over it. "Jaymar you got something sharp" Curtus asked. Jaymar reached into his coat pocket and pulled out a pocket knife. Curtus felt around the until he felt the gap between the door and the door frame. He exposed the blade and began cutting. He continued in each direction until he reached the hinges before pulling the door open and found himself in a small storage room.

From the amount of dust that was on everything Curtus could tell that no one had ventured in this room in years. The room had a table with a book in the center of it and the walls were lined with glass cabinets. Curtus walked over to the table and began fingering through the book. It was in a foreign language that Curtus had never seen before. "Hey Jaymar do you know what this is" Curtus asked. Jaymar walked over and looked over Curtus's shoulder. "No but if it is in a hidden room like this then is has to be important… Let's take it with us" Jaymar said. "My thoughts exactly" Curtus replied putting the book in his backpack.

They examined the glass cases to see if there was anything of value in them. Most of them were filled with Old World shotguns and rifles. Curtus began to lose hope until he came across a case with two swords in it. "Hey you think these are the swords that they are talking about" Curtus asked. Jaymar walked over. "I mean they are Shinwa Shirasaya Katanas" He replied. Curtus looked at Jaymar in shock. "How did you know that" Curtus questioned. "My dad was a weapon junkie. It only makes sense that his son knows every type of sword ever created" He replied sharply. Curtus opened the dusty glass case and grabbed the two swords and made their way back toward Glade and Mysuki.

They returned Mysuki's room and she had gone through a compete metamorphosis. She changed from the dingy white tee shirt and shorts she was wearing to a bright purple long sleeve shirt and black jeans. Curtus and Jaymar stood in the doorway like deer caught in the headlights. "Wow" Curtus said. "You really like it" Mysuki said. "Yes we do" Jaymar answered. Glade rolled her eye. "Did you idiots find something of use" She asked. Curtus snapped out of his trance and remembered the swords. "Oh yeah. Are these the swords you were talking about" Curtus asked holding them out in front of him. "Those are my Yuki's" She replied as the smile melted from her face. "Oh we can go look again" Curtus said noticing her attitude change. "No those are the ones I am talking about. I'm just remembering the days that she would beat and yell at me and my brother when we broke form" She explained. "Can you even still use those things" Glade asked. Mysuki crack a smirk and grabbed the swords from Curtus. Everyone took two steps back as they didn't know what was going to happen. Mysuki took the swords out of their sheath, took a deep breath and began.

It looked as if Mysuki had been trained yesterday by the effortless nature of her movements. She performed complicated maneuvers with ease precision and looked extremely comfortable doing it. She finished, dropped to her knees and let out a large exhale placing the swords on the floor. She was met with an applause from her small audience. Mysuki couldn't help but smile at the applause. "It really looked good" She asked panting. "Hell yeah. Now hurry up and put those swords back in their covers before you kill someone" Glade said peaking from behind the dresser. Mysuki sheathed he swords and pulled opened the bottom drawer of the of the dresser. "I never thought I would use this again" She said pulling a belt out of the drawer. The belt was specially made to carry the two swords. She put it on and clipped the swords on. One on each hip. "Okay now time to walk to out doom" Glade said popping her knuckles. Curtus turned around and when he opened the door Yuki was waiting on the other side.

His stomach dropped to the floor at the sight of Yuki. She looked at everyone with a smile until she got to Mysuki where her face quickly turned to one of disgust. "I should have known that the medicine you brought back was for her. You're just like your mother." Yuki said angrily. "Yeah, but I have a question who pours formula 561 in a little girl's eyes" Glade yelled. "A nosey ass girl who saw too damn much" Yuki yelled back. "Yeah you didn't want her to see what a good person you were" Jaymar said sarcastically. "You don't know me. You don't know what I had to sacrifice" She barked at Jaymar.

Mysuki got enraged at Yuki's comment about sacrifice. "What did you sacrifice" She yelled. Yuki looked at Mysuki in shock. "ANSWER ME YOU OLD BITCH. WHAT HAVE YOU SACRIFICED" Mysuki yelled. "I had to give your brother away to people who were going to help keep the restaurant open. I loved your brother" Yuki explained nervously. "BULLSHIT. When you sold Ymerel you told the man thanks for freeing me from this parasite. Does that sound like love to you?" Mysuki yelled.

The room went quiet. Everyone was awaiting Yuki's response. Mysuki had reached her boiling point. In her current state depending on how Yuki responded she could have plunged one of her swords into Yuki's chest. Yuki's looked changed from shocked to one of a person who was watching a comedy show as she began to laugh. Mysuki lost it and charged at Yuki drawing her blades. Curtus not wanting any unnecessary bloodshed grabbed the blanket off of the bed and ran in front of Yuki. He turned the blanket to diamond to prevent the oncoming slash. "What are you doing" Mysuki yelled. "I don't want you to play into her hand" Curtus replied. "You see this is why I sold that dune coon brother of hers. Her kind is born violent." Yuki said with a smile. Mysuki jumped back and sheathed her blades. "Are you guys are familiar of the Purge of 2215" Yuki began.

Curtus returned the blanket to normal and threw it on the ground behind him. "Well the government record states that 2 Arab children survived that purge. Well Curtus the day after the Purge your mother comes to me with two Arab children." Yuki said taking a seat on the bed. Mysuki looked at Curtus. "Your mother left me to rot in this hell hole" Mysuki barked at Curtus. "Well let's think logically here. Your heritage alone makes you an enemy of the state. You can't just live anywhere" Jaymar said. "Yeah and you better thank Curtus. The reason you are alive is a promise I kept to his mother" Yuki explained. "Were you thinking about that promise when you sold her brother" Glade asked. "You don't understand. They promised they would make the Smokebox a conflict free zone and that they wouldn't hurt him" Yuki explained. "And you believed that" A voice said from down the hall.

Curtus began shaking in his sneakers at the sound of the all too familiar voice. He wanted to turn around to confirm his fear, but he body was locked up. Curtus looked at Jaymar and Glade who had a fierce looks on her faces. Curtus feared that she didn't know that she was looking in the face of pure insanity. "Curtus. My Man. Sorry about the house" The voice said. The mysterious being put its hand on Curtus's shoulder waking his body up. He spun around to see his fears realized. He turned around to see none other than Leremy.

Mysuki looked at Leremy in shock. Curtus jumped in front of Mysuki activating his tonic. "Stay back. We got this" Curtus said. Leremy began to laugh at Curtus's new found courage. "What's so funny" Glade asked erecting her blades out of her wrist. "It's how confidently he said we got this" Leremy replied. He began walking over toward Curtus and Mysuki. He stopped in front of Curtus and leaned towards his right ear. "You know damn well you and your gang of tagalongs have no chance against me" he whispered in his ear. Curtus didn't generally act on emotion, but the tone that Leremy spoke with causing him to act out of character. Curtus pushed Leremy away and simultaneously charged him. "Where are my parents" Curtus yelled clutching the Bō with two hands. He swung the Bō and it when right through Leremy's torso. In his rage Curtus had forgot Leremy's Tonic power and had left himself vulnerable. Leremy faded behind Curtus and put him in a chokehold. "You know kid you're kinda ruining this family reunion." Leremy whispered in his ear.

"Family reunion" Curtus thought to himself. This had to be one of jokes that Leremy is using to get in his head. Curtus looked over at Mysuki and to his surprise she had tears running down her face. "Ymerel... what did they do to you" Mysuki asked. Leremy released Curtus from his chokehold. Curtus dropped to all fours and struggled to catch his breath. "I was reborn. The Family took me in and washed me clean of the Arab curse. They gave me a new creative name and new life" Leremy yelled. "Leremy is just Ymerel spelled backwards. It aint that creative" Glade whispered to Jaymar returning the blades into her wrist. "Ymere... I mean Leremy you look so good. How have you been" Yuki asked.

Suddenly Leremy's demeanor changed. After hearing Yuki's voice Leremy snapped. He pulled the pistol from his belt and shot Yuki in the stomach three times. Leremy looked like a completely different person with rivers of tears running down his face. "HOW COULD YOU SEND ME TO THOSE ANIMALS. DO YOU HAVE ANY IDEA WHAT THEY DID TO ME!" Leremy yelled. Yuki began coughing up blood. Though she was creeping towards death that didn't stop her from cracking a smile and getting the last word. "They made a promise that they wouldn't kill you and they kept it. *cough* And now look at you. They made you look human. You can actually go out in society and prosper." Yuki wheezed. Before she could say anything else Leremy shot her twice in the chest and once in the head.

Curtus looked in Leremy's eyes and he could tell he was looking at a different person. There was regret and pain in his eyes. "I'm sorry for kidnapping you parents Curtus but you have to believe me I had no choice. It wasn't me it was Leremy" Ymerel pleaded. Curtus looked at Leremy with confusion. He only knew him as Leremy, the mercenary that found joy in others pain and misery. Seeing him beg for forgiveness was completely out of character. Leremy looked at Mysuki. "I haven't seen you in so long. I was scared that she sold you too" Ymerel said. Mysuki put her hands over her mouth. "I always knew you were alive" Mysuki said running to Ymerel and gave him a hug. Everyone in the room couldn't help but smile at the sight of this heartfelt reunion. But the reunion would be a short one.

"Your hair needs a good washing sweetie" Leremy whispered in Mysuki's ear. Mysuki pushed him away and Leremy had his token grin on his face. "I think I see what is going on here" Curtus said. Leremy looked at Curtus. "Let see how close you get Sigmund Freud" Leremy said sarcastically. Curtus deactivated his Bō and put it back on his pack before beginning his explanation. "Well it looks seems you as sharing three separate people in one body each with their own voice and personality. Ymerel is your true personality that feels the pain and the heartbreak of being sold away. You created Leremy as a way to cope with the pain of not only the experiments they ran on you but also whatever transgression you have committed. And the third one is the violent personality. It is the person you can point a finger to whenever you do something heinous."

"DING DING GOD DAMN DING" Leremy yelled. Mysuki couldn't believe that her brother was in such a shattered state. "The third personality is named Tyrann isn't it" Jaymar yelled. "Yeah and he can sure be dickhead can't he" Leremy began. "It takes both me and Ymerel to keep him at bay, but sometime he just breaks through and if you get caught in his path well let's just say you won't be in his path for very long because he will probably be stepping over your dead body" Leremy explained.

Curtus thought back to when he was back in his neighborhood and he came back with his search party. The way he spoke was different when he came and took his parents away. He talked about not caring what the Family thought that if he found Curtus that he would just kill him.

"Well I promised Ymerel he would get to see you before we took y'all in" Leremy said. Everyone froze. "What... you thought I was just coming to visit. I'm here to take you guy in" Leremy explained. "Are we going to prison" Jaymar asked. "Oh no you guys are the first EOS's in years. The Family wants to personally meet with you guys before they execute you" Leremy replied with a smile.

Curtus began to slowly reach for his Bō. "First of all that didn't work the first time and second if you guy did manage to beat me the building is surrounded. So you best option is to come with me peacefully" Leremy explained. Curtus was going through all of the scenarios in his head and none of them surviving in the end. He looked back at everyone else. Mysuki was still in shock at what has become of her brother. Glade and Jaymar were looking at Curtus to see what their next move was going to be. With their backs again the wall Curtus had no choice but to submit to Leremy. "Alright... I guess we have to turn ourselves in" Curtus said putting his hands behind his head and dropping to his knees. "Stand up it. It's not a movie where you just pop up in the back of the car. Your ass is walking. But first" Leremy said. He suddenly whisked around the room in a cloud of smoke and the next thing everyone knew they had thin metal bracelets around their wrists.

"What the hell are these" Glade asked trying to pull one off. "This will prevent the altered cells in your body from activating. Long story short you guys are regular humans again" Leremy explained. "Well these bracelets won't stop me from cutting you down." Glade said. "Well you go ahead and shoot those blades out of your wrist. I assume you have a man-made healing factor from a reptile Tonic and those bracelets prevent you from healing. So we would just sit here and watch you bleed out. That fine by me and its less paperwork for Ymerel too" Leremy replied popping a piece of gum in his mouth. "How did you know I had blades in my arms" Glade asked confused. "Don't worry about that. Come along now, your chariot awaits" Leremy said walking out of the room.

As they exited the room they took turns looking a Yuki's lifeless body. Even after her death she had a smile on her face. Jaymar grabbed Mysuki's old white t shirt and draped it over her face. Everyone looked at Jaymar. "What, she was giving the creeps" Jaymar said before walking out of the room. Curtus and Glade looked at Mysuki as she took her last looks of the room she was a prisoner in. "You know this is all I know. We trained in here, we ate in here, we slept in here. This is my entire world" Mysuki said. Curtus walked next to Mysuki. "Trust me. There are better places in the world than this room. When we get out of this we will explore them together" Curtus said. "Oh brother! Can we get a move on here people?" Glade yelled as she walked down the hall. "Yeah we should probably get moving" Mysuki added beginning down the hall. "She isn't going to make it easy" Curtus whispered under his breath before following her down the hall.

They walked down the stairs to see the dining room in disarray. Tables were flipped over, shattered plates peppered the floor, and unconscious Duhu and Haske members were everywhere. "When did this happen" Curtus asked. "While we were talking" Leremy said picking up food off a plate. "When word got out that there were four EOS's the place became a mad house and my guys had to restore order" Leremy added. He reached down and picked a small satellite dish off the ground. "Latest from Odomtech. A device that cancels all sound in a finite space. You're familiar with this device aren't you Jaymar" Leremy said picking a plate of food up off on the ground. "Yeah. It was one of the devices you stole from me" Jaymar replied. "ah ah ah. I didn't take it Tyrann did" Leremy said patting Jaymar on the shoulder as he walked past.

They walked out of the restaurant to see vehicle that looked like it was pulled straight out of a science fiction movie. It looked to be a cross between an airplane and a helicopter. "Y'all get in the back" Leremy said pointing to the back of the vehicle. Curtus looked around and saw that there were about 25 guys standing outside. "He wasn't kidding when he said the place was surrounded" Glade said. "Ehh we could have taken them" Jaymar added. "Curtus looked toward one of men in uniform. "Hey what is that called" he asked.

"We call it the C63G-Raptor, but you'll call it your last ride now get moving" The man said shoving Curtus toward the Raptor. They were shoved in the cargo hold of the Raptor. There weren't any seats, just mesh netting and roller costars type harnesses lined the wall. Four mercenaries walked in to the cargo hold and locked each of them into a harness. "How long is this ride" Glade asked as her harness was locked into place. The men didn't reply he just glared at her. Once everyone was locked in the mercenaries walked out of the cargo hold. The Raptor's engine started with a loud roar. Then the door for the cargo hold slowly began to close.

The more the doors closed the more nervous he became. Curtus began to think about all the files that they read. All the acts against humanity that the Family has committed and they were about to meet the people who orchestrated it all. "What if my parents are already dead?" "What are they going to do with us before they kill us?" "What if Tyrann takes over midflight and just killed them all" these were some of the thoughts that were going through Curtus's mind as they sank into an abyss of darkness.

XIII

Curtus couldn't help but wonder if he made the right decision by turning themselves in. "Guys you think we messed up" Curtus asked. "Of course we did, but we aren't going to get out of this situation thinking like that" Glade said. "I just got my sight back and now I can't see again" Mysuki whispered to herself. "Okay guys it may seem bad, but look at the bright side" Jaymar said. "What is that" Mysuki asked. "We have our weapons" Jaymar replied. Curtus noticed that they didn't take their weapons or his bag from them. They just put the Tonic canceling cuffs on. "Speak for your damn self. If I use my weapons now I'm gonna die" Glade yelled. "Not necessarily all we have to do is get those bracelets off before you bleed out" Jaymar replied. "Guys we need to come up with a plan for when they land" Mysuki yelled. "I actually don't think we need one" Curtus said.

Curtus could feel everyone was staring at him through the darkness. "What do you mean. These are the most powerful and dangerous people on the Jefferson" Glade said. "Yeah and they are also your parents. That alone should by us time to formulate an escape plan" Curtus finished. "But what about your parents. That is the entire reason that we went through all of this"

Jaymar asked. Curtus hesitated in his response. "Don't think like that. They may have beat the hell out of them but they are alive. You said it yourself they are too valuable" Glade said. "Well we still need to prepare for the worst" Curtus said.

The Raptor suddenly started ascending again. The jerkiness of the flight was making Curtus nauseous. The sound of a large door opening echoed throughout the cargo hold. "So the myths are true" Mysuki said. "What myths are those" Jaymar asked. "People often talked about the sky opening up and a big metal bird flying down" She explained. "What would the metal bird do" Curtus asked. "Nothing. It would just fly in the sky watching over the people before flying away" Mysuki replied. The sound of the metal door opening finished and they begin flying again.

Suddenly there was a binding flash of light. With their arms strapped to the wall they had no way to protect themselves. The worst case scenarios was going through Curtus's mind. He thought that Tyrann had taken over midflight and threw a flashbang in the cargo hold. But that wasn't the case. What actually happened blew Curtus's mind. The walls and floor of the cargo hold seem to disappear. He could feel the wall on his back and the floor under his feet but they seemed to have become transparent. "Good afternoon first class passengers this is your Captain Leremy speaking. I hope that you enjoy our new 360 degree view window"

Leremy said over the intercom. Curtus looked around and everyone was as surprised as he was. "Now if you guys look anywhere out of the window you will see an angry mob of people who want to see you thrown off the Jefferson" Leremy announced. As he spoke the Raptor came to the surface were there was a mob with thousands of people with signs calling for their deaths.

Signs contained pictures of Curtus, Glade and Jaymar with red slashes over their faces. "I thought you said they were only airing that down in the Gettys" Glade asked. "Well I guess they aired it up here too to show what happens when you defy the government." Jaymar replied. Curtus looked into the mob to see a girl who couldn't be any older than eight years old holding a homemade posted that read "Death to the Terrorist". "If they only knew who the bad guys actually were" Curtus said looking down at the mob. Mysuki look in the mob in envy and confusion. She had never seen white people at any point in her life so she was fascinated by them. "Why are they so angry" Mysuki asked. "To be completely honest they don't even know why they are angry" Glade answered. "What do you mean" Mysuki asked. "Well they here about something on tv and without doing any research on the subject to form an opinion on it. So in our case, we were called enemies of the state on tv and now they demonize us even though we have not committed a crime" Jaymar elaborated.

Curtus sat quiet with his heart beating in his stomach. He didn't want to make a comment because he himself used to be a part of that way of thinking. He never thought about the situation the criminal might be in only the crime they were accused of. He thought people who took Tonics we nothing but deadbeats junkies that had no future. He thought all poor people were dumb and that their situation was entirely on them. After meeting Glade, Jaymar, And Mysuki and seeing the circumstances and situation in which they are living in his opinion has changed, but he still sympathized for the people who down there protesting. He sympathized with them because he knew they were scared. Nothing puts more fear in a person's heart than the unknown. Fear causes many people to listen to one side of an argument and take it as the truth.

Suddenly the room went dark again and Curtus felt his wrists slammed together in. "I can't move my arms" Jaymar yelled. "Calm down, the cuffs just magnetically locked together" Glade calmly replied. "Oh… why all the sudden did they restrain us" Jaymar asked. "Because we are here" Mysuki said. At that moment they felt the sudden jerk of the Raptor landing. "How did you know we were landing. The room is completely dark" Curtus asked. "Being blind all those years gave me enhanced hearing. I heard the people in the cockpit talk in about preparing the teleportation engine. The room went dark because the engine used all of power."

Mysuki explained. "Wow they have teleportation. We may be royally screwed" Glade said nervously. "Oh don't tell me your scared Glade" Jaymar said trying to get Glade fired up. "Let's see. An entity with infinite resources and technology versus me, almost a doctor, a comic book nerd, and a bat who is good with swords. Excuse me if I am a bit nervous" She yelled.

The harnesses suddenly released and the cargo by door began to open. Mysuki kept her eyes shut as she didn't want to be blinded by the wave of white light. Jaymar and Glade on the other hand did not prepare and their pupil were seared like expensive steaks. They both rolled on the ground with their hands over their eyes. "Come on guys you didn't learn from the first time" Mysuki asked. "Nope" they said in unison pressing their hands against their eyes. The door opened with Leremy and company waiting on the other side. "Alright now. Get y'all asses up. You're already late for dinner" Leremy yelled banging on the side of the cargo hold with his pistol. "Alright kiddos I need you to walk in a single file line. This is the most exclusive dinner on the Jefferson and you won't be embarrassing me" Leremy said waving his gun around. Curtus started the line with Glade, Mysuki, and Jaymar all filing behind him.

They walked out of the raptor to a large hanger. The walls covered in catwalks and signs with different instructions on how things worked and where things were. The hanger itself was filled wall to wall with different types of Raptors. Unlike the Raptor that picked them up these were covered in unique types of armor and weapons. "What are those for" Curtus asked. "Protection" Leremy said quickly. "You need 24 flying killing machines for protection" Glade asking. "It's better to have them and never use them then to not have them and to not need them" Leremy replied with a smile.

Leremy led them to a small elevator where the five of them plus 3 armed guards crammed inside. The elevator was easily the most beautiful elevator that any of them has ever been in. In contrast to the dull all metal hanger the floors of the elevator were made entirely of marble. The wall was a bright white with gold trim. The ceiling was a mirror that was so clean Curtus could see the pores on his face. "Are these how all the elevators are topside Dumbass" Glade asked. "This one is way nicer" Curtus replied looking around in awe. Leremy hit the button for the second highest floor and the doors slowly closed.

As the elevator began to ascend Curtus noticed that the music that was being played was none that he had ever heard before. It wasn't your run of the mill elevator music it. This elevator was playing rap music "Hey Glade have you heard this song before" Curtus asked. "No, but I know the artist" She replied. "It is C 5" One of the guards said. "Nice try. That was never released.

The artist died during the Hindsight War" Glade said. "Well just because it wasn't released doesn't mean the Family doesn't have a copy of it" The guard replied. "In my opinion it is his best work" another guard said. "Nah it's not better than his mixtapes" The third guard argued. Curtus looked at Leremy and saw that he was sweating. The arguing of the guards was enraging Tyrann and Leremy was doing everything to suppress him. His eye began to turn red and Curtus knew he was about to blow at any moment. The four of them were in a block in the back left corner of the elevator surrounded by the three guards and Leremy was in the front right by the button. Then after a slight build up, Leremy lost control and Tyrann broke free.

"SHUT UP" He yelled in a burning rage. "Get down" Curtus yelled to the other. The all huddled in the back corner of the elevator and Curtus jumped over top of them. His plan was to turn them into diamond to protect them from whatever attack Tyrann was planning. Curtus made sure he was touching everybody, he closed his eyes and began to activate his Tonic.

Curtus closed his eyes mainly because if he failed he didn't want to watch all of his friends die. "Holy crap" Jaymar yelled. Curtus opened his eye and noticed none of his friends were diamond. They all were staring at him like he had six heads. "What wrong" Curtus asked. "Nothing what you're doing is awesome" Mysuki said.

Curtus turned around and saw that there was a diamond wall behind him. "I did that" Curtus asked. "You are the only one with a diamond power" Glade said smugly. On the other side was a sea of grey smoke. They could he the screams of agony of the guards. Curtus dropped to a knee and stared at the wall of smoke. "What do you think he is doing to them" Curtus asked. "Honestly I don't care. Just as long as I'm not a part of it" Jaymar replied. The screams went on for about 15 second before the elevator became dead silence. The clouds of smoke dissipated and Leremy could be seen sitting with his back against the wall. He was breathing heavily with tears running down his face and his hands were coated with blood. "Are you done yet. Did you get your fill?" Leremy yelled. "I'm good... for now" Tyrann replied.

It was weird seeing Leremy and Tyrann have a conversation with each other. It was like a conference call on speakerphone. Depending on who was speaking the tone of voice would change. "Ymerel... what did they do to you" Mysuki whispered to herself. Curtus looked at the wall trying to figure out how he was going to deactivate it. He did it by complete accident and had no real idea how it actually worked. He pressed his hands against the wall and it shattered into a fine powder. Tiny speckles on diamond dusted down on the group like snow. "I don't know how you did that Dumbass, but good job." Glade said slowly standing up. Curtus didn't understand how he did that.

Not only has he never done that before but the Tonic negating cuffs should have prevented him from doing so. Rather than dwell on the unknown he retrained his focus to the task at hand.

They looked around the elevator for any remain of the three soldiers. "Sorry. He tends to get antsy when he goes alone time without a kill" Leremy said. "Where are the three guards" Curtus asked. "Trust me… you are better off not knowing" Leremy replied as he rose to his feet.

Noticing the blood on his hands he wiped the palm of his right hand on his black pants and reached into his pocket and pulled out a pair of black gloves putting them on. Curtus looked at Leremy's face and saw a look of fear and disgust. It looked that when one personality takes over the other two have front row seats to what the other is doing. The elevator bell chimed and the door open. "All right single file" Leremy said shakily wiping the tears from his face. Whatever Tyrann did to the guards was affecting Leremy's psych. His personality had changed from his usually charismatic self to that of a scared child.

They exited the elevator to an elegant hallway. Just like the elevator the walls were bright white with gold accents. The floors were made of a rich mahogany wood. "How much do you think these floors cost" Jaymar asked. Curtus knew a square foot of mahogany cost $2500. The hallway looked to be about 30 yards wide and it stretched as far as the eye could see. "I don't even think we could count that high" Curtus replied. They walked down the hallway and looked in each open doorway. One room contained a massive hot spring. Another room was movie theater. The amount of money that it took to make this place made Curtus's head spin. "All this money and they still have places like the Market District and the Gettys" Glade whispered in disgust. They continued down the hall until they reached two large wooden doors. Leremy walked over to an intercom to the right of the door and pressed the call button. Two tones rang from the intercom before there was a loud "Clunk" and the doors began to open.

The doors opened up to a massive dining hall. Everything was clean and white. There was a buffet with a massive spread of different types of rare food. From Old World comfort foods like Mac n Cheese, Fried Chicken, and Ribs to the more extravagant dishes such as Caviar and Filet Mignon were just some the many foods present. There was a fountain the stretched the entire back wall that shot out water that looked like gold. There was a massive stained glass window that took up the entire left wall of the dining hall. And in the center of it all was a large wooden table surrounded by the Jefferson's elite. "What is the meaning of this Leremy" A voice yelled out. "We thought that you would want to see the EOS's before they were executed" Leremy replied. "Oh these are the EOS's" The voice began. Suddenly an old man stood up from the table. Curtus couldn't tell who he was when he was sitting down but as the man got closer it became very clear who he was. It was the Captain of the Jefferson who was presumed dead 10 years ago Vladimir Don.

The four of them looked upon Vladimir in shock. "You guy look like you have seen a ghost" Vladimir said. Vladimir was a tall skinny white man with a bald head and yellow teeth. He wore a tailored pinstripe black suit with a white shirt and a bright red tie. He walked with a swagger that made the group nervous. "Yeah. Because you're supposed to be dead" Glade yelled. "Huh so it seems you guys got your hands on the Rush of 4 file. Well as you can see I am living and breathing" Vladimir said walking toward the group. He examined each of them individually giving each of them their own personalized look of disgust. "What a waste of God's clay" Vladimir spat walking toward the table. Jaymar looked at the table and locked eyes with his mother. She was a small Native American lady with dark brown skin and eyes with short grey hair. He hadn't seen her in so long he had almost forgotten what she looked like. She looked at Jaymar as if she was looking at a stray dog. That look shook Jaymar to his core and his emotions boiled over. "Why did you treat us like that Mom?" Jaymar yelled. Lisa scoffed at her son's remarks. "You guys were nothing more than means to an end. Your father had a gift and I used it to make money" She said grabbing a roll from a basket on the table. "We lived in a hole underground. You sent groups of thugs down there to beat him up for weapons. Why mom" Jaymar pleaded. "First of all it is pronounced Lisa. And second we aren't in the same class. I'm an elite. An untouchable. I was born to be followed and revered by many. You guys are vermin. Bottom feeder. Just they in case people like me need you to do something. We each have a lane to stay in. Your father wanted to leave his lane so I had to make sure he knew where his lane was" Lisa explained.

Jaymar became so enraged that tears began to run from his eye. Seeing this Curtus stepped in front of him before he did anything rash. "Remember we have to get out of here. We can't come up with a plan if we are all dead on the dining room floor" Curtus said trying reminding him of the bigger picture.

"Pumpkin it has been so long" Another voice called out. Glade's blood ran cold. Everyone in the group was looking for who the voice maybe coming from but she was well aware of whom the voice belonged to. Then walking towards them from the table was Liam Lopez. He was a large Mexican man with a bad spray tan and an equally bad toupee "Don't Pumpkin me you fat bastard. The only time you cared how I felt was when you were beating my ass" Glade yelled. Liam stopped and shook his head. "Still an ungrateful little shit I see"

Liam said with a smile. "Ungrateful?!? After I took that Tonic you sent me and mom to live in that shit hole. Do you know what she did to pay the bills? Do you know what we have been through because of you? Do you have any clue!!!" Glade yelled.

Curtus looked on and watched as these people who have failed as parents act as if they have done nothing wrong. "I sent you guys there for the good of our family" Liam began to explain. "OUR FAMILY. You didn't even come and visit. Not once. You didn't send food, money, or medicine. All you did was make money and forget about us. What kind of family does that sound like?" She yelled. Liam let out a loud sigh. "You're just as stubborn as your mother" He said shaking his head. The comment made Glades blood boil and she charged at Liam. Knowing that if she drew her blades to strike Liam she would die as well. Mysuki ran in front of Glade and knocked her to the ground. "Get off me" Glade said struggling to get free. "You'll be doing him a favor by drawing your blades and killing yourself. We need to keep a level head come up with a plan to get out of these things" Mysuki whispered into Glade's ear. Remembering the situation at hand Glade took a deep breath and reluctantly regained her composure. "Oh and by the way… mom died a year ago. I know you don't give a damn, but I just thought you should." Glade said standing to her feet. Curtus turned his focus back on to Vladimir. "Since it seems you're the one running the show I'm going to ask you this one time and one time only. Where are my parents" Curtus said sternly as he shot a fiery glare at Vladimir?

A sinister smile grew on Vladimir's face. "Not one for small talk I see. You get that from your mother don't you" Vladimir asked. Curtus couldn't understand why but he had a genuine sense of fear being the presence of Vladimir. He wasn't physically imposing, in fact he looked sickly. He was practically skin and bone, but he just had this terrifying aura about him. There is a reason that Tyrann hasn't tried to kill him yet. "Curtus Ryan Parker. 20 years old and top of his class at University Med. You had the potential to be very successful, but given your circumstances that would never come to be" Vladimir said. "And what circumstances might those be" Curtus asked. "Well your parent defied the government multiple times so like you they were enemies of the state. You think they would hire anyone who was raised by people like that" Vladimir said turning his back to Curtus.

Curtus knew his parents very well. They grew close from long nights in the lab and from them begin very hands on in his studies. "I know my parents. they have never broken the law in their lives" Curtus argued. "Well they haven't broken any written laws, but when it comes to the unwritten laws of the Jefferson they have broken plenty" Vladimir explained pacing back and forth in front of the group.

Curtus began to get angry. If they did not break any written law they should not have been arrested. They should be back at the house eating dinner talking about how close Curtus's father is to a breakthrough of some sort. Glade looked over at Curtus and noticed that he was becoming visually enraged. "Keep your cool. You said it yourself this is not the time to lose our cool" She whispered to him. Glade's words reached Curtus as he let out a deep exhale. "You guy have been a troublesome bunch" Vladimir said stopping his pace and starring at the four of them. "Where are my parents. I'm not asking again" Curtus asked not letting his anger change his tone. "You said that already, and don't worry you will see you mother soon but not right now. Your father on the other hand is right over there" Vladimir said pointing over to a door to the right of them.

The door opened and Curtus's father came stumbling out. Curtus looked in horror at the deplorable state of his father. There were no noticeable physical injuries, but Curtus being medically trained noticed some alarming anomalies. The yellowing of his skin and eye let Curtus know that he had liver damage of some sort. He was walking with a slight limp and there were holes along his top and bottom lip from his mouth being sewn shut while he was being tortured. He looked in his father's eye and saw nothing. His father pupils were completely dilated and he looked at Curtus as if he was a complete stranger. "What did you do to him" He yelled. "Sorry that is one of the side effects of the new truth serum were are testing" a voice said.

Curtus's heart skipped a beat. That voice was all too familiar to him. "Glad to see you again" Burraza said softly as she walked from behind Curtus's father. Curtus wanted to beat the life out of her for not only what he did to his father but for the MBF and playground experiment. "Don't worry if he is like the other subjects it should wear off in 10 minutes" Burraza said as she walked to the table. She pulled a chair out next to Lisa and began fixing her a plate. "How can you eat" Glade asked. Burraza stopped making her plate and looked at Glade. "Excuse me" Burraza answered. "After all the death and misery that you have caused. How are you able to eat and sleep soundly at night?" Glade asked. "I do it the same why you do. And that is the last I want to hear from you. I will not be judged by a subhuman garbage such as you" She barked at Glade.

That last comment left Curtus shook. He remembers vividly his professor telling them that all people are equal and deserve the same treatment on numerous occasions. It was comments like these why Curtus idolized his professor. But Curtus could tell by the way she talked to the Glade that she had a genuine hatred towards he solely based on her race. "Who are you" Curtus asked. Burraza finish her bite of steak and wiped her mouth before responding. "I'm the same person I have always been" She said with a smile on her face. "So all that about all people being equal was just smoke and mirrors" Curtus said. "You're young so you don't understand. Her people were violent. They were not different than a pack of wolves or any wild animal." She replied. "But what makes you so different from them" Jaymar asked.

Jaymar's mother Lisa took exception to her son speaking up. "Don't talk about stuff you can't possible understand. Everything we have done and everything we are going to do is for the safety of the Jefferson" Lisa shouted back. "You tried throw an entire race of people off of the ship. You didn't make the people feel safe. You made them fear you." Jaymar countered. "That is enough" Lisa yelled slamming both of her hands and standing up out of here seat. "I don't know who raised you but they obviously didn't teach you about respect" She yelled. "The reason you don't know is probably because you were never there" Glade said. "I don't remember asking for your opinion taco jockey" Lisa barked at Glade. "I'm an expert on deadbeat parents, trust me I have one, and you have all of the symptoms of a deadbeat mother" Glade replied. Lisa did not like Glade referring to her as a deadbeat mother. She picked up her steak knife and threw it at Glade. Glade kept her cool and tilted her head to the right letting the knife fly by her ear and stick in the wall behind them.

Curtus looked in his dad's eyes. Just like Burraza said the side effect was wearing off as the yellow in his eyes began to slowly fade. His father slowly walked over to the table and began making a plate. He walked and stood right behind Burraza. "So obedient. Like a dog" Burraza said scooping up a second helping of mashed potatoes. "Well we are going to just be going. Sorry for the interruption" Leremy said. "Yes you ruined a perfectly fine dinner bringing these deplorables" Lisa said grabbing a fresh knife and taking a seat. "Ok y'all this way" Leremy said.

As he said that Leremy grabbed his head in agony. Curtus knew that Leremy and Ymerel were doing everything to keep Tyrann at bay. Curtus looked at the table to see everyone at the table frozen in fear. They knew what Tyrann is capable of and if he gets lose their safety couldn't be guaranteed. "Leremy are you ok" Vladimir asked reaching in his jacket pocket. "Yeah... just had to calm Tyrann down" Leremy strained slowly standing tall. Curtus looked at Leremy's eyes and noticed that his right eye was bleeding. The conflict between the personalities are taking such a toll that they began to physically manifest themselves. The four of them lined up and began to walk out of the dining room. As they walked out Burraza felt the need to get the last word. "Hey Curtus. Tell your Carolyn I said hello"

XIV

Leremy walked into the elevator and hit the button for three floors down. The door closed and the elevator began to descend. The air in the elevator was stale and smelled of burnt flesh. No one wanted to say anything for fear that it would anger Tyrann. The episode he had in the dining room had everyone on edge. Curtus looked at Leremy who was wiping the blood from under his eye. His face was full of pain and fear. It seemed that the fights with Tyrann have a lasting psychological effect. The elevator came to a sudden stop and the door opened up to a dark hallway. "H… here is your stop" Leremy said shakily. They exited the elevator and bright lights suddenly flashed on. "What is up with you guys and sudden bright ass flashes of light" Glade asked covering her eyes.

The light dissipated revealing a long dungeon like hallway. The walls were lined with steel doors. Each door had a number in the center of it. The locks on the doors were tumbler based which meant that they could not be hacked by conventional means. The only way to get in and out of them was with a key. "S… She is all the way at the end" Leremy said pointed at the door at the end of the hall.

The door was the only one on the back wall. The number 87 was painted in the middle of it in yellow paint. Curtus made a mad dash for the door. After reading what these people are capable of he feared the worst had happened. "Oh god I hope she is okay" He thought to himself as he sprinted down the hall. He reached the door and slid open a small hatch towards the bottom of the door. He looked in and saw a woman laying on a cot. "MOM" he yelled into the cell. The person flinched before slowly sitting up. She turned around and looked at Curtus with pure joy. "Curt I knew you would come" She said with a smile. Curtus looked at his mom and noticed her face was covered in cuts and bruises. Leremy and the rest of the group walked up behind him. Curtus snapped his head around. "OPEN THE DAMN DOOR" He yelled. "O… Okay" Leremy said putting the key in the lock. The moment her unlocked the door Curtus threw the door open and ran and gave him mother a hug.

While Curtus was hugging her he could tell something was off about his mom. There was a weakness to her body that was unfamiliar to him. It was as if he was giving a hug to a dying 79-year-old woman. "Mom what did they do to you" Curtus asked. He pulled back and looked in her eyes. Her pupils were fluctuating in size and the white in her eyes were now a brownish color. "They injected me with a serum and now my body is slowly eating away at itself" Carolyn explained. The others walking in and immediately noticed the worry on Curtus's face. Leremy closed the door behind them locking them in the cell. Carolyn looked at the group and smiled, "Looks like you made new friends. Hi I'm Carolyn Curtus's mother" she said in a soothing motherly voice.

Curtus had never heard her introduce herself as Carolyn before, yet it wasn't weird to him. She said it with confidence, comfort, and no hesitation. She looked at Leremy and kept her same smile. "Ymerel I knew you were in there" She said. Everyone looked at Leremy and saw a tears running down his face. "I'm so sorry" He said as he began to weep. "It's okay. With what they did to you I'm surprised your even remotely sane" She said. Mysuki looked over at Leremy and notice that he didn't have the same look in his eye. His eyes had a softer more vulnerable look to them. She was certain that her actual brother was here and not one of his other personalities.

Curtus looked back at him mom. "Mom do you know why they kidnapped you" Curtus asked. Carolyn cleared her throat before she began. "Their supply of Beast Tonics had run dry. After many failed attempts of trying to reverse engineer it they chose to abduct me the only one with the formula to make it. When I got here I told them there is no chance that I would make them any. So they injected me with advance aging serum and said they would only give me the cure when I agreed to make them their Tonics" She explained.

Curtus looked at the state of his mother's body. The serum seemed to break down the muscle and bone tissue first before it acted on her organs. From the look of her she didn't have any more than two days and that's if she is lucky.

Suddenly there was a knock at the door. Ymerel unlocked the door and opened it to see Curtus's father on the other side with a bag in his hand. "Honey do you have the gauntlet" Carolyn asked. "It is all here along with the transfer module" Kirkland replied. Carolyn looked over at Ymerel. "How much time did they give you" She asked. "10 minutes" Ymerel said. Mysuki walked over to Ymerel and grabbed his hand. "It has been so long since I got to hang out with my brother" Mysuki said with smile. "I know. I'm sorry they are so strong and they said I couldn't go see you" Ymerel said. "Well at least we have these 10 minutes together." Mysuki said hugging her brother.

Curtus's father opened the bag to reveal a gauntlet and a bunch of wires. The bracelet was about 8-inch-long and contained a screen in the center of it much like the pipboy from the fallout videogame series. "Curtus let me see your left arm" his father asked opening up the gauntlet. Curtus hesitated before extending his arm. His father put it on his arm and locked it into place. Then Curtus felt several needles burrowing into his arms. The pain from the needles brought Curtus to his knees. "Stay strong. This is the worst part" Carolyn said. Wave after wave of intense pain came throbbing from his left arm. Then just as quickly as it came the pain subsided. He looked up to see everyone looking in shock and Glade trying to hold back a laugh. "How are you feeling Curt" His father asked. "Weird, the pain is just gone" He said. "Good that means it successfully linked with your central nervous system" Carolyn said. She looked at Kirkland. "Let's start the transfer" she said.

Kirkland walked over to Curtus and began attaching wires to the gauntlet. Then he plugged all of the wires into the base of a cylinder with a long needle at the other end of it. Once all the wires were plugged in Kirkland put the device down and began rummaging through his coat pockets. "We don't have time for an epidural. Just do it" She said putting her hair over her right shoulder exposing her neck. Kirkland took his hand out of his pockets and picked up the device. He took a deep breath to steady his hand and stuck it in base of her skull.

Carolyn lightly groaned in pain. She refused to show her son she was hurting. Everyone looked in horror as Curtus's father drove the long needle deep into his mother brain. "Dad what are you doing" Curtus asked. "We are going to transfer your mother's consciousness into the gauntlet" He replied. Curtus's eye shot at his mother. "I know it sounds farfetched but your father is telling the truth" Carolyn reassured him. "Believe me. Some of the stuff we have seen in the past couple of days. Nothing is farfetched to us anymore" Glade replied. Curtus's mother began to chuckle. "Your friend is funny" She said with a smile. The sight of his mother's smile gave him a sense of comfort in their dire situation.

Curtus watched as his father began pressing button on the cylinder. "Mom are you sure this is going to work" Curtus asked. "In theory it should" She said. There was an uncertainty in her voice. "We don't have to do this. All we need to do is get these handcuffs off and we can fight our way out of here" Curtus pleaded to his mom. "Curt. You guy are part of a bigger plan." she said putting her hand on his cheek. "Bigger plan. What do you mean?" Curtus asked. Carolyn let out a deep sigh. "You thought the clues we left were for you to save us if The Family abducted us. No they are part of a larger plan by the Kryll to take down The Family" Carolyn explained. The room fell silent. No one thought for a second that there were going to be a part of an operation to topple The Family. "Curt Listen carefully. You are going to need to board the Skytrain in the hanger under the Loraine building. The coordinates should already be set so all you have to do is fire it up and take it to Shangri La. Once you are there you will go to a place called The Well. There all your questions will be answered" She explained. Curtus looked at his mother and saw a fire in her eyes that he had never seen before. "But you said you were going to answer my questions" Curtus said shakily. "And I'll be with you every step of the way. You know I never break a promise Curt" She said. If there was one thing he knew about his mom, it was that she always kept her promises. .

She turned and looked at the rest of the group. "Thank you for keeping my Curt safe. You guys didn't have to" She said. "Don't worry about it Mrs. Parker" Jaymar said. "Actually to be honest we needed him more than he needed us" Glade said with a smile. "Yeah we need to be thanking you for having such a wonderful son" Mysuki added. Carolyn looked back at Curtus. "Seems your friends really like you. These friends seem like the ones that would do anything to keep you safe. Make sure you do the same for them" She said. "Carolyn we are running out of time. We need to start" Kirkland said. Curtus could tell from his father's voice that this wasn't easy for him. He was in essence killing his wife for a result he probably will never see.

Before they began the consciousness transfer something dawned on Carolyn. "Hold on Kirk I have to tell Mysuki something" She said quickly. "Ok but do so with haste" he replied. Carolyn looked at Mysuki. "If you are going to leave the Jefferson I want you to do so with the name your mother and father gave you" She said with a smile. Mysuki's face lit up. She had always had her doubts about her name, but never wanted to question. "Really" She asked putting he hands over her mouth. "Yeah it seems wrong to let you go around with fake name born out of hatred" Carolyn said. "What is my name" Mysuki said wanting to waste no time. "Isis Yara" Carolyn replied. Mysuki smiled from ear to ear hear her actual name for the first time. "Isis Yara" She kept repeating to herself trying to get used to the name. "Okay Kirk. Let's get this show on the road" Carolyn said.

The process was a lot quicker than everyone expected. Curtus's father pressed a button on the base of the needle and it was as if they took a battery out of his Carolyn's back as her body immediately fell limp. Kirkland turned away immediately after he pressed the button to avoid the sight of seeing his wife fall to the ground. Curtus stared at his mother's lifeless body in horror. Every second that passed felt like its own individual lifetime. Curtus waited for anything to happen but nothing did. Curtus's eyes snapped to his dad. "What did you do" Curtus yelled. "I was doing what you mother told me ok" he yelled back. "Don't worry Curt I'm okay" Carolyn said.

Curtus froze. He could have sworn that he had heard his mother's voice. He looked back at his mother's body which remained lifeless on the ground. "Did you guys hear that" Curtus asked. No one responded but he could tell from the confused looks on their faces that they did not hear it. "No only you can hear me sweetie. The gauntlet is linked to your central nervous system. Think of me like a second conscious" She said. Curtus let out a sigh of relief. "Don't worry guys it worked. She is in my head" Curtus said with a smile.

Then Ymerel grabbed at his head in agony. "What's going on" Isis asked. "It seems that Ymerel's personality is being phased out" Kirkland said. Isis looked at Ymerel. "Can you hear me. It was good to see you again even if it was for a short time" Isis said. "Yeah I was beginning to think that I would never see you again. Now I can final go in peace" Ymerel strained. Through his immense pain he was still able to put a smile on his face.

A single tear ran down Isis's face. She gave her brother one last hug as she knew that this was the last time she would be with him. He dropped to a knee and began to yell out in agony. Kirkland pulled the needle out of Carolyn's neck and removed the cords from Curtus's gauntlet. "I need to get back. If I'm gone too long they will get suspicious" He said. Even though his tone of voice was monotone Curtus could tell his father was afraid. Afraid of the unknown. Afraid of failure. Afraid what was going to happen to him when they found his wife dead in her cell. Afraid of his only son getting hurt or worse once while venturing into the world. Curtus walked over to his dad and gave him a hug. "Don't worry. I will be alright" He whispered in his dad's ear. His father froze for a second before giving him a strong hug. "I love you. I always have and always will"

Kirkland said with tears pooling in his eyes. "I know dad I know" Curtus replied. "You be safe out there Curt" Kirkland said before letting go of Curtus and exiting the cell.

Ymerel continued to yell out in agony until he suddenly fell silent. Everyone stared at him in fear of which person they would face when he came to. If it was Tyrann they would be out of luck and their mission would come to a violent end. He stayed on a knee like a statue for roughly 30 seconds before he jumped in the air and landed on his feet with a big smile on his face. He was breathing heavy as if he had been in a 12 round boxing match. "What did I miss" Leremy asked. He looked down and saw Curtus's mom laying on the ground. "Aww I always liked her" He said reaching in his pocket. He shuffled around in his pocket until he pulled out the key that would unlock the Tonic suppressing cuffs. "You're letting us go" Jaymar asked. "Yeah me and the big guy thought it would be best to let you guys go" Leremy said unlocking everyone's cuffs. "Why are you doing this" Curtus asked. "We have been waiting for an opportunity to take down those elitist pricks for what they did to us, and you four are our best chance at good old fashion revenge" Leremy explained. "Okay we are free so what is the next part of your plan" Glade asked. "I'm going to lock you in this see and go upstairs and say you killed Carolyn. They will send two guards here to take you to an expedited execution. Once you handle those guards you will go up to the dining room and confront Vladimir. While you guys have him distracted I will come in from behind and end him" Leremy explained. "Seems easy enough he's an old man how tough can he actually be" Jaymar said configuring the Omnitool. "Don't underestimate him. He is the leader of the Family for a reason." Leremy warned.

Leremy walked out of the cell and closed the door behind him. As he was locking the door Isis ran up to the door. "What happened to Ymerel" she asked through the food slot. Leremy locked the door and took a deep breath. "Are you sure you want to know kid" Leremy asked. Isis hesitated before saying "Yes". "Well to calm Tyrann down enough to reason with him Ymerel sacrificed himself to feed his lust" Leremy explained. Isis's blood ran frigid. "So your telling me" She began. "Yes your brother is dead" Leremy quickly stated. "He wanted me to tell you that he never stopped loving you and wants you to be safe. And I can attest that he talked about you every single day since I met him" Leremy said. Isis noticed the look on Leremy's face was one of sadness. It was the type of sadness that could not be faked. It was the same sadness one has when they lose a family member or a close friend. Isis felt herself getting choked up. It felt like she was swallowing a golf ball holding back her tears. All she wanted to sit in a corner and cry, but she knew that it would only put the group in danger. She took a deep breath and turned around to the face the others. "Come on you guys. Let's not let Ymerel's sacrifice go in vain"

Everyone could tell that Isis was hurting. Her eyes were red from holding back tears and she would occasionally space out. But through this sad time Isis's true strength came out. The fact that she didn't just shut down after the loss of her brother and only living family shows how mentally strong she truly is. "So… what is the plan" Isis asked. "We are going to have to split up" Curtus said. Everyone looked at him in confusion. "Guys hear me out" Curtus said trying to explain his reasoning. "He said they would send down two guards. Two guards who think we can't use our Tonic powers so we have the element of surprise. Two of us will 1 v 1 the guards while the other two will go up and scout out what is ahead" Curtus explained. Everyone looked at each other and nodded in agreement. "Wow they seem to really believe in you" Carolyn said. "Trust me mom it didn't come easy" He replied. "Now who is taking on the guards and who is going ahead" Jaymar asked. "Me and Dumbass will scout ahead. He can't really fight so he will be a liability if we leave him back here, and with my camouflage ability I naturally should be on the recon mission" Glade said. "That works for me" Jaymar said. "I agree this way I can start to get back at the people who killed my brother" Isis said grabbing her swords. "Okay then it is settled. When they open the door you two will jump on them and we will sprint to the elevator" Curtus began. Suddenly there was a loud bang at the door. "Good because there is no turning back now" Curtus said looking at the door.

XV

"What the hell is going on in there" A voice on the other side of the door said. Curtus and Glade got behind Isis and Jaymar. Curtus's heart was racing. He knew that if this plan failed not only would his father be killed but everyone else's life was in jeopardy. There was a loud "clunk" and the door slowly swung open. Once the door was fully opened Jaymar and Isis pounced on the two guards. Curtus and Glade hurdled over them and sprinted to the elevator. Curtus looked back to see both Jaymar and Isis getting thrown off the guards. When the guards stood up Curtus's stomach dropped. He assumed that when Leremy said they would send guards he meant just regular guards. These guards were part of the elite squad Tyrann brought to the comic book story. "They'll be fine. You have to trust them" Glade said trying to reassure him. "Are you sure" Curtus asked. "No, but sometimes you just have to have faith in people" She replied stepping on the elevator. Curtus stepped on the elevator and turned around to see the four of them preparing for combat. "You have to have faith in them" Glade said. "Okay"

Curtus replied pressing the button. Curtus watched them charge at each other as the elevator doors closed.

The match ups for Jaymar and Isis were pretty even. Isis found herself up against a Tonic Trooper named Spine. She was a shorter white woman with half shaved head of blonde hair and her eyes were pitch black like the back side of an 8 ball. She had the power of a porcupine and could sprout razor sharp spines from anywhere in her body. Jaymar got his long awaited fight with Spitter. He had been waiting for this since their run in at the store. Isis lunged at Spine with a two sword overhead downward slash. Spine sprouted two long spines from the palms of her hands and blocked the attack. Her momentum carried over Spine and she went crashing into the wall. Isis quickly popped to her feet to see Spine charging at her. In the blink of an eye the tables had turned and Isis found herself on the defensive. Spine came with what seemed like an endless barrage of slashes and stabs and all Isis could do was block and evade.

Jaymar and Spitter stood face to face. He was a tall lanky white man with silver hair. The white in his eye had turned to an orange red and his pupils resembled those of an iguana. They were stood at the ready waiting for the other to make the first move. Jaymar had a good idea of what his power was and knew he had to keep his distance until an opening presented itself. Spitter stared at Jaymar with an arrogant smile. It was the smile your older cousin gives you when you challenge them to a game they knew they are better than you at. "What's so funny" Jaymar asked. "You think you have a chance to win. That is what is funny" Spine replied back arrogantly.

All the memories of what happened in the shop were now coming back to him. "What you still mad about the books. They are online get over it" Spitter said beginning to laugh. When he began to laugh Spitter closed his eye and leaned his head back. Jaymar knew that this was his best opportunity to strike. Wasting no time, he took the Omnitool with his left hand and fired the grappling hook. The hook whistled past Spitter's and landed in the wall behind him. Spitter opened his eyes to see Jaymar flying toward him with his fist clenched. Using the speed from the grappling hook Jaymar landed a vicious punch directly on Spitter's nose.

Isis continued her strategic retreat. During which she got a chance to see the resilience of Spine's spines. The point of the spine was so sharp it pierced and slashed through the steel walls with relative ease. Spine was very disciplined in her fighting style and wasn't giving her an opening to counterattack. "What happened. You came out with all this fire now you're just running" Spine asked. The moment she began talking to Isis noticed something. While she was talking he form would briefly become sloppy. The untrained eye wouldn't catch this, but for Isis, who had been training to fight from a very young age, this was an eye sore. All she had to do is keep Spine talking and striking when her form began to break down.

Jaymar's punch carried Spitter all the way to the wall. The punch was so powerful that it left a sizeable dent in the steel wall. "Get over that" Jaymar yelled. Then Jaymar suddenly felt his hand get hot. It took him a split second to realize what was going on and pull his hand away. He reeled the hook from the wall and jumped back. He looked at his hand and saw that his glove had been burned through and his knuckles were bleeding. Jaymar then returned his focus to Spitter. Though his face was in disarray Spitter continued to smile. Jaymar's punch did do some damage but it wasn't enough to bring any alarm to Spitter. "You got me good there bud" Spitter said slowly rising to his feet. As he rose blood and teeth began falling from his mouth. Jaymar was in shock. He was certain a punch like that would have put him down. "Using the grappling hook to increase your punch speed was a stroke of genius" Spitter said dusting himself off. Then Jaymar dropped to a knee clutching his hand. "Oh my spit tends to do that" Spitter said cracking his neck. Jaymar's hand was in so much pain that he couldn't move. He looked at his hand to make sure it wasn't on fire and when he looked up he saw Spitter's boot hurtling toward him.

Living in the Market District Jaymar had been in his fair share of fights, but he had never gotten hit with the force that came from Spitter's boot. The kick landed square in the center of Jaymar's chest sending him flying into a cell door behind him. Jaymar immediately began coughing up blood as the kick broke several ribs some of which splintered into his lungs. "C'mon is that all you got kid. You're good for one good punch" Spitter asked. Jaymar tried to reply but he was too busy catching his breath. "Look at you. Just like a wounded animal. The only humane thing to do would be to put you out of your misery" Spitter said popping his knuckles as he walked toward Jaymar. He knew he needed to come up with a plan quickly or this hallway would be his coffin.

Continuing to block and evade Isis had to come up with something that would get her talking. "As she spoke Isis noticed that she seems to be a touch too confident so acting nonchalant would be the best way to get under her skin." Isis thought to herself. "Hey how long are you gonna warm up" Isis asked. She looked at Spine and her face told the story. "You want me to go all out. You got it" Spine yelled. While she yelled Isis noticed her window to strike. She was doing an overhead dual downward slash which left her torso exposed. Isis tightened her grip on her sword and was going to cut Spine down at the waist. As the blades flew through the air Isis was certain that this blow would end it and she would be able to help Jaymar who sounded like he was having trouble with Spitter. But her plan quickly turned to a failure when Spine blocked her attack.

Spine had moved the blades from her hand and made the protrude from her armpits going straight down the side of her body blocking the attack. "You almost had me there. But look you left your head exposed" Spine said. Isis was so focused on not missing her window she left herself completely defenseless. Then Spine did a front flip and preformed a downward axe kick to the top of Isis's head. With no way to protect herself Isis's head went crashing to the ground. She hit the ground so hard that she almost bounced back on her feet. Isis opened her eyes to see the bottom of Spine's boot heading straight toward her face.

Jaymar stumbled to his feet struggling to catch his breath. Spitter continued menacingly walk toward him. He kicked Jaymar in the air before grabbing him by his ankles and slamming him into a nearby cell door. "I thought you would be more of a challenge seeing as I am the guy who burned your dad precious collection" Spitter said kicking Jaymar in his ribs. Jaymar continued to cough up blood as he slid down the hall. He needed to buy some time and come up with a plan of attack or he was done for. He reached in his coat pocket and pulled out homemade smoke bombs. They wouldn't do any damage but they would allow him to get away from Spitter.

He threw them at the ground and within seconds a dense cloud of white smoke engulfed them both. "You're desperate if you're pulling out gimmicks like this" Spitter said. Jaymar was desperate, but the smoke bombs were part one of his endgame plan he was coming up with on the fly. He fired the grappling hook up to the ceiling pulling him above the cloud of smoke. Using the ability from his Tonic he was able to slowly float down keeping him at the high vantage point he needed to begin part two.

Not being around people most of her life, Isis didn't have the opportunity to get into many fights so she wasn't familiar to the feeling being knocked unconscious. One moment she was staring at the sole of Spine's 9.5 and the next she is sitting with her back against the wall with blood dripping from her nose and mouth. She looked up and noticed something weird. When Spine would talk she heard what she was saying before her lips would move. It was as if her eyes were on a second delay from her ears. This must have been a side effect of her being blind all of these years, but that wasn't the case. She was seeing things in real time, but she had developed such a keen sense of hearing that she could hear what she was saying before it left her throat. "Let me try something" she thought to herself.

She closed her eye and to her surprise she was still able to see, but as opposed to when her eyes were open everything was in sync now. Her ears had become so powerful that from the sound around her she was able to know where everything in the room was. It was as if her eye were open but the only thing missing was colors. She rose to her feet keeping her eyes closed. She saw the outline of Spine walking toward her, but when she opened her eyes Spine was two steps behind.

Isis was in shock. Her hearing was so precise she could hear Spines muscles fire and her brain processed those sounds to predict her movements. It was as if Isis could see into the future. She took a deep breath and closed her eyes. "Don't tell me you're going to fall asleep on me" Spines said jokingly. "Don't worry about me. It you who needs to be worried" Isis replied. "Oh and why is that" Spine asked. "Because in about 10 seconds I am going to have beaten you with my eyes closed" Isis replied.

Step two was a simple two-part plan. The first part was that he was going to activate his thermal scope and shoot Spitter with the grappling hook to get him in the air. Then when he was helpless in the air hit him with a barrage of attacks. As he prepared the Omnitool something came flying out of the smoke screen. A rope of saliva came flying out of the cloud directly at Jaymar. He had seen firsthand what Spitter saliva can do and this was well on its way to burning a hole in Jaymar's chest. "Oh this is it" Jaymar thought to himself. With the power of the Tonic slowing his decent Jaymar was a sitting duck. Jaymar thought about blocking it with the Omnitool but then he would have no way to defend himself. Jaymar closed his eyes and began thinking of a plan.

Jaymar always wondered why he wasn't able to fly with his Tonic. In theory it should give him all of the powers of a hawk. He has the eye sight and the hovering ability but he wasn't able to fly. "What am I missing" he thought to himself. He began to think about all of the birds that he had seen fly and the answer hit him in the face. It was so obvious that Jaymar was slightly embarrassed that he hadn't figured it out sooner. He clipped the Omnitool to his belt, took a deep breath, brought his hands to chest level and thrusted his palms towards to the ground. He opened his eyes to see the saliva flying under him.

With her eyes were closed Isis was seeing clearer than clearer. With sounds and visuals were now in sync and now she was ready to go on the offensive. Spine moved the blades from her armpits to the palms of her hands. Her plan was to plunge the two blades into Isis's chest. Before the Spine could begin her stabbing motion her body was in 4 separate piece. While she was drawing her arms back Isis hit her with three lightning quick slashes. Two which cut off each of her arms and one that cut her down at the waist. Spine found herself with her back laying on top of her legs and her arms falling to her side. Isis let out a long quiet exhale and put her swords back in their sheath.

She opened her eyes and looked down upon Spine's dismembered body. To her surprise Spine bled very little for the severity of her injuries. Isis shook her head and began to walk away in the direction of Jaymar and Spitter. "You're just going to leave me here to suffer. Finish what is on your plate" Spine yelled. Isis stopped and looked over her shoulder. The blood was beginning to pool around Spine's body. "I'm not a murderer" Isis said. "Well if you think you're some kind of hero then come save me" Spine yelled. Isis stared at Spine for a couple seconds before responding. "I'm no hero either, so I'm not obligated to save you" Isis replied. "Well at least put me out of my misery" Spine pleaded. Her tone quickly changed from arrogant to scared. Isis turned to face Spine. "Let me ask. Did you put my people out of their misery before jettisoning them from the Jefferson" Isis asked? Spine fell silent. She knew that the truth would only put her in a deeper hole. "I'll take your silence as a no. So I'll show you the same amount of mercy you showed them" Isis said and continued towards Jaymar. Tears began to fill Spine's eyes as she realized that this hallway would be her final resting place.

Jaymar smiled ear to ear at the discovery of his new found ability. It felt as if he was pushing up a ledge when he pushed toward the ground. His mind raced with the possibilities of with what he could do with his powers. "I can fly. I can really fly" he thought to himself. He unhooked the Omnitool and continued with phase two of his plan. He looked down the thermal sight and fired the grappling hook which found a home in Spitter's chest. Spitter yelled out in agony as he tried to pull the claw of the grappling hook out of his chest. Then Jaymar squeezed the trigger tighter and he pulled Spitter out of the smoke where he met by Jaymar's fist.

Jaymar punched him square in the face breaking him free of the claw's grasp. "I'm not done yet" Jaymar yelled. He quickly reeled in the grapping hook and shot it into Spitter's abdomen. Spitter groaned in pain as the blades from the grappling hook sunk into his stomach. He opened his eyes and shot three more spit bullets at Jaymar. Jaymar kicked down at the ground and moved out of the way to dodge the bullets. He kicked off the air like he was kicking off of a wall. "You can fly" Spitter groaned through his teeth. "I know it's awesome right" Jaymar replied. He reeled him in and kicked him in the side sending him crashing against the wall. Jaymar kicked toward the ceiling propelling him toward the ground. He shot the grappling hook one last time grabbing him by the hip. He spun around in the air sending Spitter crashing head first into the ground. Jaymar reeled the hook in as he looked at Spitter laying lifelessly on the ground.

"Paralysis... you're just as cruel as I am" Spitter said. "Don't compare you to me" Jaymar said clipping the Omnitool to his belt. "You are going to leave me here to die over some damn books written in a foreign language" Spitter asked. "They were just books to you... they were the last memory of my father to me" Jaymar said staring at him.

Jaymar looked over to see Isis walking over. "I didn't hear any commotion so I just assumed you had it under control" She said. As she got closer he noticed how bruised and bloodied her face was. "She really did a number on you" Jaymar said with a smile. "I can say the same about you" Isis replied. She looked past Jaymar to see Spitter laying face down on the ground. "Did you..." She began. "If you are going to ask if he killed me the answer is no. He would not give me the luxury of an honorable death" Spitter answered before she could finish. Jaymar looked at Isis. "What happened to that girl" He asked. "She is over there in four pieces" Isis replied. "Damn" Jaymar and Spitter said in unison. "Yeah I had to do what I had to do" She added. "Come on. Let's not keep Curtus and Glade waiting" Jaymar said. They both took a second to get themselves together before making their way to the elevator.

XVI

It hadn't dawn upon Curtus until he was in the elevator that he had actually failed on his mission. The entire reason he turned himself in was to save his parents. Even though he is able to still talk to his mom he will never be able to physically contact his mother ever again. He slammed his back against one of the elevator walls and slowly slid to the floor. Once his butt hit the ground he began to break down. Overwhelmed with guilt tears began stream down his face. "What's wrong" Glade asked with concerned tone in her voice. She knew they were about to take on possibly the most powerful group of people on the Jefferson and everyone needed to be sharp. "I failed… I wasn't able to save my mom and they still have my dad prisoner waiting for a reason to kill him" Curtus sobbed. "Curtus you didn't fail. You said it yourself the transfer worked and your mom is in that watch thing" Glade said pointing to the gauntlet on Curtus's arm. "I know I can hear her, but I can't see her. I can't have dinner with her any more. I can't save her from going out in public in a terrible outfit. Hell I will never be able to hug my mom when I have a bad day anymore" Curtus explained wiping tears from his face.

Suddenly Curtus felt a warmness on his shoulder. He looked over to see his mother sitting next to him with her hand on his shoulder. Curtus was at a loss for word. He thought the last memory he would have his mother would be of her laying lifeless on the floor. "Curt just know that I will always be here. Whenever you need me just call me and I will be there" Carolyn said with a smile. She gave him a hug and then stood up. Curtus wiped the tears from his eyes and rose to his feet. "Are we good now" Glade asked. Curtus's nodded his head continuing to wipe the tears from his eyes. He thought his mother would only be a voice in his head but it turned out to be more than that. Similar to the Ymerel situation there are two separate people sharing the same body, but unlike Ymerel the two people are not in conflict for control. A chime went off in the elevator and the door slowly opened. "Well whether you are good or not we are here so let's get a move on" Glade said.

The two exited the elevator to the hallway Leremy took them to when they first arrived. This time around it was almost unrecognizable. The once vibrantly lit hallway was now only lit by emergency light. They walked down the hall they would hear the sounds of breaking glasses and footsteps from each of the rooms. "Where do you think we should go" Glade asked. Curtus looked around at the bottom of each of the door to see any light. "Go back to the Dining Room" Carolyn said appearing next to Curtus. Curtus looked over at her. "For you guys to get to the Skytrain you need to get the Omnitool to the Dining Room and use it to get to the Lorraine building. That is the only way" She explained. Curtus nodded and looked back at Glade who was staring at him with a confused look on her face. "Talking to your mom" She asked. "Yeah how could you tell" Curtus asked. "There is nobody over there" She replied. Having no response Curtus began to walking toward the Dining Room. "That is going to take some getting used to" Glade whispered to herself before following after Curtus.

They arrived at the Dining Room with the door cracked opened. The two of them pushed the door open enough for them to squeeze though. The dining room had undergone the same dark makeover as the hallway. The table had been removed and replaced with a lone chair with a mysterious man tied to it. "Mom who is that" Curtus whispered trying not to make the situation uncomfortable for Glade. Curtus's question went unanswered. "Mom who is that" He whispered again and still there was no response. Curtus looked over to see if his mom was still there. She was standing to the left of him with her hands over her mouth in shock. Curtus's stomach sank. There was only one person here who could cause her to react like that. Curtus looked at the chair again and upon second glace Curtus realized his father was tied to the chair.

Throwing all situational awareness out the window Curtus ran towards his dad. Glade looked around and realized something was truly wrong. This was all way too easy. This is the most well-guarded building on the Jefferson and they were walking around like they owned the place. It wasn't until Curtus began his sprint that she realized it was a trap. She sprinted behind him and tackled him to the ground. "What the hell are you doing" Curtus yelled. "It's a trap" Glade yelled. "What do you mean. No one is here get off me" Curtus yelled. As Curtus pushed off Glade a cage erupted from the ground clamping down like a crab claw and trapping them inside.

They both rose to their feet and looked around at the cage. "I would like a written apology and sign it Dumbass with a Capital D" Glade said wiping the dirt off her sweatshirt. Suddenly the lights switched on and Curtus and Glade found themselves temporarily blind. As their vision began to come back they began to make out some figures that were not there before. He recognized the chair as his dad, but there were 3 new figures all behind him. Curtus closed his eye and rubbed them in an effort to regain his vision faster. When he opened his eyes the figures were crystal clear. The three figures were Vladimir Don, Alyson Burraza, and Liam Lopez.

"Glad you guys could join us. You're just in time to witness the greatest scientific achievement in human history" Vladimir said with a sadistic smile. Curtus wasn't focused in Vladimir or anything he was saying. He was too focused on Burraza. She was carrying her old beat up briefcase that she took to work every day. She looked at Curtus with her lazy day smile. It was the same smile she gave when they were watching a film or if she was going to cut class short. That smile used to bring Curtus joy. Now that smile took on entirely different meaning. "Curtus, what he has to show you is pretty spectacular" Burraza said. "Don't say my name you demon" Curtus yelled back.

Burraza was taken back by Curtus's sudden outburst. Even though Curtus was known around University for being outspoken in her class Curtus was known as the quiet genius. He sat in the back and didn't really talk to people. When it came to grading his work it would always be graded in the top 5% of his class. "Okay. Then what would you like to call you then huh. Dumbass?" Burraza asked. "Hey lady that's trademarked. Make up your own name" Glade said. "Burraza would you be a doll and set me up" Vladimir asked. "With pleasure" She replied. She dropped to her knee and gently laid the briefcase on the ground. She opened it and pulled out a pair of gloves. There were several things about these gloves that made Curtus and Glade nervous. The first was the amount of pride that Burraza and Lopez looked at this pair of gloves. It was as if they had finished building a car from scratch. The second was the amount of circuitry on the gloves.

There was wires and circuit boards everywhere in the glove except the palm. Vladimir carefully put on both pairs of gloves. Then Burraza pulled a vest covered in power cells out of the briefcase. Vladimir put the vest with the same care as someone trying to defuse a bomb. Once he got the vest on both Burraza and Lopez helped in putting wires in the right spots. "Hey Glade. Do you know what that is" Curtus whispered? "Not a clue. Then again he also kicked me out when I was young so he has had plenty of time to come up with ideas" Glade whispered back.

Once everything was properly wired Burraza switched the vest on. The vest beeped three times and wires glowed a bright deep green. "I apologize for the ugliness of this model. It's our first prototype so we were going for more function not fashion" Lopez whispered to Vladimir. "Well if this test is a success then I might be able to overlook the rough atheistic" He replied. Vladimir began to walk toward Kirkland. Curtus grew more nervous with each step he took. He walked until he was standing right in front of Kirkland. "Curtus are you familiar with temporal distortion" Vladimir asked. He had heard the phrase one time his theories class but wasn't sure what it meant. "Like time travel" Curtus replied. "Well you have the time part correct" Vladimir replied beginning to pace. "You see, what we have done something that people only thought was possible in science fiction films. We now have the power of time and gravity at the palm of our hands" Vladimir explained looking at both of his palm. He took his right hand and placed it on the top of Kirkland's head. "You guy have front row seats to the moment when I become a god" Vladimir said looking at Kirkland.

What happened next left both Curtus and Glade speechless. It was as if Vladimir was sucking all of the water out of his father's skin. Kirkland began to wrinkle and his hair began to turn white. In a matter of 15 seconds it looked like his father aged 25 years. Vladimir took his hand off of Curtus's father ending the aging. "What did you do to him" Curtus yelled grabbing the bars of the cage. "Why do you ask questions you already know the answers to" Vladimir asked. "You should really listen better" Burraza added. "I told you we now control time. All I did was make your father a touch older" Vladimir replied. Curtus looked at his dad again. His body had become frail and was shaking like an autumn leaf. "You guy need to smile more. You two were just witness to a scientific achievement that many thought was impossible" Liam said.

The sound of her father's voice began to make Glade's angry. "Why the hell are you here" She asked. "Excuse me" Liam replied. "You're not a scientist and had no part in creating the technology that made this possible so why are you here. Because you sewed the batteries to the vest?" she yelled. Liam was becoming enraged.

"Listen here. You are not going to talk to me any kind of way" He began. "And you are going to quit talking to me like you're my father" She yelled back. Curtus looked at Glade, whose face had become red. "Aww your about to cry. Now that brings back some good memories" Liam said with a smile. "Liam enough. What is your status" Vladimir asked? "The invasion force and awaiting you command" Liam said. "Invasion force" Curtus asked. "Yes… believe it or not I do more than just sew batteries on vests" Liam said. "Yeah Liam is the General of the Family Army" Burraza said.

A look of shock came over Glade's face. She had no idea that her father was the general of anything. "You look surprised" Liam said looking at Glade. "They must have read the files in my office" Burraza said. "Oh… well at those events that you read about it was my army that made them happen" Liam said.

All of the events they read about in Isis's room began flashing back into Curtus's head. The Purge of 2215, Mexican Blood Flu, The Rush of 4. Glade's father had a hand in all of these event. "Proceed with the invasion as planned" Vladimir said. "Ask him about the invasion plan" Carolyn said. Curtus looked over to see his mother outside of the cage. "He doesn't think you guys are going to make it out of here. I guarantee he will tell you what it is and that way we can buy some time and plan a way out of here" Carolyn said with a smile. "Hey! What invasion are you talking about" Curtus yelled?

The group seemed shocked that Curtus asked about the invasion even though they didn't make an effort to keep it secret. "They aren't going to make it out of here alive so I guess we can tell them" Liam whispered. Burraza and Vladimir both nodded in agreeance. Vladimir walked over to the cage and looked Curtus directly in the eyes. "You look scared Curtus" Vladimir said. Curtus wanted to say something slick and witty, but his blood came to a complete stand still. No matter how hard he wanted to breathe his body just wouldn't. Was this true fear. Fear to the point that your body shuts itself down in the presence of it? "You need to breathe son, before you pass out" Vladimir said. "Come on Curt you got to breathe!" his mother pleaded. But her plea fell on deaf ears as his body wouldn't respond. It wasn't until Glade slapped him in the back of his head that he started breathing again. "C'mon Dumbass this isn't the time for your ass to get tight. We will have plenty of time for that later" She said. "Well yours and my perception of plenty of time are very different" Vladimir said turning his back to the cage. "Liam head to your command ship and lead the attack on Shangri La." Vladimir ordered.

An evil smile grew on Liam's face. "The first wave will be there in 24 hours" He replied. "Excellent. I have faith like all of your other operations that this one will be a success" Vladimir said. Liam reached on his belt and pressed a button and disappeared in a blinding flash of white light. Curtus looked at his mother who had an expression of shock and utter defeat on her face. "24 hours. The quickest we can get there is in a month and that is if everything goes perfectly. This is really bad." she muttered to herself. Vladimir turned his focus to Burraza. "What is the status of [Project M41M1]" He asked. "Everything is in place. Lisa is there now fixing the teleportation unit, but once that is done we will be awaiting your order to start phase two" Burraza explained. "Don't wait any longer. Once the teleportation unit is finished begin phase two" Vladimir said. An expression of childlike joy came over her face. "I promise I won't let you down" She said. "You better not" He replied.

Vladimir looked back at Curtus and Glade. "Oh yeah I was telling you the last good story you will ever hear" Vladimir said. He cleared his throat before he continued. "Well from intel we were given from a reliable source there is a thriving city on the surface. This may come a shock to you but there have been rumors about this for a long time and now we know where it is" He began to pace back and forth. "In the Tran-Mexican Volcanic belt there is an inactive volcano known as Citlaltepetl which reaches over the Rad Clouds and on the top of it is the city of Shangri La." Curtus looked toward his mother and the expression on her face let Curtus know that everything he was saying was 100% factual. "The city was rumor to be as the last Kryll stronghold and is housing servers with all recorded human history on it. The plan is to go take that server as well as squash the last of the resistance. Once we have the servers in our possession we will be able to rewrite history in any way we see fit." He finished.

Curtus always wondered what happened in the final days on the surface. When did they build the Jefferson and how did they go about choosing the people who got on? "If they get to the Well all is lost" Carolyn said. She walked and stood next to Vladimir. "Curtus change of plan you need to stop them from getting to the Well at all cost" She yelled. "Wasn't the original plan to get on the Skytrain" Curtus asked. "Oh yeah I'm getting ahead of myself. You need to get to the Skytrain ASAP" Carolyn said. "Question is how do we get out of here" Curtus asked. "Let's hope your friends are on their way" She replied nervously. Curtus could tell that the magnitude of the situation had increased exponentially. Two days ago his main goal was to find and save his parents. Now it just grew to him saving all of human history.

"Now it is time for the best part of my evening, how will I dispose of you two" Vladimir asked himself. Curtus looked at his father who was sitting in the chair barely clinging to life. "He probably has 15 minutes' tops. In our test it seemed that it wasn't the physical aging that killed people but the rapid aging of the brain. The brain would overwork itself trying to keep up it would just overheat and eventually give out" Vladimir explained. Curtus's heart skipped a beat. "He is doing better than most subjects though. All the other ones would be screaming out in agony from the pain" Vladimir said with a sadistic smile. "Do you hear yourself. You're a monster" Glade said. "If it takes a monster to ensure the survival of the human race then call me the goddamn boogeyman" Vladimir said.

Vladimir looked back at Curtus's father who was swaying side to side. "Maybe I should just put him out of his misery" Vladimir said walking toward the chair. A wave of hopelessness came over Curtus. He was about to watch his father be murdered in front of him and he could do nothing about it. "Don't worry Curt your father was ready for this outcome from the very start" Carolyn said in a soothing voice. Then all of the sudden the cage fell apart. It was as if an electric current that had been holding it together had been severed. Without hesitation Curtus charged at Vladimir. He clenched his right hand into a fist activating his Tonic. "Wait Curt the glove" his mother yelled. But Curtus couldn't hear her. He was so focused on protecting his dad that all outside noise was drowned out.

Vladimir turned around just in time to see Curtus winding up his punch. As he threw his punch he activated his Tonic creating a diamond glove. Vladimir stuck his right hand up and caught the punch before it could hit his chest. "So long Curtus" Vladimir said. He squeezed Curtus's fist activating the aging process. He squeezed his hand for five seconds but nothing happened. "What is going on. Why aren't you dead" Vladimir said. While he was trying to figure out what was going on Curtus came around with his left arm and caught Vladimir across the jaw sending him flying across the room. Vladimir grabbed his jaw and looked at Curtus in shock. "Why didn't you age" He asked. "It's actually elementary science. Diamonds get harder with time and pressure" Curtus said popping his knuckles. Vladimir reset his jaw and squeezed it with the time gauntlet for a second to heal it. "Now this is for all the people that you guys tortured and killed" Curtus said.

XVII

Isis and Jaymar exited the elevator to an unfamiliar hallway. "Where are we" She asked looking around the dusty corridor. "The hell if I know. I thought you knew where we were going" Jaymar replied. "I just got my sight back like four hours ago… how would I know where I am going" She asked. "You do make a valid point" Jaymar said. "I think we might have went up one too many floors" Isis said. "Let's just hop in the elevator with haste" Jaymar said jokingly. Suddenly the door of the elevator slammed shut and they heard the elevator go crashing down the shaft. "Good thing we didn't hop in with too much haste" Isis said jokingly. "Well looks like we need to find another way down" Jaymar said.

They walked down the hall until they reached a large wooden door much like the one for the Dining Room. It was apparent the door hadn't been touched is a long time from the thick layer of dust and the number of cobwebs surrounding it. "Nobody's been in this room in ages" Jaymar said dragging his finger along the door. Isis looked at the door and a queasy feeling began to build in her stomach. "Maybe we should find another way" She said. "Nonsense the quickest way from point A to point B is in a straight line" Jaymar said grabbing the dusty knob. He twisted it and with both hands pulled the heavy wooden door until the opening was big enough for them to walk through. "After you madam" Jaymar said. Isis drew one of her swords before entering the room.

What awaited them on the other side of the door was nothing short of disgusting. The large door led to a museum holding all of the Family's sick and twisted accomplishments. Little things that were not stated in the report were brought to light in disturbingly high definition. The first exhibit was dedicated to the Purge of 2215. The report only told them the finished result but the exhibit showed everything else. Massive pictures of battered and beaten Middle Eastern people being paraded half naked down the street covered the walls. Isis's grip on her sword became tighter as she walked through the exhibit. "Killing them wasn't enough they had to humiliate them first" Isis whispered to herself. As Jaymar was looking around he caught a glimpse of Isis. He could feel the rage oozing from her pores. "I probably should get her out of her" Jaymar thought to himself. As he walked over to Isis he saw a picture of an eight-year-old girl yelling and throwing rocks at the people as they walked by. He looked at the picture and felt nothing short of pure sadness. "At that age you have no hate in your heart. Her parents failed her" He whispered to himself.

He walked to Isis to find her crying. It wasn't the conventional sob. It was if everything was normal and she had rivers of tears running down her face. He put his hand on her shoulder in an effort to comfort her. "So this is it huh" She began. "What do you mean" Jaymar asked. "This is how my heritage died. They were treated like something less than human. They were paraded through the city half-naked to be lead to their slaughter like animals. And they laughed and smiled and acted like what they were doing was for the greater good" Isis finished. Jaymar was at a loss for words. He had no idea how to explain such and evil act. "Men, woman, and children all treated like animals.

How can a human treat another human like that?" She asked looking at Jaymar.

Jaymar took a moment to gather his thoughts before responding. "Fear... Fear is the strongest emotion and also the most artificial emotion too. Fear will make us do things we didn't think we could do. It has the power to push all other emotions to the side in order and take control of you. It will also make you believe in just about anything. If it has a chance to make what you afraid off disappear fear will make you gravitate to it. And at the end of the day Fear isn't real. Most of those men, women, and children in those pictures aren't inherently evil people, they are just scared of what they don't understand." Jaymar explained. Isis wiped her eyes and gave Jaymar a hug. "And don't say your heritage is dead. It is not dead because it lives on in you" Jaymar whispered in her ear. Isis took a step back and looked at Jaymar with a smile. "We have to see the good in people even if they can't see it in themselves" Jaymar finished. "Thank you. If you guys would have never saved me I could have ended up like the rest of my people." She said wiping the last of the tears from her eye. "Now come on this place is giving me the creeps" Jamar said.

As they were exiting the exhibit there was one small glass case. Inside was the was a mannequin head wrapped in a head scarf made of a beautiful purple fabric. On the glass of the case was a plaque that read

"Yari Rose... The last of them." Without hesitation broke the glass with the back of her sword and pulled the mannequin head out. After studying the way, the hijab was wrapped on the mannequin Isis wrapped it on her head the same way. She tightened her new head wrap and looked at Jaymar. "Now we can go."

They exited the exhibit and enter a shrine of some sort. The shrine was sent up like a church. There were rows pews on each side of the massive room. Fountains squirted different colored liquids from the wall. The shrine itself was a massive bronze statue of an old man. They walked down the center of the of the room looking in each individual pew for a clue of what this place is for. It looked like the place had been looted as each pew was empty. They reached the statue and read the golden plaque underneath it. "Donald Romano (He is our father and we are his children) 1946-" Jaymar whispered. "That's weird there is no death date" Isis said. "He had to be dead. He would be like 260 years old" Jaymar replied. "You guys also thought Vladimir was dead too. I don't know how it could be done but what I have learned is the Family can make anything happen." Isis said.

Behind the statue was an office that like all of the other places on this floor had been abandoned. Jaymar pushed the door open to find a room with the walls and the ceiling painted black with a desk in the center of the room. No other furniture was in the room and nothing hung on the walls. Jaymar walked into the room and opened the only drawer in the desk to find a flash light. He picked it up and examined it quickly. "This room is too eerie for this to be the only thing in it" Jaymar said. He activated his Tonic and examined the walls. Isis looked in awe as she saw Jaymar's eyes change colors. The white of his eyes turned black and his irises turned yellow. "Do your eye always do that" She asked. "Do what" Jaymar replied keeping his focus on the walls. "Do they change colors like that" She said rephrasing the question. "I didn't know they changed colors… Do I look like a badass" Jaymar asked with a smile? "More scary than badass" She replied. "Works for me" Jaymar said returning his focus to the wall.

Jaymar was looking for abnormalities about the wall. He scanned the wall until he saw the glimmer from a top layer of paint. It wasn't anything visible on the wall but his enhanced vision was just strong enough to spot it. He looked at the flashlight and he notice something odd about it. When he examined it with his normal eyes it looked like a normal flashlight but with his Tonic active he could see there was a filter on the lens. He deactivated his Tonic and looked at Isis. "Close the door" He said. She nodded her head and closed the door making the room pitch black.

Jaymar turned on the light and the walls lit up with pink lettering. The walls and ceiling were covered with disjointed phrases, words, and numbers. "Whose ever office this was... must have been completely out of their mind" Jaymar said pointing the flashlight around the room. "Well I wouldn't be surprised. Look at the type of people we are dealing with" Isis replied.

Without prior information or notes to go off of Jaymar tried to find things that appeared one multiple walls. "What do you make of all of this" Isis asked. "Your guess is as good as mine" He replied continuing to analyze the walls. After a thorough inspection Jaymar found five phrase that appeared on all the walls. "Well we don't have time to figure this out, but I noticed some phrases appear on all the walls" Jaymar said. Isis took he sword and cut a square piece out of the wooden desk. She sat on the ground and placed the tip of her sword on the slab ready to carve the words. "Alright tell me" She said. "New Pangea, Miami Fl, MKUltra, Deacon X, ABZ43Z" Jaymar said. He watched as she effortlessly carved the five phrases into the wood. She stood up and put her sword back in the sheath. "Okay let's slide. This place too spooky" Jaymar said. "Yeah I think I saw a door on to the left of the shrine." She replied.

As they exited the office they both noticed something was off. It was as if someone had moved the pews around slightly. The room was cold and a white fog that covered the ground. Then they began to hear heavy footsteps and chains coming from the doorway across the room. They looked over to see what looked like a large man walking his dog. The man stood around eight feet tall and was a large muscular build. His eyes were blood red and his skin was paper white. He had a chains around his neck, wrists, and both ankles. His dog had white fur with grey spots and blood red eyes like his owner. It stood on two legs like a person and was being held back by a flaming leash. "This is a warning." The mysterious man began. He had a deep bellowing voices that shook both Jaymar and Isis ribcages. "What you have inhaled is fear toxin created by Alyson Burraza." The man explained.

Suddenly the office made sense. Whoever was in there was a test dummy for the gas and they lost their mind. "The goal of the gas was to get people to tell the truth and show who they really are on the inside, but the major side effect is people go criminally insane. It puts your mind in this pocket dimension while your body does what it wants. I got to you guys just in time." The man finished. "Criminally insane. The people running the Family seem to be all the way together in the head" Jaymar replied. "Insanity comes in many forms." The man answered. Isis began to think of some of the other words that were on the wall. "Purge, MBF, cleanse" She thought to herself. "While under the influence of this drug this you will see what torments you the most. You can say they aren't real as much as you want but they will have the ability to kill you if you are not careful" The man finished.

Once the man was done speaking the man's dog walked over to them and handed them two syringes. "These will bring you back to reality" The dog said. "Why are you helping us" Isis asked grabbing a syringe. "As time has gone on I have gotten sick of watching people suffer. In the past I would have observed from afar and watched you slip into madness. I think I have reached my limit. A person can only watch so much pain before they break" The man explained. "Wait so you were a real person" Jaymar asked. "In a past life… I had a wife, children, even a real dog. Then they captured me and trapped me in this pit" he replied. They watched as dog returned to the man's and jumped on his back like a monkey. "She needs to be stopped. If she is able to finish her research she will become a force than even the Family can't control" The man said. He pointed to the right wall of the shrine. "There is a secret door behind this wall. Press the discolored brick and it will open" He said. "Okay before you disappear and never see each other again. What is your real name" Jaymar asked? "In my past life my name was Chris… Christopher Perkins and this is my dog Peaches, but now they know me as the red eyed man and his hell hound. And if you and your friends do try and stop her we will meet again" Christopher said. They looked at each other before inserting the syringes in their arms at the same time. "Until next time Chris" Isis said with a smile. They pressed down on the back part of the syringe injecting the mysterious fluid into their system.

It was as if they just come back from a daydream. They found themselves standing outside of the office looking out at the pews. Isis looked at her wrist and found no syringe. Jaymar turned back and looked in the office. He saw that in the ceiling of the office was a vent where the toxin was being pumped in. He looked at the door and saw that on all four edges on the door was pieces of rubber to make the room air tight. Jaymar grabbed the door and slammed it shut. "You saw that too right" Isis asked. "You mean the red eyed dog owner talking about the secret door" Jaymar replied. "Okay so it was real" Isis said running over to the wall Christopher pointed to. She looked around the wall until she found one brick that was slightly brighter than the others. She pushed it in and it open a hatch in the middle of the church. They looked down the hatch to see a rusty ladder. "Ladies first" Jaymar said nervously. Isis gave him a nervous look before she began down the ladder.

The ladder put them in an armory with piles of weapons scattered across the floor. The room had all weapons from conventional firearms such as rifles, pistols, and shotguns to the more obscure such as sword, crossbows, and halberds. From the layout of the room this was a room not meant for people to go into as there was not type of organizational system. "These must be the weapons they confiscated" Jaymar said. Isis looked at him. "What do you mean" She asked. "While I was reading the file about the Purge of 2215 the first thing they did was take the weapons away from the people. They said they were taking them to be put in a registry and that everyone on the Jefferson was abiding by the new code, but they never got their weapons back. With no way to protect themselves so they began getting attacked. This them until someone snapped and fought back giving them a reason to be called violent and be jettison them" Jaymar explained. He looked around the room and saw a door on the other end of the room. "There is out way out" he said beginning to make his way to the door.

On the way out of the armory one of the weapons caught Jaymar's eye. It was an engraved Bō staff sitting on a pile of rifles. "Why would a Bō staff be confiscated with rifles?" Jaymar thought to himself. He climbed the mountain of weapons and picked up the staff. He ran his hand across the wood and could tell there was something special about the staff. "What are you doing" Isis asked. "I don't know, but I just have this feeling I need to get this to Curtus" Jaymar replied picking up the staff. He slid down the plie 3/4th the way down the pile before jumping off and landing next to Isis. "That is what you were getting. What is wrong with the one he has" Isis asked. "There is nothing wrong with that one. But there is just something about this staff. I need to get it to him" Jaymar explained. They waded through the sea of weapons until they reached the door on the other side. They open the door to find themselves in a back hallway. As they made their way through the hall when they saw an open elevator and in the elevator was none other than Alyson Burraza.

Burraza's eye filled with fear as she stood defenseless in a cornered in the elevator as she began to furiously mash the door close button on the elevator. Jaymar wasting no time dropped the staff and reached for the Omnitool. As he was trying to unhook it from his belt Isis grabbed his hand. "What are you doing" He yelled. Jaymar looked at the elevator and watched as the doors closed. "Look now she got away" Jaymar yelled. "If you kill her now. He research can still continue. To truly defeat her we have destroy her and her research" She explained. "And how do we find the source" Jaymar asked. "I don't know but I'm hoping one of these phrases can give us some answers" Isis said holding up the piece of wood. Jaymar took a deep breath and picked up the staff. "Well we aren't getting any closer to the others standing here" Isis said.

They sprinted down the hall until the found another door. Seeing no other doors on the way to this had to have been where Burraza came from. The door was locked by a numerical turn lock with the dial was surrounded by the numbers 1 through 9 "Of course there is a lock and scanning for prints won't do me any good" Jaymar said. Isis looked down at her plank of wood. Her eyes were immediately drawn to the sequence ABZ43Z. "It's T9" She whispered to herself. She walked over to the dial and turned the dial clockwise three times before beginning the sequence. "2-2-9-4-3-9" She said as spun the dial back and forth. When she was finished a light above the dial turned green and the door unlocked. Jaymar looked at her with a surprised look on his face. "How did you know" he asked. "Blind faith… and before I was blind we had a safe that used T9 for all he codes. Yuki wrote down her passwords the same way." She said with a smile. "Well let's hope they aren't dead" Jaymar said pushing the door open. They burst through the door to see Curtus charging at Vladimir and Glade untying Curtus's father.

XVIII

"Be careful Curt we don't know was the other glove does" Carolyn said. Curtus took heed of his mother's words. He knew that his right glove had the ability to accelerate time, but he had to always be aware where that left hand was. Curtus's plan was to be the aggressor keeping Vladimir on the defensive so he wouldn't be able to get off an attack. As threw his endless barrage of punches he noticed Vladimir casually blocked and deflected all of his attacks with a smile on his face. "Hand to hand is not your specialty.

Why don't you get that Bō so we can really go at it?" he said with an arrogant tone. Curtus knew that he wasn't very proficient at hand to hand combat. He was just good enough to defend himself but not good enough to overwhelm and defeat a skilled opponent. Curtus wanted to get to his Bō but the ever present threat of his gloves made Curtus hesitant to grab it. During the bombardment of punches Vladimir side stepped causing Curtus to lose his balance.

All it took was a touch from his right hand and it would be all over. Curtus flexed his back muscles creating a diamond turtle shell. Before the shell was finished Vladimir snatched the staff from his backpack. Curtus stumbled but managed to keep his balance. He quickly turned around to see his Bō staff rusting in in Vladimir's hands. "Now isn't that a shame. Like most machines they get rusty when you need them most" He said as the Bō quickly withered into a cloud of orange dust. "I told you to be careful" Carolyn said. "You're really not helping" Curtus replied. "Why would I help you. We are fighting each other right?" Vladimir asked.

A wave of embarrassment came over Curtus. He didn't realize he spoke out loud. "What are you going to do" Carolyn said. "Don't worry mom I got this far. I'll figure something out" Curtus silently replied. Carolyn had never seen this side of Curtus before. She had never seen this level of confidence from her son and that brought a smile to her face. Suddenly Jaymar and

Isis came bursting through the door Burraza exited through. "Yo Curtus catch" He yelled throwing him the wooden Bō. "See mom I told you I'd figure something out" Curtus said catching the with his right hand.

Holding the wooden staff in his hand brought a smile to Curtus's face. This was the type of Bō he was used to. Curtus looked at Vladimir and noticed something different about his face. He no longer had that confident smile on his face. He looked nervous and uneasy. Curtus looked at the staff again. Even though on the outside it looked like a regular wooden staff it had a strong aura to it. "Mom what is up with this Bō. It is like he is scared of it" Curtus asked. She walked over and looked at the staff and she too had a look of shock on her face. "That is Methuselah" She said. That name was very familiar to Curtus.

On the Jefferson there are a rumored 3 legendary weapons. The rumor has it if the wrong person had all three they would be an unstoppable one-man army and kill everyone on the Jefferson. The first of these weapons was the Omnitool which was in Jaymar's possession. The Second was a two sword set called Aonoror and Orfa. And the third was Methuselah which Curtus now had. "You don't need to coat that in diamond because the wood it is made of doesn't age and is already hard as diamond" Carolyn explained.

"Really" Curtus replied. He twirled the staff in his hand twice before charging at Vladimir.

Jaymar and Isis ran over to help Glade. She was struggling to untie Curtus's father. "Nice of you guys to show up" Glade said struggling with the wire. "Here let me help you with that" Isis said pulling out one of her swords. She carefully put the blade in between the Kirkland's hands and cut the wire that was binding his wrists. The moment the wire snapped Kirkland grabbed Isis's arms. Isis saw a bright flash of light.

The light disappeared and she found herself in a grass meadow. The sun setting over the horizon painted the sky a deep orange. The meadow was full of beautiful flowers and grasses as far as the eye could see. "You're Isis huh. My wife has said a lot about you and your brother" A voice said. Isis turned around and saw Curtus's father was sitting on a bench next to a road. Isis walked over and sat next to him. She looked at him and saw he was noticeably younger than when they first met. He had a high top fade with a blonde white patch in the front with a thin goatee. "Where am I" She asked. "Oh this place. This is a bridge between life and death" Kirkland replied. "Why am I here" She asked. "Because I have to give you a gift and this is the safest place I can give it to you." He replied. "A gift for what. You've only known me for an hour" She asked. "All you young people are just full of questions aren't you. It is to keep you safe on your journey" He said reaching in his pocket. He pulled out a napkin with a cookie in it. "This is the Lightning Tonic my wife made. It is the most powerful Tonic she has ever made" Kirkland said.

Isis grabbed the cookie and stared at it. "Why are you giving this to me" She asked. "Because if I don't pass it on to someone it will remain in my body. This will give the Family a chance to extract it and reverse engineer it and if you thought they were bad now imagine them with an army of people who can control lightning" He explained. Isis looked intensely at the cookie. "How do I even use it" She asked. "Don't worry about that. When the time is right you'll figure it out" he began. "And if you worried about if it is going to taste good it is going to taste like whatever you want it to taste like" Kirkland said with a smile. Suddenly a bus pulled up to the bench. "Well this is for me. Let hope the big man has mercy on me. He knows all the vile things I have done" Kirkland whispered to himself. He put his hand on Isis's shoulder. "Once you finish the cookie you will be returned to the real world. Sorry about forcing this on you" Kirkland said with a smile. He began to board the bus but stopped halfway up the stairs and turned around. "Hey Isis can you do me a favor" Kirkland asked. "Absolutely" She replied. "Please let Curtus know how proud I am of him. Even though we didn't get to change the world together I know he will change the world and make it a better place" Kirkland said. "I'll tell him." Isis replied. Kirkland smiled as the bus doors closed.

The air brakes of the bus let out a loud puff of air before the bus took off for the horizon. Isis looked at the cookie for a second before eating it all in one bite. The cookie had a sweet cinnamon sugar flavor like a snickerdoodle. The moment she swallowed the cookie she snapped back to reality. Kirkland laying on the ground, Jaymar trying to perform CPR, and Glade yelling at Jaymar to put more force into his chest compressions. She looked at Kirkland and noticed that he was smiling with the same smile he had when the bus doors closed.

Trying to get the jump Vladimir Curtus planned on attacking while he was busy messing with his glove. Vladimir was so focused on his glove that he didn't see Curtus coming. Curtus was able to get a clean hit on Vladimir's left ear causing him to stumble. Curtus got behind Vladimir and poked the back of both of his knee making him to drop to the ground. Then he finished the brutal combo by turning the Bō to diamond, grabbing it with two hand, and like a baseball player swung it the Bō hitting him in the right side of his jaw sending him flying across the room. Curtus was breathing extremely heavily. The onslaught of wasted punches plus that combo and the about of time he was using his Tonic had Curtus feeling drained. He looked over to where his father was sitting to see everyone gathered around him. The way they stood around him Curtus knew something bad had happened.

When he got over to the group he saw the manifestation of his worst fears. His father was lying dead on the ground. "I'm sorry Curtus I couldn't save him" Jaymar said. "We never wanted it to happen like this" Carolyn said. Curtus looked at his mother. "What do you mean" Curtus asked. "When we were planning we tried to make a plan where all three of us would make it off the Jefferson. But every time we thought we had a plan we either got caught or all of us got killed. So your father decided he would sacrifice himself for the sake of humanity" she explained. Tears began to roll down Curtus's face. Carolyn took notice and reminded Curtus of the magnitude of the situation. She grabbed him by his shoulders and turned him to face her. "Curt we have the finish the mission. There will be plenty of time mourn Kirkland, but now we have to stay focused" She said. Curtus looked at his mom and saw the pain in her eyes. He could tell that she was truly hurting, But along with the pain in her eyes was strength. Curtus wiped the tears from his face and turned his focus back to Vladimir.

He was slowly getting up of the ground bleeding from his ear and mouth. His jaw was hanging lifelessly after being completely broken from Curtus's attack. "You guys think you can actually make a difference. We will hunt you down like dogs" He yelled stumbling to his feet. His speech was muffles from his mouth being filled with blood. The four of them began to walk over toward Vladimir. Unable to keep his balance Vladimir dropped back to the ground and began to crawl backward in a seated position. "Stay back" He yelled with blood dripping from his mouth. The group continued to walk toward him. Suddenly a smile appeared on Vladimir's mangled face and he extended his left arm with the palm facing them. "You guys should have escaped when you had the chance" He said pressing a button on his left wrist.

The tables turned the moment he pressed that button as they found themselves suspended in midair. "These gloves are the most powerful thing created by man. In one hand I have the power to control the flow of time and in the other I can control gravity" Vladimir said adjusting his jaw. He turned his left palm up and sent them flying high into the air. He quickly reset his jaw with his right hand and accelerated time so it would heal, and then stuck his left palm at them to catch them. He turned his palm down and sent them crashing into the floor. "You guys are helpless. As long as you are in control of my gravity glove" Vladimir said arrogantly. Curtus began to think that all that he had done was for nothing. They weren't able to do anything to him because he would just make you float, grab you and hold on until you were nothing but dust. It was as if they were fighting a god. All was lost. "Hey guys I think I found a flaw in his system" Jaymar whispered

Everyone looked to the left to see Jaymar with a smile on his face. "I think I know how to beat him" He whispered again. Curtus looked over at Vladimir. He was busy talking about how he had defeated them that he wasn't focused on them. "Well spit it out" Glade whispered. "When he sent us flying he reversed the flow of gravity. I felt the force of gravity pushing us up. But when he went to heal his jaw for a split second I didn't feel that force. We were just working off our momentum. He isn't able to power both gloves at the same time" He explained. "So what you're saying is we have to come at him from more than one angle to defeat him?" Isis inquired. "Bingo" Jaymar replied. "Only problem is that we have to get free of this gravity blanket" Glade said. "How do you think we do that" Isis asked. Everyone turned and looked at Curtus. "What are you looking at me for" He asked. "Well you're not saying anything so I guess we thought you were coming up with a plan" Glade replied. Curtus needed to think of something quick so he didn't look like he was a burden. "Leremy is coming" He said nervously.

Everyone looked at Curtus with a look of disbelief. "You have got to be kidding me. That is your plan" Isis whispered. "Now give him a chance to explain himself" Jaymar said. "Well Leremy is going to come and distract him long enough to for us to escape this trap" Curtus explained. The three of them just stared at Curtus shaking their heads. "Dumbass… that has to be the worst plan you could have come up with. That man is probably in a hallway somewhere having a conversation with himself" Glade said. "I have to agree her on this on. That is pretty bad" Jaymar added. Suddenly there was a loud knock on the door. It was a loud deep knock like there was something massive on the other side of it. There were two more knocks before the door was blown of the hinges. A cloud of dust filled the doorway from the crashing door. When the dust settled to everyone's surprise Leremy was standing in the doorway.

Vladimir glared at Leremy. "Leremy what is the meaning of this" He yelled. "You can stop giving me orders old man" Leremy yelled. He began to walk toward them. "That kid is the son of the lady who saved us. Without her we wouldn't be here. This is our way to repaying her" Leremy yelled beginning a sprint toward Vladimir. "Did you really plan this" Jaymar asked. "I told you guy he was coming back. You guys just didn't believe me" Curtus replied. Curtus never in a million years thought Leremy would come back and didn't understand why he was here. His mother saved Ymerel and the part of them that is Ymerel no longer exist. Glade looked at Curtus with the "You know you just got lucky" look on her face. "You guys get ready because you don't know how long our window will be to move" Curtus said.

They watched as Leremy ran by them and leaped in the air. He drew his arm back and it disappeared in a cloud of smoke. Curtus was becoming nervous due to the expression on Vladimir's face. He was about to be attacked by his top assassin and he doesn't look the least bit nervous. He quickly turned his left palm of his glove toward Leremy trapping him in midair.

The group popped to their feet and all became extremely lightheaded. Being under intense gravity for an extended period of time the sudden change didn't give their brain enough time to adjust. Jaymar dropped on all four and began to vomit. "Oh get a hold of yoursel…" Glade began. Before she could finish her sentence she dropped to her knees and began to vomit as well. Seeing the current state of the others Curtus and Isis chose to remain silent and let it pass.

Vladimir shook his head in disappointment. "I always had my doubts about you" he began. Leremy tried to throw his punch but the gravity was so intense it locked him place. "You were the strongest in the academy, you fought with this anger that we loved, but we always thought there was always a chance you could turn on us" Vladimir said beginning to pace. He reached in his pocket and pulled out what looked like a stick of chapstick with a button on top. "Goodbye old friend" He said pressing the top of the button. The button triggering an explosive at the base of Leremy's skull causing his head to explode. Isis looked in horror as her brother's headless body fell lifelessly to the ground.

He looked at Isis with a sinister smile. "No matter how white we made his skin we knew what he was and we knew we would eventually have to eliminate him for the greater good of the Jefferson" he said. "Keep your cool" Curtus said. "I just have one question. How does it feel to be the last of your kind?" Vladimir asked

Isis snapped drawing both of her swords and charging at him. Curtus knew she had no chance against him one on one. "Jaymar zip over to the left of him and give Isis cover fire" Curtus yelled. Jaymar unclipped the Omnitool and shot a zip line to the wall behind Vladimir. Curtus looked at Glade. "We have to keep attacking him and create an opening" Curtus said. "We have gotten this far. Let's see it to the end" She replied back erecting her blades. Glade's words came as a shock to Curtus. All the things they have been through this was the first time that Glade had genuine faith in him. Curtus smiled and nodded before sprinting toward Vladimir with Glade closely behind.

Isis drew the swords behind her head in preparation for an overhead slash. Vladimir smiled as prepared his left hand to gravity trap her. As he was about to use his gravity glove he saw Jaymar out of the corner of his eye. He was flying parallel to the ground looking down the scope of the Omnitool. He knew that if he trapped

Isis he would get hit by whatever attack was planning to launch.

Though Isis's slash and Jaymar's cover fire were synced up perfectly Vladimir managed to dodge them both. He first sidestepped the two sword slash before ducking under the bullet. Jaymar sliding on the ground continuing to shoot at Vladimir. All he had was non-lethal bullets so he was using them as a decoy. He fired 19 more shots before his clip ran dry. "What out of bullets" Vladimir asked. "You shouldn't get too comfortable" Curtus said swinging a diamond Bō at his legs. Vladimir jumped just in time to avoid what would have been a shin shattering strike. "This doesn't seem fair" Vladimir said. "We aren't here to play fair we're her to beat you" Curtus said.

Jaymar looked through his inventory and found a small taser in his pocket. It wasn't a very powerful taser but it was strong enough to stun the average man for a second or two and it was small enough to be fired by the Omnitool. He loaded it, looked down the scope and saw that Vladimir was up in the air. He took a deep breath in, held it for a second, and pulled the trigger. The Omnitool fired the taser right into Vladimir's neck. Vladimir, who was getting ready to make Curtus celebrate 70 birthdays at one time found himself locked in place. "Now" Curtus yelled. Glade who was running behind Curtus jumped off his back. With her erected blades she stabbed Vladimir straight through both hands. Vladimir yelled out in agony as Glade's blood began to eat at the flesh and wires around the blades. "It's all on you now" Glade yelled. Vladimir looked to see Isis sprinting at him. A sense of hopelessness came over Vladimir. He was in the air and unable to defend himself. This was checkmate. With one swipe of her swords his arms were in six separate pieces cutting him just above and below the elbow. He dropped to the ground and rolled on the floor in agony. Glade landed softly next to Vladimir. She looked at the two lifeless hands on her blades. "I think these are your" she said letting them slide off and land next to him.

Curtus looked at Isis who was sheathing her swords. "Why didn't you kill him" He asked. She looked at Vladimir watching as his blood began to pool around him. "Because I want him to suffer like Ymerel did" She said walking away. Curtus put the Bō back on his bag and grabbed the chair his father was sitting in. He walked over to the massive window and slammed the chair into the bottom of it. The window slowly cracked from where he hit the window to the ceiling before slowly raining down in a multicolored snow flurry. "It's time to free the people of their ignorance" Glade yelled. Curtus looked back and saw Glade smiling ear to ear. Curtus took off his backpack and open the pocket that contained all the files in it. Curtus was about to empty his bag when his mother grabbed him by the shoulder. "There are certain things people are just not ready to hear" She said. "Mom they need to know what is going on. Right now they are in this mental cage thinking that the Jefferson is this utopia. They need to know the Family is real and how evil they actually are. That is the only way they can truly fight for their freedom." Curtus replied. His mother smiled. "I wish your father was here to see you right now. He would be so proud" She said letting go of his shoulder. He as he walked over Glade stopped him before he could pour the files. "What are you doing" Curtus yelled. "No that is a question you should be asking yourself" Glade said as she pulled the massive diamond out of his bag.

Curtus was shocked that Glade put that in his bag. "Why did you keep that" Curtus asked. "Because if we ever need money we will have this to sell. And plus I'm not just going to live the biggest diamond in the world I would never forgive myself" She replied. Curtus was surprised with Glade's forward thinking. Where every they were about to go they would most likely need money, and being wanted criminals doesn't make it easy for one to get a job. "Now what are you waiting on Dumbass enlighten the people" Glade said pushing him toward the window. Curtus took a deep breath before turning his backpack over and letting all the file rain out.

Hundreds upon thousands of pages of reports rained down on the people of the Jefferson. Curtus shook the bag to make sure all of the files were out of his bag. He grabbed the diamond from Glade and the plank of wood from Isis and put them in his bag. "Do you know what you just did" Vladimir screamed. "Besides littered" Glade said. Vladimir glared at Glade quickly before looking up at the ceiling. "Computer execute Protocol 8809 Password Maureen" He yelled. Suddenly the lights went out and the ground began to shake. The lights came back on and everyone looked at Vladimir who had a sinister smile on his face. "What did you do" Curtus asked. "I did nothing… You on the other hand just killed everyone on the Jefferson"

XIX

Glade picked up Vladimir by his collar. "What the hell did you do" She yelled. "You guys tipped the balance of power too far in one direction. So I took it upon myself to restore order" Vladimir said. "What do mean restore order" Curtus asked. "When those papers reach the people they will panic and revolt" Vladimir began. "Yeah against you guys" Isis said. "Yes. The group that has kept the Jefferson afloat for hundreds of years" Vladimir said. "Stop beating around the bush and answer the damn question" Glade said shaking him. "Because of your actions the only way to preserve the American values it in the pages of history. I set the engines of the Jefferson to overload one at a time causing a slow decent. They will only think that we are hitting rough air and the radiation should make their deaths relatively painless" Vladimir explained.

Everyone was speechless. One second he was talking about how they kept the Jefferson afloat for hundreds of years and now he is set to kill everyone on it. "How is this saving them" Curtus asked walking toward Vladimir and Glade. "The Family's intentions were never to preserve the American people that is obvious from the files you read. We have two goal. Preserve America's core values and ensure the preservation of the human race" Vladimir replied. "How can you preserve the human race by killing millions of people" Jaymar asked. Vladimir began to chuckle. "There is so much about this world you kids don't know about. The Family is much bigger than you know. The Jefferson is just a fraction of the Family" Vladimir replied. He turned his gaze to Curtus. "Isn't that right Carolyn. I know she found a way to cheat death" Vladimir yelled. Curtus looked at his mother who had a concerned looked on her face. She was shaking nervously. Curtus could tell that her plan was completely ruined by Curtus's actions. "Mom don't worry your plan is going to work" Curtus said in a calming voice. "How we won't be able to get to the Skytrain before the Jefferson sinks below the clouds" She replied nervously. Curtus put his hand on his mother's shoulder. "Well then I guess we should get going" Curtus said with a smile.

Curtus looked at Glade. "Put him down we are moving" Curtus said. "What, we aren't going to finish him off" Glade asked. "Look at him. He will probably bleed out before we get to the Lorraine building" Curtus replied. Glade gave him one last look before dropping him in a pool of his own blood. The group gathered at the open window. Curtus looked across the way at the Lorraine building. It was much farther than he anticipated. "Dumbass I hope you got a plan for how to get across" Glade said. Jaymar knew this was a perfect time for his new ability, but he didn't know if he could make it that far a distance. "Mom any ideas" Curtus whispered to himself. "I actually do have one, but I'm going to need to take control" She said. "Take control" Curtus thought to himself. "Don't worry it will be quick" She reassured him. She gave him a motherly smile before stepping into his body.

What came next took Curtus by surprise. His body began to move without his permission. "Whoa" he said. "Don't worry. I'm won't put your body in harm's way we just need to hurry." He mother said in an effort to calm Curtus down. On the outside Curtus moved with an urgency and precision that none of them had seen before. He snatched the Omnitool off Jaymar's belt and began pressing button. "What are you doing" Jaymar yelled. Carolyn ignored and continued working on the Omnitool. He continued pressing buttons until a secret compartment opened with a second grappling hook. Jaymar worked with the Omnitool for 14 hours and not once did he come across that compartment. Curtus pulled out two harpoon tips and attached on to each end of the line. He closed the compartment and aimed the Omnitool at the Lorraine building. Curtus pulled the trigger and both ends of the line fired out. The backend anchoring thin the ceiling of the dining room and the front end anchoring at the far end of the Lorraine building.

Just as quickly as Curtus lost control of his body, he was back. His mother stepped out of his body. She was breathing heavy but she was smiling. "Wow that was a rush. It felt good to be alive again." She said. She looked at Curtus. "What are you waiting on. Get your ass over there" She yelled. Curtus had to get his bearing. His body was rebooting and his mind had to sync with his muscles. He looked and saw his mother had created a zip line leading directly to the roof of the Lorraine building. "I don't know have you did that but I'm glad you did" Glade said. She broke one of the legs off the chair and jumped on the zip line with no fear. Isis, though she was more hesitant, followed Glade's lead breaking off a second leg. Jaymar walked over to Curtus and grabbed the Omnitool from Curtus. "After this we are going to have a talk about boundaries" Jaymar said. Curtus tell by the look on his face that he was genuinely embarrassed that Curtus knew more about the Omnitool than him. The irony in that is Curtus knew absolutely nothing about the Omnitool. "Hey man I'm..." Curtus began. "Not now, but later"

Jaymar replied. Curtus nodded his head and grabbed one of the remaining legs of the chair. He looked back to take one last look at Vladimir. He didn't have the look of someone who was about to die. He just sat in calmly. His smile resembled the smile of Pennywise from the 2017 remake of the movie IT. "Until next time kid" He said in a chillingly clam voice.

The ground began to shake again. Another engine had overloaded bringing them closer to the irradiated clouds below. Curtus ran to the window and jumped out and began down the zip line.

Curtus looked down at the city below and to see the consequences of his actions. What he thought was a heroic deed brought nothing but destruction and pain to the people of the Jefferson. The streets below him looks like a scene out of a war movie. The air was filled with screams, smoke, and agony. People were fighting, looting, and setting building on fire. "This is all my fault isn't it" Curtus said. "No it isn't" His mother replied. He looked to his right to see his mother flying next to him.

"All you did was provide them with information. It is on them how they react to the information given to them. They could either take it as truth or take it as fiction. They could've come together to solve the problem or act on individual whims and destroy each other." Carolyn said. "But why did they chose to attack and steal from one another" Curtus asked. "In times of crisis people's true colors begin to show. As Americans we grow and are taught that capitalism is the greatest thing since bottled water. The basis of capitalism is to benefit off of other people. How is this any different. The person benefiting is the looter or the aggressor and the person losing is the store owner or victim. We also grow up with this romanticized outlook on violence which just add fuel to the fire. It's actually kind of sad really. They're stealing things for the present not knowing the true level of danger that awaits them in the near future." She explained. Curtus looked at his mother. "Is there anything you can do about the engines" He asked. "Even if I could do anything about the engines, I wouldn't be able to do it before the clouds engulfed the entire city" She replied.

Curtus continued down the cable until he reached the roof of the Lorraine building. Glade and Isis were waiting at the base of the cable. "So where do we go from here" Glade asked. "If you open the elevator shaft there should be four cable. Slide all the way down those to the hanger bay at the bottom" Carolyn said. "Follow me" Curtus said.

They opened the elevator door and just like his mother said there were four cables waiting for them. "This shaft used to house two elevators but they were taken out when the building was condemned" She said. "Why didn't they just tear it down" Curtus asked.

"There is a finite space on the Jefferson. There isn't enough room for you to knock it down or blow it up. So the best thing to do is condemn it and seal it off from the public" She replied. "So we just slide down these right" Jaymar said walking up behind the group. Everyone looked at Curtus. Seeing as it was his plan they wanted him to call the shots. "Yeah. We ride these cables down to the hanger bay at the bottom" he replied. He slowly walked over to the edge of the shaft and looked down to the endless darkness. He took a deep breath and look at Jaymar. "You got a light in that jacket of your" He asked. Jaymar reached in his coat pocket and pulled out the light he pulled from the desk in the chapel. "Yeah here" He said handing Curtus the light. Curtus turned on the light and jumped in the shaft descending down one of the cables.

The light wasn't very strong but it was enough for Curtus to see what was below him. Being the only one with a source of light Curtus knew the others were depending on him for guidance. As he made his way down the shaft he began to notice something strange. As he made his way down the shaft an occasional pink splatter would pop up on the wall. It was as if someone took a bucket of paint emptied it recklessly on the wall. After noticing the anomaly Curtus slowed down to allow the others to catch up. Once the whole group was together again Curtus began to question Jaymar about the flashlight. "Jaymar where did you get this flashlight" Curtus asked. "We found it in a weird chapel back in the Keep. Why?" He replied. "Because as I was looking at one of the walls a splattered began to glow" Curtus answered. Glade looked at the walk and noticed another splatter on the wall. "There. There goes another one" Glade said pointing it out. "Yeah in the office we used the flashlight to read secret writing on the wall" Jaymar said. Curtus looked down as saw the were about to reach the bottom of the shaft. "Alright guys I see the bottom. Time to slow it down" Curtus yelled. Curtus grabbed the cable with two hands and began to slow himself down.

They jumped of the cables and found themselves in a dark room. The ground violently shook again almost knocking everyone over. This one felt more violent than the first one because they were closer to the engines. "You need to get moving. Through that door" Carolyn said pointing to a door to their right. Curtus ran to the door and tried to pull it open with no luck. "Damn the door is locked" Curtus muttered to himself. He looked back to see everyone smiling. "Well instead of everyone laughing can one of you guys help me" He yelled. "Chill out" Glade said walking over. She grabbed the door handle and gently pushed the door open. She stood in the door way and pointed up at the edge of the doorframe. "If there are no hinges that means it is a push not a pull Dumbass" Glade said chuckling as she walked through the door. Jaymar and Isis looked at Curtus and chuckled as they walked past. "I got your hinges. Your asses won't have any light"

Curtus muttered to himself. "Dumbass hurry up its dark in here" Glade yelled. Curtus snapped out of his daze and ran to catch up with the others.

Curtus walking into the hall and the once the light entered the hall, the walls and floors lit up like fireworks. Fluorescent splatters covered the walls, floor, and ceiling. The four looked on in horror as they walked down the hall. "What exactly does that light show" Glade asked. "I honestly don't know. Let's just hope it is paint" Jaymar replied. "It's blood" Carolyn said. A chill ran down Curtus's spine. He looked over at his mother. "What do you mean" Curtus whispered. "What is splattered on the floor and walls is blood" She reiterated. Curtus wanted to tell the others what it was, but he didn't want to cause a panic. "Make a left up there" She said. "How do you know that is blood" Curtus asked. "I don't think now is the right time for this. We are in a bit of a hurry" She said. "Well then make it short and sweet" Curtus said sharply. Carolyn let out a deep sigh. "Let's just say me and your father were the reason that this building was condemned" She said.

Curtus's world had been turned upside down over the past couple of days. He told his parents everything thinking that in return they would tell him everything in return. His outlook on his parents as well as the world in general has completely changed. A week ago he would've have never thought that his parents could be a part of carnage like this, but now anything is possible.

They walked until they reached a fork in the road. Both hallway was dark and it was up to a coin flip on which way they would go. "Alright we go left" Curtus said "Why do we go left" Glade said. "Yeah we should put it to a vote" Isis said. "There is no time to vote. My mom knows this building better than any of us and she told me to get left" Curtus said. Isis looked at Curtus with a worried expression on her face. "Curtus your mom is gone. We all watched her die" She said in a calming voice. "No she isn't she is talking to me, and she said to go left" Curtus pleaded. "Shine the light down the right hallway" Carolyn said. Curtus walked over to the right hallway. "You guys want to go this way go ahead" Curtus said shining the light down the hallway.

Expressions of disgust and horror were painted on their faces. The wall and ceiling was covered in old blood and the floor was covered in assorted human remains. The body parts still had flesh on them giving the indication that the activity down here was recent. "What the hell did you guys do down here" Curtus whispered to himself. The ground shook violent again almost knocking everyone over. "So we can either go this way and take on whatever did that or listen to my mom and go left" Curtus said. Without a word everyone started walking down the left hallway. Before he followed the group he noticed something odd on the ground. It was a hospital wristband all patients get when they are checked in. Curtus walked over and picked up. His soul left his body as he read the name Maria Sanchez. "Curtus we need light" Jaymar yelled. He put the wristband in his pocket and ran to catch up with the others.

They continued walking until the hallway opened up and tripled in size. The doors on the right side were the size of the warehouses from the Ghettys. "Okay the Skytrain will be in hanger three" Carolyn said. "Okay guy it is in hanger three" Curtus yelled out beginning a jog. Without question everyone started jogging after him. The doors were counting backwards from 9 which meant they had a way to go until three. Curtus looked over to see his mother running with him step for step "Seems you have gotten them to believe in you" Carolyn said with a smile. "Yeah it seems like it… thanks for the help mom" Curtus said. Curtus wanted to bring up the wristband but thought with the current situation the timing wasn't right. "Okay I'll see you guys in the Skytrain" She replied before fading into the background. They ran until they reached a massive with the number three paint on the middle of it. Though the power was cut to the building due to the failing engines. The shock from the explosions had jarred the door open.

They enter the hanger to see that I was dimly lit with emergency lighting. They looked in the center of the hanger to see the mechanical marvel that was the Skytrain. This was the thing that his parents sent Curtus to go find when they were captured at the house. Curtus imagined what it might look light and real thing lived up to his imagination.

They walked over to it to take a closer look. "It is the type of stuff you see on the history channel" Jaymar said. Curtus walked to the front and opened the door. Once he stepped in the CPU of the train activated. "Welcome back Carolyn" the computerized voice said. The dashboard, floor, and ever the walls lit up a beautiful light blue. Then a pillar sprouted from the ground and stood at about belly button level. "Please insert your gauntlet Carolyn" The CPU said. The other enter the Skytrain and their eyes too filled with awe and wonder. Curtus walked over to the pillar. In the top of it was a hole that was the perfect size for the gauntlet. He took a deep breath and plunged his are into the pillar. The pillar began to beep which Curtus took as it processing information. Then suddenly the Skytrain went dark.

"We came all the way here for you to break the damn thing. Way to go Dumbass" Glade said sitting down in one of the chairs. "He didn't break it I'm just taking over the CPU" Carolyn said. Everyone looked up in alarm. "Y'all heard that too right" Jaymar said pointing to the ceiling. The room lit up pink and a hologram appeared in the middle. Curtus couldn't help but smile at everyone seeing that he wasn't crazy. "The consciousness transfer was a success and I was being housed in the gauntlet's CPU. Since the gauntlet was connected to his central nervous system I was able to communicate with him and guide your steps through him" She explained. "So that thing with the Omnitool" Jaymar began. "Yup that was all me" She said with a smile. Jaymar let out a massive sigh of relief. Carolyn looked at Curtus and unlocked his arm. "Now that I'm in the CPU I don't need the gauntlet anymore" She said. As she said this the gauntlet unlocked freeing Curtus's arm. The ground suddenly shook again. "Okay you guy get that door open while I start this baby up" She said.

Curtus stomach dropped to his ankles. He had forgotten that he had to get the hanger door open and he didn't have the slightest idea of hove he was going to do it without power. "Uhhh how do you plan on doing it without any power. That door weighs like 50 tons" Glade said. "49.75 to be exact and I know you guys will figure it out. You guys did confront the Family and survive" she said. She walked over to the pillar and screens suddenly started popping up out of thin air. Isis looked at her hands and remembered he encounter with Curtus's father. "When the time is right you'll figure it out" Kirkland's words rang through her head. Everyone was beginning to panic when she rose to her feet. "I got this" She said stepping off the Skytrain.

XX

Isis walked over to the power box to the right of the door. She could hear the whistling of the outside air though the door. The others watched her work through the windshield of the Skytrain. She drew one of her swords and pierced the cover of the power box. She took a deep breath and began to focus. She tried to think of things related to electricity to activate her Tonic, but nothing happened. "Uhhh no rush but we are currently falling out of the sky" Glade yelled out. "NOT HELPING" She yelled back. "Okay just thought you needed a friendly reminder is all" Glade replied. Isis began to think of things trying to get her body to react. She was going every type of emotion to see if any of those had any effect. She began to think of things that made her angry like Yuki, but that too had no effect. Same happened for disgust, fear, sadness. It wasn't until she started think what made her happy was when something happened.

It was a tingling feeling in her stomach as she started thinking of things that brought her joy. She was going through fun times she had with Ymerel in her early life, though it got a reaction it wasn't enough to make a real difference. Then she was going through her teen years when she realized she didn't remember much because she was blind all of those years. Then she got to when she met Curtus and the others and her whole body began to tingle. That was the first genuine connection she had after years of abuse, isoslation and imprisonment. She went through her memories with her new friends which were mainly conversation because she was still blind until she got to Curtus restoring her eyesight. Suddenly a surge of energy rushed to ever cell of her body. "Ok now focus" She whispered to herself. She focused on moving the energy to her hands and like an obedient dog the energy flowed where she told it to. Then she took another deep breath and focus the energy out of her hands and to the sword.

The energy jumped from her hands to the swords and within seconds the hanger was fully functional and the door slowly began to open. She pulled her swords out of the power box jogged back to the Skytrain where she was met with a hero's welcome. Everyone was clapping and patting her on the back. Even Carolyn stopped what she was doing to clap her holographic hands. "So what did you think about" Carolyn asked. "What do you mean" Isis replied sheathing her swords. "I created the Tonic so I know the key to activating it is joy. So what made you genuinely happy" She asked again rephrasing the question. She didn't want to say

Curtus in fear of what everyone would say and for Curtus to be weirded out. "Oh it was just one of the few good childhood moments I had" Isis lied. Carolyn could tell she was lying by she nodded and returned to work.

She kept on pressing the screen until the engine fired up. "Okay now we are in business" She said to herself. She turned around and looked at the group. "Okay everybody, buckle up. The initial takeoff is always bumpy" Carolyn warned. Everyone sat down in a seat and strapped themselves down. The seatbelt consisted of 6 different straps connecting to a piece that sat in the middle of a person's chest. The ground shook again and with the hanger door open they could watch themselves sinking toward the irradiated clouds. They were one engine away from being under the clouds. "Alright kiddos. Let's get jiggy with it" Carolyn said. Even in hologram form his mom found a way to embarrass him.

She pressed a couple of buttons on one screen and then turned a dial. Once she turned that dial everything began moving in slow motion for Curtus. Turning the dial caused the Skytrain to shoot forward without any warning. "Wait what the hell are you doing" Glade yelled. "You just have to trust me" Carolyn said with a smile. "Trust you. Lady I just met you!" Glade yelled grabbing onto her harness. "What are you afraid of heights" Jaymar said. "No I'm afraid of dying" Glade yelled. The Skytrain flew until the momentum ran out and gravity began to take effect. Curtus closed his eyes in fear that the Skytrain would malfunction and they would all die crashing into the ground. He kept his eye shut until he felt what felt like jumping in a boat. He opened his eyes to see they had stopped falling.

Curtus undid his harness and began to walk toward his mom. Everyone else sat in their seats unconscious. He looked at Jaymar who was drooling all over himself. "You were talking trash and now you are drooling all over yourself" Curtus whispered to himself. He walked over to his mom who was at what looked like a small conference table in the back of the cockpit. "So what is this" Curtus asked. "This is the only vehicle on the planet that can traverse these clouds safely" She said. Carolyn looked around frantically. "This view is horrendous. Let me fix that" She said. She swiped in front of her and a control pad popped up. She turned two dials and Curtus felt them rise. He looked out the windshield and saw the were rising above the clouds. She pressed two buttons and the walls of the Skytrain disappeared. "Now we are completely invisible and we have a 360 view" She said cheerfully.

Curtus looked around and took in the sights. He was always able to look at the night sky from his house but never had he seen the horizon before. Unless you had the money to live in one of the expensive penthouses your view was obstructed by the wall of the Jefferson.

Curtus focus on the horizon as he spun around. "It stretches so far" He whispered to himself. He continued to spin until he saw behind his mother the Jefferson slowly sinking beneath the clouds.

In the time they entered the Lorraine building the city had taken a turn for the worse. Massive fire now covered the outer shell of the Jefferson. The fires were so powerful it colored the clouds a mixture of red and orange. Several stacks of smoke came from city itself fluttering in the wind like a dingy wash cloth hanging on the line. The others slowly began to wake up to the same dismal sight. "All of those people" Isis said putting her hands over her mouth. "There was no way we could have saved all of them" Glade said.

Carolyn turned and faced the group. "That right there is why we fight the Family. Because they will do anything for power. If feel that they are losing power they will do anything to make sure no one else gets it, including killing millions of people to make a statement" She explained. She looked out at the group to see everyone was a defeated expression on their faces. They were disappointed in themselves. They felt that all of this death was caused by them. "Don't beat yourselves up. They could have done this at any time for any reason. Now what you have to do is make sure their sacrifices mean something." She said. "You saw what technology they possess we have no chance" Jaymar said. "Yeah they have created a way to control space and time" Glade said. "Yeah but you guy are going to master your Tonics." Carolyn began. This caught everyone's attention. "It doesn't matter how much technology you have, if you don't have to skill to use it is all for nothing" She finished. "How do you plan on doing that" Isis asked. "I created them so I know what they are capable of, and what part of the brain to tap to activate them" She said. "So you are going to train us" Curtus asked. "You bet. By the time you get to Shangri La you guys will be an unstoppable 4-person army" she replied.

She tapped the table and a blue virtual keypad popped up out of it. She typed in a sequence of numbers and a video feed popped up. The feed was of a destroyed conference room. The chairs were thrown all over the room and the table was in five separate pieces. She typed in another sequence of number and it was from a security camera outside a building. The feed had people running while this militia chased after them with guns shooting into a mob of civilians. Curtus recognized the uniforms on the men firing on the mob. They were wearing as they were the same ones Leremy was wearing when they abducted his parents. "Shit they got there sooner than I thought" Carolyn said to herself. She swiped and feed disappeared. She looked at everyone and noticed that they had new fire in their eyes.

Carolyn knew they were going to do what it took to see the mission to the end. "How long until we get there" Curtus asked. "The trip is 30 days. We want to make sure we get there undetected to keep the element of surprise. By the time we get there they would have locked the place down so you guys need to be ready." Carolyn replied. "Well then you set the course and tomorrow we begin our training" Curtus said. Carolyn smiled. "Alright you guys have had a rough go of it and earned a good rest. But when that sun comes up be ready for work. A month from now you guys begin the fight for the freedom of the world"

Thank you

If you are reading this, that means you have reached the end of the first part of Curtus's journey. I want to personally thank you for picking it up in the first place. There hundreds upon thousands of books you could have chosen from and the fact that you took a chance on mine means the world to me. If you didn't like it I apologize, but I tip my cap to you for at least giving my book a shot. Whether you loved it or hated it just know this is only the beginning!!!

I also want to thank everyone who had a hand in helping me manifest my dream. It has always been a dream of mine to write an I couldn't have done it without y'all. Whether it was giving me advice on where I should take the story to just telling me to keep working hard all of it helped and for that I say Thank You!!!

Stay Blessed, Stay Creative, and Stay True to who you are

-Avery Justin

Made in the USA
Lexington, KY
05 March 2018